"The best historicals, the best romances. Simply the best!"
—Dallas Schulze

"Bronwyn Williams was born and raised at Harlequin
Historicals. We couldn't have asked for a better home or a
more supportive family."
—Dixie Browning and Mary Williams,
w/a Bronwyn Williams

"I can't believe it's been ten years since *Private Treaty,* my
first historical novel, helped launch the Harlequin
Historicals line. What a thrill that was! And the beat goes
on...with timeless stories about men and women in love."
—Kathleen Eagle

"Nothing satisfies me as much as writing or reading a
Harlequin Historical novel. For me, Harlequin Historicals
are the ultimate escape from the problems of everyday
life."

—Ruth Ryan Langan

"As a writer and reader, I've always felt that Harlequin
Historicals celebrate a perfect blend of history and
romance, adventure and passion, humor and sheer magic."
—Theresa Michaels

"Thank you, Harlequin Historicals, for opening up a 'window into the past' for so many happy readers."

—Suzanne Barclay

"As a one-time 'slush pile' foundling at Harlequin Historicals, I'll be forever grateful for having been rescued and published as one of the first 'March Madness' authors. Harlequin Historicals has always been *the* place for special stories, ones that blend the magic of the past with the rare miracle of love for books that readers never forget."

—Miranda Jarrett

"A rainy evening. A cup of hot chocolate. A stack of Harlequin Historicals. Absolute bliss! Happy 10th Anniversary and continued success."

—Cheryl Reavis

"Happy birthday, Harlequin Historicals! I'm proud to have been a part of your ten years of exciting historical romance."

—Elaine Barbieri

"Harlequin Historical novels are charming or disarming with dashes and clashes. These past times are fast times, the gems of romances!"

—Karen Harper

LORD
OF THE
MANOR

SHARI
ANTON

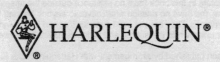

HARLEQUIN®

TORONTO • NEW YORK • LONDON
AMSTERDAM • PARIS • SYDNEY • HAMBURG
STOCKHOLM • ATHENS • TOKYO • MILAN • MADRID
PRAGUE • WARSAW • BUDAPEST • AUCKLAND

To Ray and Jean Antoniewicz,
with love.

ISBN 0-373-29034-9

LORD OF THE MANOR

Copyright © 1998 by Sharon Antoniewicz

All rights reserved. Except for use in any review, the reproduction or
utilization of this work in whole or in part in any form by any electronic,
mechanical or other means, now known or hereafter invented, including
xerography, photocopying and recording, or in any information storage
or retrieval system, is forbidden without the written permission of the
publisher, Harlequin Enterprises Limited, 225 Duncan Mill Road,
Don Mills, Ontario, Canada M3B 3K9.

All characters in this book have no existence outside the imagination of
the author and have no relation whatsoever to anyone bearing the same
name or names. They are not even distantly inspired by any individual
known or unknown to the author, and all incidents are pure invention.

This edition published by arrangement with Harlequin Books S.A.

® and TM are trademarks of the publisher. Trademarks indicated with
® are registered in the United States Patent and Trademark Office, the
Canadian Trade Marks Office and in other countries.

Printed in U.S.A.

Richard came toward Lucinda with long strides.

A tall, muscled warrior, strong of body and purpose. His arms swung at his sides in rhythm to his footfalls, and his hands were clenched. Hands that could skim over her with serene tenderness or stroke her with urgent hunger. Either way, guiding her to beyond the heavens.

She'd come to envy his inner tranquillity, admire his calm but firm treatment of his vassals, appreciate his effort to give her son a noble's education, and cherish the time he spent with her alone.

She couldn't have selected a better man to act as protector.

Or found a better lover. Or chosen a better man to love.

The realization severely tested her already fractured composure. But there it was. Undeniable. She loved Richard.

And he must never know....

Chapter One

England, 1109

Richard stepped back and sucked in his gut to avoid the whizzing tip of his brother's broadsword. The gasp of the crowd encircling the castle's practice yard confirmed how close the sword had come to nicking his navel.

He grinned. As always, Richard had let Gerard, his elder half brother and Baron of Wilmont, set the pace of the session. Allowed Gerard to probe for weakness in his defenses. That mighty stroke, clean and swift—and close—proclaimed Gerard hadn't found one.

Richard returned the compliment with a stroke that would have disarmed a lesser man. Gerard absorbed the blow like a huge boulder, half buried in earth, not budging a mite.

"Ready to halt?" Gerard asked almost casually.

"Not until you sweat," Richard answered, having noted the lack of a sheen on Gerard's bare chest. 'Twas now a matter of pride to make the wavy blond hair at Gerard's temples curl from dampness, as his own did.

In truth, neither brother would win this contest. He and Gerard were too evenly matched, from their skill at swordplay to the strength in their broad shoulders. From the green of their eyes to the flaxen color of their hair. Each even bore a long, jagged scar across his chest—Gerard's earned many years ago while defending Everart, their now-dead father; Richard's earned more recently, when he'd been mistaken for Gerard.

When mounted on war horses and sheathed in chain mail and helmet, 'twas nearly impossible to distinguish the Baron of Wilmont from the bastard of Wilmont. Usually, the resemblance provided amusement for the brothers—until the fateful day in Normandy when their likeness had spared Gerard the injury that had nearly cost Richard his life.

The man who ordered Gerard's murder, Basil of Northbryre, had paid for the mistake with his lands and his life. Gerard had then rewarded Richard by granting lordship over part of the lands won as a result of Basil's downfall.

Richard owed much to Gerard—whose raised sword was about to cleave him in two if he didn't pay better heed.

The clash of steel on steel reverberated through the yard as Richard met Gerard's vigorous downstroke. The force of the blow numbed Richard's hands and sent a wave of shock up his arms. He knew Gerard felt the shock, too. Gerard just didn't have the decency to show a reaction.

Blade ran along blade. Richard stepped forward to come chest-to-chest with Gerard, and shoved hard to force his brother out of that irritating, rock-solid stance.

Another gasp rose from the crowd, but he paid little heed to the onlookers. Instead, he focused on Gerard's narrowed eyes and feral grin. Richard knew that look, and prepared for the flurry of sword strokes sure to follow.

He reveled in the power of each blow, in how his muscles responded to the command of his will, in the simple pleasure of pitting his skills and wits against Gerard's. 'Twas the foremost reason he returned often to Wilmont, where he'd been born of his English peasant mother and raised by his Norman noble father. Where he'd experienced both love and scorn as a child. Where he now commanded respect as a man.

A piercing whistle brought Richard to an immediate halt. As the tip of his sword dropped, he glanced toward the keep. Stephen, his younger half brother, pushed his lean, lank frame through the onlookers and briskly walked toward him and Gerard.

While one could tell at a glance that Richard and Gerard had been sired by the same father, that couldn't be said of Stephen. Not only was he shorter and more slender, he bore the olive skin and black hair of Ursula, Stephen and Gerard's mother.

Richard beckoned forth the young soldier who held his and Gerard's tunics.

"Hellfire," Gerard said under his breath as they exchanged weapons for tunics.

"Hellfire, indeed," Stephen said with a teasing grin. "Ardith heard what you and Richard were about, Gerard, and that neither of you used a shield nor wore a hauberk. I fear you are in for a tongue-lashing."

Gerard's wife was one of the gentlest women Richard knew. When provoked, however, Ardith had no qualms about expressing her displeasure. This wouldn't be the first time that Gerard caught hell for engaging in swordplay without protection.

Gerard huffed. "So she sent you out to halt us."

"A woman in delicate condition should not push her way through crowds or get in the middle of swordplay. So I offered my services. Besides, I hoped you would now explain why you summoned Richard and me to Wilmont."

Gerard pulled his tunic over his head. "In good time."

Stephen rolled his eyes. "I have been here for two days, waiting for Richard to arrive. He came this morn. 'Tis now nearly time for evening repast. How much longer must we wait?"

"Until after I calm my wife, wash the sweat and dust from my body, and eat," Gerard said, then turned and headed for the keep.

"That man is infuriatingly stubborn," Stephen complained, glaring at Gerard's back.

Richard eased into his tunic. "Patience, Stephen," he said, knowing it would do no good. Stephen always wanted to be where he was not, do something other than what he was doing. His rush into adventure often got him into trouble, but that never lessened Stephen's eagerness for the next exploit.

"I have been patient," Stephen declared. "Are you not curious about Gerard's summons?"

"Aye, but I am content to wait until he is ready to explain."

"Humph. Likely, he will do so two words at a time and drive me insane."

Richard laughed lightly and chided, "Come now, Stephen. When Gerard chooses to, he can talk endlessly."

"Truly? When did you last hear him utter more than two sentences at a time?"

Richard well remembered standing beside Ardith in Westminster Hall while Gerard proclaimed innocence concerning the death of Basil of Northbryre. "At court. During Gerard's trial for murder. He presented his case to King Henry in eloquent fashion."

Stephen sighed. "I missed the trial, as you know. I was here at Wilmont, preparing for the war that would have followed if Gerard had lost. You are forgetting, Richard, that Gerard did not win against King Henry with words, but through ordeal by combat."

Gerard had almost lost the ordeal against the king's champion. If Ardith hadn't thrown a dagger onto the field of combat, within reach of Gerard's hand, Gerard might have lost Wilmont and his life.

"The how of it does not matter. Gerard defended his barony and honor, and we all kept our lands."

"There is that," Stephen conceded.

Richard slapped Stephen on the back. "Come. Let us see what wines Gerard has managed to import from France. Mayhap the drink will loosen his tongue."

The evening repast turned out to be a pleasant affair.

Gerard had placated his beautiful wife, Ardith. She sat next to him at the high table, on the dais in the great hall of Wilmont, serenely sharing his trencher. Stephen shared a trencher with Gerard's illegitimate son, Daymon, a boy of six. Little Everart, now three and Gerard's heir, ate with Ursula, his grandmother.

Ursula had once been the bane of Richard's existence. Over the years, her sharp tongue had dulled somewhat. Richard knew, however, she still couldn't look at him without remembering her husband's infidelity.

Not wishing to cause Ursula more painful memories than his mere presence always did, Richard shunned the high table in favor of a trestle table, on the pretense of visiting with the castle's older knights.

Later that evening, after most of the folk had taken to their beds or pallets, Richard sat across from Gerard at that same trestle table while Stephen paced around them.

Pouring sweet French wine from a silver pitcher into gold goblets, Gerard said, "On Whitsunday, King Henry holds court at Westminster to settle the conditions of Princess Matilda's betrothal to the Emperor."

Stephen sat down beside Gerard, straddling the bench. "You wish us to accompany you to court, to witness the royal betrothal?"

Gerard placed the pitcher on the table within easy reach of them all. "I chose not to go, so I am sending the two of you in my stead."

While Stephen jumped for joy, Richard winced. He hated attending court, disliked the crowds of nobles and their incessant political maneuvering. And though no one would say so to his face due to their respect for Gerard, the nobles tolerated his presence as the bastard who enjoyed his brother's goodwill. Never mind that his holdings far exceeded what many men could hope to gain, or that the court accepted King Henry's multitude of bastards. Those bastards enjoyed favor simply because they were royal bastards.

Richard took a sip of fortifying wine before he asked Gerard, "Why do you not attend?"

"Each time I show my face at court, Henry's ire flares and he gives me a duty which keeps me from Wilmont for months. Ardith is due in two months and I wish to be home when she gives birth."

Stephen nodded. "Wise of you, Gerard. Come, Richard. Do not look so glum. We will have a fine time! On the grand occasion of his daughter's betrothal, the king will spare no expense on food, drink and entertainment."

Richard ignored Stephen. "Then why not send only Stephen? My face is too like yours, Gerard. Henry's ire may flare when he sees *my* face."

"'Tis possible, but for all the king's faults, he is usually a fair man, and he is not angry with you as he is with me. Too, I want both of you there, as my eyes and ears."

Gerard didn't lack for staunch allies at court. Richard could think of several who would gladly give Gerard detailed reports. While Richard could see the sense in one of them attending court to establish a Wilmont presence, why Gerard would wish to send both of his brothers was beyond him.

"Why? What do you think will happen?" Stephen asked.

Gerard leaned forward. "All know that Henry will be generous at this court. He will hear all petitions, from those for land to requests for heiresses. The balance of power within the kingdom will shift, and 'tis important I know in whose direction the favor tilts. We can be sure it will not tilt in our favor, and must protect what is ours."

Richard frowned. "You think Henry might yet have his eye on Wilmont holdings?"

"Possibly."

Stephen waved a dismissing hand. "I doubt Henry would do anything to test Wilmont's power. You have too many strong allies, Gerard. Do you know which heiresses are available? Ah, Richard, think! We could both come home rich!"

Richard laughed, at both Stephen's sudden change of subject and his optimism. "You, mayhap, but me? Doubtful."

Richard knew the chance of his being granted an heiress was almost nil. The great heiresses of England were given to men of high standing and good name, not to bastards—unless they were royal bastards. Still, if something could be done to soften Henry's ire against Wilmont, there might be the slimmest chance of gaining favor, and mayhap a less wealthy heiress.

With the wealth that an heiress would bring, he could expand his holdings. In land was power, and the more he controlled, the greater his standing, bastard or no.

"What say you, Richard?" Gerard asked. "What harm could come from looking?"

Richard finally understood Gerard's maneuvering. Once more, Gerard was opening a door for him. Aye, Gerard might wish to be at Wilmont when Ardith gave birth, but he was staying away from court to give Stephen and Richard the chance to gain favor on their own, without reminding the king of past hard feelings.

No harm could come from looking. While he looked, he also might find a way to help mend the rift between two men who had once been very close—Gerard and King Henry.

"I daresay I should go, if only to keep Stephen out of mischief."

While Stephen sputtered a protest, Gerard nodded slightly and took a sip of wine from his jewel-encrusted goblet. His failed effort to hide a satisfied smile wasn't lost on Richard.

On her knees beside Hetty's pallet, Lucinda bent low to hear the old woman's whispered words.

"Take the boy away, dear," she said. "Go now, before the sickness claims you, too."

Lucinda placed a cold, wet rag on Hetty's fevered brow. This sickness had swept through the village at a frightening pace. Infants and the elders seemed particularly vulnerable. Few survived.

Lucinda knew Hetty spoke wisely. Philip was but six. She should remove her son from harm's way, but she couldn't leave Hetty alone to battle the illness.

Hetty and her husband had taken Lucinda and Philip into their home and cared for them for the past three years. Leaving would be a betrayal of their kindness. Even if she did flee, there was no surety that she and Philip wouldn't succumb while on the road.

"Hush, Hetty, save your strength," Lucinda said.

Hetty grasped Lucinda's hand and squeezed. "I know I am dying, and would go quickly to join my Oscar. Have they buried him yet?"

Lucinda shook her head. Oscar had died yesterday, but too few of the village men were well enough to dig graves for those poor souls who had already departed this mortal life.

"Good," Hetty said on a relieved sigh. "Then they

will put us in the same grave. 'Tis fitting I should spend eternity with my husband."

Hetty and Oscar's devotion to each other had always amazed Lucinda. Their marriage had been a joy to them, so unlike the horror of her marriage to Basil. The only thing Basil had done right in his whole miserable life had been to warn her to flee the castle at Northbryre, to go to his family in Normandy, before his downfall. Of course, he hadn't been concerned with her safety, but with that of Philip, his son and heir.

She'd fled Northbryre, but hadn't gone to Normandy.

Lucinda glanced about the one-room hut built of wattle and daub. It had become her refuge, a place to hide from both Basil's enemies and his family.

If she did flee, where would she go? She yet possessed a few of the coins she'd taken from Northbryre's coffers. Were they enough to get her and Philip to another village, enough to entice some other kindly couple to shelter a woman and her son?

"We will stay here with you, Hetty," Lucinda said. "When you are well—"

"Go to the king. Petition for Philip's due."

Lucinda closed her eyes and bowed her head. She and Hetty had argued over Philip's inheritance before. In all of the village, only Hetty and Oscar knew her identity. They had explained her presence in their home as that of a niece come to live with them after suffering widowhood. These kind, gentle souls had taken in the widow of a man considered a traitor to the kingdom, the son of a man whose cruelties were well known, and shielded them from those who would shun them.

Hetty insisted that since Philip was noble, he should take his rightful place among the nobility, no matter that his father had been the devil himself.

Basil's downfall had been almost total. He'd lost his life, and the king had divided Basil's English holdings between himself and Gerard of Wilmont in restitution for Basil's treachery. She highly doubted that King Henry would restore those lands to the son of a man who'd tried to convince England's barons to revolt.

Basil's holdings in Normandy were now, probably, controlled by his family, who would loathe giving them up. To regain control of the Normandy holdings, Philip would have to become the ward of a noble strong enough to demand their return.

Lucinda couldn't bear the thought of giving Philip over to someone else to raise, especially not any noble she knew. The thought made her shudder. Her son was all she had left in this world.

Hetty squeezed her hand harder. "You shiver. Are you ill?"

Aye, she was sick, but of heart, not of body. The concern in Hetty's eyes nearly tore her apart.

"Nay, I am fine. As is Philip."

Lucinda glanced at the corner of the hut where her son had curled onto his pallet to nap.

Basil's visits to her bedchamber had been the most horrifying experiences of her life, and Philip's birth the most painful. Yet, Philip was her one true joy. He no longer remembered his father, or the castle at Northbryre, and truly thought of Hetty and Oscar as relatives. He mourned Oscar as a beloved uncle, and would need comforting when Hetty died.

There. She'd finally admitted the unthinkable.

Hetty was about to die. Probably within the hour. Then what?

Go to the king.

Was she wrong to raise her son as a peasant, forsaking all noble connections? Maybe if she could get back to Normandy, to her own family…no, her father would turn Philip over to Basil's family without second thought.

So might the king. Henry was not only the King of England but the Duke of Normandy.

Hetty had fallen asleep, a sleep she might not wake from. Lucinda unclasped her hand from Hetty's and stood up. On her way to the door, craving a breath of fresh air, Lucinda stopped to push a lock of Philip's black hair back from over his eyes. He'd inherited her hair color, but under his closed eyelids lurked Basil's gray eyes, so unlike her own unusual violet ones. Hopefully, his eye color was the only thing he'd inherited from his father.

Could disdainful disregard for one's fellow man be passed along bloodlines? Surely, proper guidance shaped a person's character more than the blood in his veins. But there were those who would never see past Philip's heritage, would judge him as tainted because of his sire.

She opened the door to brilliant sunshine and a warm breeze. 'Twas sinful that so much unhappiness could occur on such a beautiful day.

Few people roamed the road. Most everyone had shut themselves away in their hovels, to either avoid or contain the sickness. The church's bell hadn't pealed the hours for two days because the priest was ill. How many would die on this glorious day? How many tomorrow?

Lucinda crossed her arms over her midriff and leaned against the oak tree just outside the doorway where she would hear if either Hetty or Philip stirred.

Philip.

Nothing remained for her and Philip here. Once again she would be fleeing for her life. She'd managed to find a haven once. She could find another.

On Whitsunday, only a sennight hence, the king would hold court at Westminster. Passing travelers and peddlers had brought tidings of the princess's betrothal to Emperor Henry. A celebration would be held. Feasting. Dancing. The nobility would flock to court to pay homage to the king and to witness the royal betrothal. King Henry would hear petitions from all comers, noble and peasant alike. He would be in a generous mood, strive to please each of his subjects if he could.

She looked down at her gray gown of loosely woven linen and tried to imagine standing before the king in peasant garb, begging for favor. Humiliating, considering that she'd once curtsied low to the king in a gown of silk.

Basil had taken her to court only once, but once was enough to know how people dressed there, to learn the proper decorum when in the royal presence. She'd been raised in a noble house, brought up as a lady. She knew how to conduct herself and could teach Philip.

But how did one teach a little boy to ignore the insults that he would surely hear? How did one explain that he must hide his feelings behind a mask of indifference and trust no one?

Sweet heaven, was she really considering going to court?

"Mother?"

Lucinda spun around to the sound of Philip's voice. He stood in the doorway, tears streaming down his face. She held out a hand, inviting him outside. He didn't move, except to look over his shoulder—back to where Hetty lay.

Lucinda took a deep breath, knowing what she would find when she went back into the hut. She could no longer do anything for Hetty, but she could for her son. Was she going to court? She wasn't sure, but knew she must leave the village or risk her son's life.

Slowly, she approached Philip and put her hand on his small shoulder. "I want you to stuff all of your garments into a sack," she told him, amazed that her voice didn't tremble. "I'll see to Hetty, then we must leave."

He stared up at her for a few moments, then nodded. The trust shining in his eyes was nearly her undoing.

Chapter Two

Lucinda tugged on the rope to coax the mule along. After four days of travel, she hadn't decided if the beast was more a bother or a blessing. The mule carried all her possessions, including Philip, who thought the ride great sport. The mule thought it great sport to impede their progress. Without him, however, she might not have made it this far.

Leaving the village had been hard. She'd made sure that Oscar and Hetty would be buried, ensured their sheep and oxen would be cared for, packed what little food lay about the hut, then set out on the road.

"Mother? I thought that last village nice."

Philip had thought "nice" each village that they'd passed through. He was right about the one they'd visited this morn. The people smiled as they went about their work. The condition of their homes said they prospered. However, the village's overlord happened to be Gerard of Wilmont. While the baron might never learn of her presence there, she couldn't risk that he might hear of it and take exception.

"The people were pleasant enough, but no one had room for us to abide there permanently," she said.

"Could we not build our own hut?"

If he hadn't been so serious, she might have laughed at the suggestion. Philip desperately wanted a new home. He hadn't taken well to traveling without a fixed destination. She also suspected he very much wanted off the mule, despite his initial exuberance.

"I fear you must grow first before we attempt such a feat. Neither you nor I possess the strength or the skill. Our hut would likely fall down about our heads." She patted his knee. "Be patient for a while longer, Philip. The Lord will provide."

She hoped, and soon.

Philip looked over his shoulder. "Someone comes."

Lucinda turned as the jingle of a horse's tack and the thud of heavy hoofbeats grew louder. A large party approached, judging from the size of the dust cloud hovering over it. She wrapped her woolen scarf around her head to cover her hair and the lower portion of her face, to block the road dust from her mouth and nose and to conceal her features.

The chance of recognition was slim. She'd spent her entire married life buried at Northbryre—save for a single visit to court—then hidden away in a small village after her husband's downfall. Few would remember her as Basil's wife, but those who would were of the same nasty disposition as Basil. She had no wish to acknowledge their acquaintance.

Lucinda pulled the mule to the edge of the road to let the oncoming party pass by.

"Remember what I told you," she said to Philip.

"I will not stare or speak," he said, then drew a long, awed breath. "Oh, is he not wondrous!"

Lucinda knew he meant the destrier that led the company. Shiny black, his head held high and proud, his tack studded with silver that glinted in the sunlight, the war horse was indeed magnificent.

To her chagrin, she noted the destrier's master was also a wondrous sight to behold. He guided his horse with reins held loosely in his right hand—the left rested on his hip—as though he commanded the road.

Even at this distance she could judge him tall. Beneath a black cloak he wore a chain mail hauberk, the mark of a warrior noble. No coif covered his shoulder-length, flaxen blond hair. He carried no shield, but a huge broadsword hung at his side.

He seemed oblivious to the troop of men-at-arms who followed in his wake—some mounted, some walking—each carrying a shield and spear. Behind them lumbered two wagons.

Nowhere did Lucinda spy a woman, a lady who might object if her lord's men became unruly. Remembering her husband's favored guards, she scoffed. Those rough, uncouth mercenaries had treated her no better than a mere woman who happened to share their lord's table and bed. Any objection she might have made to their behavior would have fallen on deaf ears.

"Philip, face forward. Pay them no heed."

She had to shake him to gain his attention.

"Some day I want a horse like that," he declared, and then obeyed.

Aye, 'twas her son's right to one day own the trappings of nobility, among them a destrier. That could happen only if she went to court and the king took pity on the widow and son of one of his most treacherous subjects. For every reason that came to mind why she should petition the king, she could think of another why she should not.

She had time yet to decide. For now, getting safely through the next few minutes took precedence.

Lucinda considered leaving the road entirely, but that would mean going into the forest. Not a safe place, not with a stubborn mule, not knowing if one of the men would take her action as an invitation and decide to pursue. Best she stay on the road, as close to the edge as possible, and pray that none of the men took it into his head to harass a poor peasant woman and her little boy.

The earth fair shook as the noble overtook them, passed by on his magnificent steed, giving her a clear view of his back. He was, indeed, a tall and broad-shouldered warrior and, to her relief, no longer a danger.

The men-at-arms, in a double column, marched past. She put her hand to her nose against the dust. The company consisted of twenty armed and likely well-trained soldiers. She let out the breath she'd been holding as she sensed a break in the retinue. All that remained to pass by were the wagons.

Philip wiped his nose with his tunic sleeve. He sneezed hard, kicking the mule. The mule brayed and shifted, nearly knocking Lucinda off balance.

Then Philip sneezed again. The mule bolted, jerking the lead rope from her hand so fast it burned.

"Hold fast, Philip!" she shouted, and began to run with a speed she'd never known she could attain. Sweet Jesu, she'd never seen that mule move so fast. Philip bounced and swayed, but he held on.

One soldier almost snared the lead rope as the mule

sped by. Two others dropped their spears and shields to give chase.

Lucinda followed, damning the mule to perdition, praying that Philip could hold tight a while longer. If Philip were injured…no, she couldn't think of that now, just concentrate on getting to him.

Too late, she saw the bump of a tree root in the road. Her foot caught, sending her tumbling. Gasping for air, ignoring her scraped hands, she tried to rise. Pain shot from her ankle. She swore, a foul word she'd learned from Basil's mercenaries.

Lucinda flinched when a hand clasped her shoulder.

"Can you get up?" the man said.

Admitting weakness to a man wasn't wise. A lone woman amid so many men would do well to keep her vulnerability a secret. Unfortunately, her injury would show the moment she put weight on her ankle. She looked up into the face of an old soldier, his warm brown eyes and puggish nose surrounded by a bushy, graying beard.

"Mayhap, with your aid," she said.

As he helped her to stand, the soldier said, "Worry not about the boy. Even now Lord Richard chases the mule."

Indeed, the commotion drew the attention of the noble who led the company. Effortlessly, his destrier kept pace with the mule. Lord Richard shouted down to Philip, then reached out and plucked her son from the mule's back.

A cheer laced with laughter went up from the soldiers. Lucinda sighed with relief, not having the breath to cheer. This lord who had snatched Philip from the threat of harm was due her gratitude.

The lord wheeled his horse around. Philip sat on

the man's lap, safe. The lord said something to his two soldiers who had given chase. They nodded and continued up the road, but at a slower pace. She assumed they'd been ordered to find the mule. If not for the precious packs on the beast's back, she'd have told them not to bother.

Lord Richard was riding slowly toward her, bearing Philip back to her. Lucinda shook the worst of the dust from her gown and straightened her scarf, hoping she could adequately express her thanks for his rescue of her son.

Her heart stopped when she recognized the man she'd seen but once, at court, lo those many years ago. Basil had pointed out each member of the family he so despised: Everart, Baron of Wilmont, whose lands Basil coveted; the heir Gerard and the youngest son Stephen; and Richard, the middle son—the bastard.

Philip was sitting on the lap of Richard of Wilmont, who had been severely wounded and nearly died because of Basil's treachery.

Richard ruffled Philip's hair, talking to him. Philip smiled up at Richard and answered. Lucinda bit her bottom lip. If Richard spoke to Philip in Norman French, the language of the nobility, Philip would answer in his native tongue, which no mere peasant boy would know. It would be a clear sign that she and her son were not who they appeared to be.

Oblivious to the danger, smiling hugely, Philip rattled on and on, his hands gesturing as he spoke. Richard commented occasionally, with only one or two words.

Though she couldn't hear what they said, one exchange didn't need to be heard to be understood.

Richard's lips clearly formed Philip's name, and then hers, Lucinda, drawn out as if he savored the word.

She shivered. Surely, now, Richard knew who she was, realized whose son he held firmly in his grasp. Or did he? True, Everart would have pointed Basil out to each of his sons so they would know their enemy. Had she been with Basil at the time? Would Everart have bothered identifying Basil's wife? Would Everart even have known her name?

Lucinda took a deep breath and squared her shoulders. Whatever was to come next, she had to face it. She couldn't run, not with her injured ankle, not with a small boy in tow. Nor would she cower. She knew how to face angry, abusive men and retain her inner dignity.

Lucinda allowed herself a small show of a mother's concern for her son as Richard reined his horse to a halt. She looked Philip over, head to toe, searching for signs of injury. She found none. That done, she smoothed her features into the impenetrable mask that had served her well for so many years.

"Lucinda," Richard said from the great height of his destrier.

Her name, spoken in his low, rumbling voice, sounded odd, almost beautiful. 'Twas a pleasant sensation, but she refused to allow the feeling to linger or cloud her judgment. Too often she'd seen nobles, no matter how seemingly charming, turn beastly.

As a peasant woman, she should bow low before Richard. But if she tried, her ankle would crumble. She gave him a slight bow and hoped he wouldn't take offense.

"This boy, Philip, claims to belong to you," he said before she'd finished the bow. She'd expected haughtiness or derision, not the hint of humor in his voice. And, thank the Lord, he spoke in English.

"He is my son, my lord."

He grasped Philip around the waist and lifted him. "Then I shall return this outstanding mule rider to your care."

Lucinda knew that Richard expected her to come forward to claim Philip. To her relief, the old soldier who had helped her to stand walked over to fetch her son. As soon as Philip's feet hit the road, he ran to the invitation of her open arms. She wanted to bend down and pick him up. Afraid she would fall on her face if she tried, she put her hands on his back and head and held him firmly against her.

"I give you my thanks, my lord, for your timely and gracious rescue," she said.

He nodded. "Is your mule always so skittish?"

"Nay, my lord. He is usually well-mannered—for a mule."

Richard glanced over his shoulder. "Ah, even now the beast comes. Having had his run for the day, mayhap he will be calmer now."

"'Tis hoped for, my lord," she answered, her fears fading. Surely, if Richard had recognized her he would have said so by now, not rambled on about a skittish mule. Perhaps she and Philip would escape this encounter unscathed.

Deftly, Richard nudged his destrier to the side, allowing the soldier who led the mule to pass by him. With the rope again in her hand, Lucinda gave the soldier a gracious smile, feeling ever more confident that she worried for naught.

"Philip," Richard called out, "have a care not to sneeze loudly again."

Lucinda held tight to Philip's shoulders as he turned around to answer, "I shall try, my lord." Then he tilted his head up to ask her, "Must I get on that beast again? My arse is well sore!"

Richard's smile widened. The soldiers about her chuckled.

She strove for a light tone. "Mayhap I will ride and let you walk, for a while."

Richard gathered up his horse's reins. "I wish you both a pleasant journey," he said, but before he could turn his horse, the old, grizzled soldier put a hand on Richard's leg.

"Beg pardon, my lord," the soldier said.

"What is it, Edric?" Richard asked.

Edric rubbed at his gray beard. "Whilst you chased the boy, the woman took a hard twist to her foot. I do not think she can walk. If the boy walks, they will not get to the next village afore nightfall. 'Tain't room on the beast for the two of them and the packs. Spending the night on the road would be dangerous."

Richard looked back at her, questioning.

Lucinda quickly said, "'Tis a small hurt, my lord. Nothing to trouble yourself over."

With a sigh of impatience, the first he'd displayed, Richard dismounted and tossed the reins to Edric.

Lucinda strove to tamp down the panic that threatened to overpower her as Richard of Wilmont came nearer. He halted a few feet away from her and crossed his muscled arms across the wide expanse of his chest.

"Edric is a well-seasoned soldier who has suffered many an injury. If he believes that your ankle will not support you, I will not doubt him. I offer you a

seat in a wagon and the protection of our company,"
he said.

"A kind gesture, my lord, but not necessary."

"Can you walk?"

"Well enough," she lied. Putting weight on her
ankle was like dipping it into fire.

Richard tilted his head. "Well enough to reach the
safety of the next village before nightfall?"

"That would depend on how many leagues to the
village."

"Too many if you cannot keep the mule moving
at a quick pace." He glanced down at her hands.
"Your hands bleed. Can you hold the rope se-
curely?"

She'd forgotten her hands. Not until he'd called her
attention to them did she notice the blood smeared on
Philip's tunic.

"Mother?" Philip said, concerned.

"My hands are but lightly scraped. Truly, my lord,
there is no need—"

"Walk to me," he ordered.

His tone brooked no disobedience. About her stood
a troop of men, Wilmont soldiers, waiting to see if
she would defy their lord. Richard was giving her no
choice but to accept his challenge.

Six steps would bring her to within Richard's
reach. Surely she could complete three or four. The
sooner done, the sooner Richard of Wilmont would
be on his way.

She handed the rope to Philip and gently pushed
her son aside. The first steps were tolerable, the third
step nearly brought her to her knees. Sweat broke out
on her forehead. Her leg trembled. She stood still.

Lucinda expected to see triumph in Richard's expression. To her surprise, she saw admiration.

"A gallant effort, Lucinda," he said, then signaled the wagon's driver to come forward.

She couldn't accept his offer. The longer she stayed in his company, the more risk was involved. She began to utter a protest. He stopped her with a forefinger to her lips. A soft touch. A spark of heat. A devastatingly effective maneuver that stole her words. Shocked, she stood still, unable to move even if she could have.

He frowned, looking intently at his finger on her parted lips. Very slowly, gently, he stroked to the corner of her mouth and across her cheek before he blinked and drew his hand back.

"I understand your reluctance to travel with a troop of men," he said. "I swear on my honor that you need not fear for yourself or your son while in our company. We will see you safely to wherever it is you wish to go."

He thought she feared as any woman would fear. Richard didn't fully understand at all, but she no longer had the strength to argue, didn't possess the physical ability to fight. Her whole body shook from the effort of having walked three measly steps. It took a fair amount of effort to hold back her tears. She nodded her surrender.

He offered his arm for support. Chain mail met her touch, but beneath the cold metal lay strength and warmth. She was careful to keep her bloody palms from wetting his hauberk.

"Philip, bring that beast over here and we will tie him to the wagon," Richard ordered.

The wagon driver pulled up within inches of where they stood. Without warning, Richard's hands encircled her waist. Instinctively, she grasped his shoulders. He lifted her up, effortlessly, until she hovered a few inches from the ground.

She stared straight into his green eyes, his wondrous green eyes. Flecks of gold shimmered within their depths.

He set her down on the wagon bed.

"Such beautiful eyes," he said. "I do not think I have ever seen their like before. Like violets they are."

Only a true dolt would respond to such flattery, but she'd been deprived of compliments for so long her vanity got the best of her.

"Not so very uncommon, my lord."

"Rarer than you might imagine."

Richard seemed to realize at the same time she did that they hadn't let go of one another and were staring into each other's eyes like moonstruck lovers. He let go and backed a step.

He crossed his arms again and looked down at her feet dangling over the wagon bed. "Do you think it broken?"

"Not likely," she answered truthfully. "Had it broke, I could not walk on it at all."

"Should we bind it?"

"Nay. My boot holds it fast. If I took my boot off, I might not get it back on my foot again."

He looked over his shoulder and smiled. "Philip and that mule do not get on well."

Poor Philip. He pulled on the lead rope with all of his might but the mule wouldn't budge. Lucinda's frustration bubbled up.

"More than once I have taken a switch to the beast to get him to move."

"You have come far with him?"

"Too many leagues."

"How many yet to go?"

She didn't know, because she didn't know where she would call her journey to a halt.

"Too many. I thank you for your kindness, my lord. Mayhap you could stop at the next abbey. I could beg hospitality from the monks for a few days while my ankle mends, then Philip and I can be on our way again."

Richard nodded. "We shall be in Westminster day after next. I know the abbot well. You will receive good care there." Then he turned and headed toward Philip.

The abbey at Westminster? She hadn't known she was that close!

Granted, she'd thought to go to Westminster, but now that it was close at hand, she must make her decision. The thought of going to court still didn't fully appeal, but her options were running out.

Nor did she wish to spend two days in the company of Richard of Wilmont. Thus far, he'd been kind to a woman he thought a peasant, but that would change if he learned she was Basil's widow.

For all Basil had hated every Wilmont male, Lucinda had to admire Richard. Merciful heaven, she was even physically attracted to the man. How very odd. This man who was her enemy had touched her, but her stomach hadn't churned in revulsion.

Who is she? Richard wondered again, as he had for most of the day and into the evening.

Standing in the open flap of his tent, he could see Lucinda sitting just outside the brightness of the campfire, with her back against a tree and her foot propped on a rolled blanket. Philip sat nearby, as did

Edric, the captain of his guard, who seemed to have appointed himself the protector of the woman and boy.

Lucinda and Philip weren't peasants, though they were garbed in peasant clothing. He'd seen through the ruse within moments of rescuing Philip. Hoping to calm the boy, Richard had spoken comforting words to Philip in peasant English. Philip had responded in kind, but as he'd become more excited while relating his tale, the faint lilt of Norman French became more pronounced. The longer the boy talked, the more Richard became convinced that the boy's first language wasn't English.

The names Lucinda and Philip weren't common names among peasants. If he were right, if these two had ties to Norman nobility, then why were they on the road with no escort, disguised as peasants? Where was her husband, the boy's father? Or their male guardian?

'Twas really none of his affair. Lucinda must have her reasons, and he had no wish to become involved in her life. His offer of an escort was simply a kindness extended to a woman in need, no more.

A beautiful woman.

Raven hair, woven into a single plait, hung low and shining against her gray gown. Her features were sharp, but not harsh. The tilt of her chin and cool set of her mouth warned a man to expect no warmth from her, but her husky, honey-warm voice beckoned a man to search for her heat.

He shouldn't have touched her. Then he wouldn't know that her lips were warm, her cheek soft, her waist slim, her hands gentle. He'd been on his horse at the head of the company, she in the wagon at the very end of the line, and he'd been achingly aware of her the whole time. He wouldn't now want her if he hadn't touched her.

Richard took a deep breath and glanced about the campsite. His men had eaten and would soon make up their sleeping pallets or take their turn at guard duty. Tomorrow would bring another long day on the road. If he hoped to join Stephen at court day after next, his company could waste no time.

In typical fashion, Stephen had rushed from Wilmont with little preparation, leaving Richard to haul chests of clothing, extra food and drink and Wilmont's gifts to the princess. Likely, Stephen now enjoyed the luxury and freedom of having Wilmont's chambers in Westminster Palace all to himself. Richard didn't doubt that Stephen had found a willing wench—or noble lady—to share his bed.

Richard looked at Lucinda. In his place, Stephen wouldn't hesitate to invite Lucinda into his tent to share his pallet of furs. He wouldn't care what his men thought, or that she had a small son curled up at her side, or that her ankle pained her. Or that she might have a husband. Stephen would note only that his loins grew heavy with desire, and that the woman seemed to share the pull of physical attraction.

So why do I hesitate?

Lucinda looked at him then. She studied him, her violet eyes drawing him in, inviting him to linger and learn her secrets.

If he learned her secrets, she might learn his.

He acknowledged her with a slight nod, then stepped back and closed the tent flap.

Chapter Three

"He is truly wondrous," Philip said.

"That he is," Richard agreed, giving a silver disk on the horse's bridle a last buff with the sleeve of his silver-trimmed, black silk tunic. On this last morning of his journey, he'd made a considerable effort to ensure his entrance into Westminster would be impressive.

Satisfied with the horse's appearance, and his own, Richard gave the destrier a pat on his gleaming black neck.

"Has he a name?" Philip asked.

"Odin."

When another question didn't immediately follow, Richard looked down. Philip stood unusually still for a boy of his age, his hands clasped behind his back, his bottom lip sucked in, pure awe on his face. The boy yearned to touch the horse, just as Richard, as a child of about the same age, had once stood beside his father admiring one of the beasts, wishing the same wish, wary of getting too near the horse's hooves.

Richard put his hands out in invitation. The boy

hesitated but couldn't resist. Philip put one arm around Richard's neck and with the other reached out to stroke Odin's neck. Sheer delight beamed from Philip's face.

"Odin is an odd name," Philip said.

"Have you never heard of Odin, the Viking god of war?"

Philip's small brow scrunched. "There is another god besides God?"

"So the Vikings believe. They worship many gods."

"Who are Vikings?"

Every Norman's heritage was ripe with Viking ancestry. Before the Normans had conquered England, the Vikings had made many raids on English soil. Every noble or peasant child should have heard of the Vikings.

"The Vikings are warriors who believe the only honorable death is to die in battle, so they can go to Valhalla, their vision of heaven."

Philip absorbed that piece of information, then asked, "You are a warrior?"

"Aye."

"Are you a Viking?"

"I have some Viking blood in my veins."

As do you, probably more than I, Richard wanted to add, but didn't.

Over the past two days he'd watched Lucinda and Philip closely and become more convinced that both were Norman. For some reason, Lucinda wanted all and sundry to believe that she and her son were English. It seemed foolish to Richard, for anyone who took the time to study them would see through the ruse just as he had.

Lucinda was also overprotective of Philip. She rarely allowed the boy to wander far from her side, and never out of her sight. Richard looked around and, as if his thoughts had called her, Lucinda was walking toward him. Her ankle had improved, though she yet walked gingerly and with a limp.

"Do you wish to die in battle?" Philip asked, his concern over the possibility seeping into the question.

Richard had once come within a gnat's breath of dying from a battle wound, and preferred not to repeat the experience.

"'Tis my wish to live a very long life and die peacefully in my bed," he assured the boy.

Philip laid his head on Richard's shoulder and whispered, "That is how Oscar and Hetty died. They got sick and went to sleep and never woke up."

A multitude of questions begged answers, but the boy didn't need questions now. He needed comfort.

Richard wasn't sure how to react to Philip's sorrow, how to comfort a hurt of the heart. True, he'd once held Daymon to stop the flow of tears when his nephew had scraped both hands and knees during a nasty fall. Richard knew he would do almost anything for Daymon.

The bond Richard had formed with Daymon was a natural one. Bastards both—English and Norman both—Richard had tried to prepare his nephew to one day cope with the attitudes of people outside of the family circle. Thankfully, Daymon's life would be less harsh than Richard's had been, simply because Ardith accepted Daymon as Gerard's son, and loved and nurtured him as she did her own son.

Philip and Daymon were of an age, and a hurt was a hurt.

Richard tightened his hold on Philip and lowered his head until his cheek touched Philip's brow.

What could he say to a boy who had obviously lost two people whom he cared about, Hetty and Oscar, to sickness? Recently? Were they friends, perhaps? Or a brother and sister? Maybe that was why Lucinda fairly hovered over the child. Maybe that was why these two were on the road, escaping a sickness that had ravaged their family.

Richard groped for words. "Their death made you sad," he finally commented.

Philip nodded.

"Does it help to know that Oscar and Hetty are now in a better place, in heaven with God?"

"Nay."

The boy's honesty echoed Richard's beliefs. In truth, he'd never been able to take comfort in religion. Oh, he believed in God and Christ, but Ursula had always made sure that he knew that God had no use for bastards.

Lucinda finally made her way to where he stood.

"Philip, you must not disturb his lordship this morn. He has preparations to see to before we leave," she said in that lyrical, husky voice that invoked visions of disheveled fur coverlets and the heady scent of coupling.

Philip stiffened at his mother's rebuke. Richard put a hand on the boy's back, holding the child still.

"He does not disturb me," Richard told her. "When Philip came to admire the horse, 'twas my notion to pick him up so he could touch Odin."

She glanced at the horse. "I see."

Lucinda was nervous, upset. Richard saw no outward sign of it. She neither fussed with her clothing

nor wrung her hands. Her voice didn't shake. Somehow, though, he knew without a doubt that she didn't
like Philip's nearness to the horse, liked even less that
Philip was in Richard's arms.

"You are generous, my lord, with your time and
patience for a small boy," she said. "I imagine Philip
asked all manner of questions."

"Not so many," Richard said.

"That is good," she said, her relief clear. "Edric
tells me we are almost ready to leave. Philip and I
must take our place in the wagon." Then she took a
slightly deeper breath. "I understand your wagon
driver will take Philip and me to Westminster Abbey.
Since we shall probably not see you again, my lord,
I would give you my thanks now for your assistance."

The arrangement made sense. He simply didn't like
it, though he couldn't for the life of him explain why.

"I had thought to ask Philip if he wished to ride
with me for a while on Odin," he heard himself say,
though he hadn't thought of asking Philip any such
thing. "What say you, lad?"

Philip's head popped up. "Oh, aye!" he said, then
turned to ask Lucinda, "May I, Mother? May I
please?"

Sensing that Lucinda was about to withhold permission, Richard tossed Philip up into the saddle.

"Of course, you may," he said. "Your mother will
be glad for some peace this fine morn, will you not,
Lucinda?"

Lucinda knew she would have no peace for the
entire ride into Westminster, not if Philip rode and
talked with Richard of Wilmont.

For the past two days she'd lived in fear that Philip

would say something to alert Richard to his identity. She'd kept Philip close, cautioned him to say nothing to Richard or his soldiers of where they had come from or where they were going. Philip didn't understand why, but she couldn't explain without either lying or telling him about his father and the hatred that existed between Northbryre and Wilmont. She'd succeeded in keeping Philip within earshot until this morning when his awe of the destrier had drawn him from her side.

She nearly panicked when Richard had hefted Philip into his arms. Seeing her son in Richard's grasp caused her stomach to churn and her heart to constrict. Thus far, Richard had been friendly and gentle with Philip, to the point of giving him a brief hug. If Richard learned that Philip was the son of Basil, the man who'd caused Wilmont no end of suffering, surely his gentleness would vanish.

Richard already suspected that she and Philip weren't who they pretended to be. Time and again she'd caught him staring intently at either her or Philip, a puzzled look on his face, as if he'd seen them before and was trying to place where.

At other times Richard's scrutiny had been for her alone, as a man looks at a woman. It always sent a tingle up her spine. Thankfully, he'd never acted on his obvious interest.

Right now he stood stoic, waiting for her to capitulate over the matter of where Philip would complete the final leagues of their journey.

Philip looked utterly joyous sitting atop the destrier. She couldn't very well deny a lord's wishes without his questioning a peasant's audacity. Resigned, she put a hand on Philip's leg.

"You must behave for his lordship," she said. "Do nothing to startle the horse. Nor will you bore Lord Richard with your chatter. Understood?"

Philip looked down at her from the great height— too high, in a mother's opinion, for a little boy to be off the ground. His joyous expression faded to thoughtfulness.

"Aye, Mother," he said, then glanced at Richard. "Mayhap his lordship will do all the talking. I would like to know more of the Vikings."

Richard chuckled. "Viking tales it is, lad."

Lucinda thought it a safe subject of conversation, with one reservation. "A mother would hope that the tales are not too gruesome."

Richard looked comically offended. "One cannot tell a proper Viking tale without some blood and gore."

She crossed her arms. "Mayhap not, but one could tell the tales without ensuring bad dreams."

He shrugged a shoulder. "One could try, but one gives no assurances, my lady." With a grace that belied his size, Richard swung up into the saddle behind Philip.

My lady.

Had the honorific been a slip of the tongue, or a warning that her disguise hadn't fooled him for long?

Having related every Viking tale in his memory, Richard considered returning Philip to his mother. The boy made for fine company, but Richard didn't want to enter Westminster with a peasant-clad boy on his lap. This visit to court was too important to risk that some noble would notice his unusual riding companion and start speculation on the boy's identity.

Too, Richard hadn't found a natural opportunity to explore the child's past. 'Twas likely knavish to wrest the tale from an unsuspecting child, but Richard knew he would get no answers from the mother.

"I have told you many a tale of Vikings, Philip," Richard said. "'Tis now your turn to tell me a tale."

Philip laughed. "All the tales I know of Vikings are those you have just told me! I know no others."

"Have you a tale of adventures, then? I know you had an adventure on your mule two days past. Surely, you have had others."

Philip was silent for several heartbeats, then said, "I caught a frog once."

"Did you? A big frog?" he asked, having a good idea of the tale's outcome. He'd caught a frog or two during his childhood, and done his utmost to frighten at least one kitchen wench with the slimy creature before being forced to release it back into the pond.

Philip didn't disappoint. He exaggerated the size of his prey, told of soaking his shoes and tunic in the pond and, upon successful stalk and capture, carrying the frog home.

"I would wager your mother forbade the beast in the hut."

"She did," Philip said on a sigh. "Mother did not think Hetty and Oscar would like a frog hopping about their feet. She told me to take the frog back to the pond."

"Of course, you obeyed her," Richard said, his tone conveying that he knew Philip probably hadn't. He smiled when Philip squirmed. "Never tell me you took it into the hut!"

Philip leaned over and looked back at the men-at-arms and wagons following them.

Richard chided. "Your mother cannot hear you, Philip. She is too far away."

Philip straightened, but tilted his head back so he could look up at Richard. "I did!" he said, grinning. "For the whole of an afternoon I kept the frog hidden in a bucket." He giggled. "Then Mother grabbed the bucket to fetch water and the frog jumped out. She screeched like a banshee!"

He couldn't imagine the cool-headed, reserved Lucinda screeching even if frightened, but kept the thought to himself.

Instead, he suggested, "Mayhap you should have asked your father if you could keep the frog."

Philip shook his head. "I have no father. He died when I was so little that I do not remember him."

Richard noted the lack of sorrow in Philip's statement, just as Richard felt no sorrow when the subject of his mother, who'd died giving him birth, arose.

Lucinda must be a widow of several years, then.

"This Oscar you spoke of, mayhap he would have let you keep the frog."

"Not Oscar. He never went against Mother's wishes. Nor did Hetty. I wish…"

True grief had crept into the boy's tone. Richard gave Philip a gentle squeeze. "What do you wish?"

"I wish they had not been so old, because then they might have survived the sickness in the village. Mother tried every potion she knew of to help them get well, but none worked."

"Were you sick, or your mother?"

"Nay." Philip sighed. "Mother thought it best that we leave the village before we got sick, too. She looks for a new home for us, but has not found one that suits her. I hope she finds one she likes very soon. I tire of riding on that mule.''

He knew of a suitable home for mother and child. His manor, Collinwood. The people had suffered greatly under the lordship of Basil of Northbryre. Since being awarded the land, Richard had done his best to improve his vassals' lot. If Lucinda possessed skill at caring for the sick, his vassals would accept her gladly.

He needed to talk to Lucinda about the prospect, but first he must find Stephen and begin his task of gathering information for Gerard. He wouldn't need to inquire about which heiresses would be granted in marriage. Stephen would already know.

Lucinda's ankle had healed somewhat, but he suspected the monks at Westminster Abbey would advise her to rest well before resuming her hunt for a home. He could visit her—and Philip, of course—at the abbey on the morrow.

The only problem with this whole plan of taking her home with him lay in his attraction to Lucinda. He had but to look at her to feel a tug on his innards.

However, resisting the temptation of her would be easier if he took a wife. An heiress. A noblewoman to share his bed to assuage his physical needs and bear his children. An heiress who brought with her enough wealth to raise his status and pay for the betterment of his lands.

For those reasons alone, he could resist temptation.

Richard reined Odin to a halt. He lowered Philip to the road with an order to return to his mother.

"'Tis not broken,'' the red-faced monk declared.

Lucinda hid her amusement at the monk's embarrassment. Brother Ambrose had touched her hose-covered ankle as briefly as was possible to confirm the wholeness of her bones.

"You must rest your foot until the swelling is gone," he prescribed as a cure. "I will have space prepared for you in the ladies' court."

"And my son?" Lucinda asked.

The monk glanced over at Philip, who was intrigued by the array of jars neatly arranged on shelves in the abbey's infirmary.

"He is young enough to stay with you, I would think, if we can arrange for a cell for the two of you. However, sleeping space is dear. The child may have to sleep on a pallet in the dormitory."

That didn't surprise her in the least. The streets of Westminster overflowed with people, making passage slow, and therefore dangerous. At Richard's order, half of his soldiers had surrounded the wagon that carried her and Philip. The escort hadn't left her until she, Philip and the mule had been safely inside the abbey. A few of the nobles streaming to Westminster would likely take refuge at the abbey until finding other lodgings.

Lucinda struggled to put on her boot.

She'd feared recognition by Richard, but that fear had deepened upon entering Westminster. Now, in close quarters to members of the court and their families, someone was sure to recognize her as Lucinda of Northbryre.

Thus far she hadn't seen a familiar face. To her knowledge, no one had turned to stare at her, marking her presence. Which shouldn't surprise her. Few nobles would deign to notice a peasant woman with a small boy in tow. Not even Richard had given them a second glance until that unruly mule took flight with Philip on its back.

Then Richard had taken too much notice. He looked too hard, and too long. She'd taken far too much pleasure in feeling the heat in his gaze. He'd despoiled her belief that she would never again wish to be held, much less touched by a man. After all she'd suffered from Basil, she'd thought herself cured of wanting any man. Richard of Wilmont had proved her wrong with merely a lustful look and a gentle touch.

After the morrow, Richard would not look on her in that way again, for on the morrow he would learn the truth of her identity. On the morrow, she would petition King Henry for a protector for Philip.

By placing Philip within a noble house, under edict from King Henry to safeguard the boy, she could ensure Philip's safety from not only Basil's family but his enemies. Most notably Gerard of Wilmont—and his kin.

Her brush with Richard had emphasized the extent of her vulnerability. She possessed neither the physical might nor the power of wealth to protect Philip from anyone who wished him ill. Had some unscrupulous Norman come upon her on the road, she and Philip would have been in deep trouble.

"Brother Ambrose, I am willing to pay for our sleeping space. Would the donation of my mule to the abbey cover lodging and meals for two days?"

The monk rubbed his chin. "I should think the mule more than fair payment. I will ask the abbot."

After the monk left the infirmary, she patted the bench beside her. "Come sit, Philip."

Reluctantly, he left his study of the jars.

"Why did you give away Oscar's mule?" he asked.

"We shall not need the mule any longer. I think Oscar would approve of donating him to the monks."

"We will stay here, in Westminster?"

She shifted on the bench to better look down into her son's face. What she would propose affected him most of all, and she wanted to witness his honest opinion.

"You would like to own a destrier."

With a sharp nod of his head, he said, "Like Odin."

"What would you say if I told you I might arrange that? Not anytime soon, you understand, but when you are old enough to control such a beast."

His gray eyes went wide. "Truly? How?"

"By making you a ward of a nobleman."

Philip expression didn't change, not understanding. She'd never explained the ways of nobles to him. 'Twas her own fault that her son now had much to learn in a short time.

"The noble would be your protector. He would see to your training in the ways of the court and the skills of a knight. I thought to petition the king for a protector for you."

He thought that over for a moment, then said, "Then we would have a home. We would live in the lord's castle, and I could have a horse!"

No, not we—you.

Lucinda realized how little thought she'd given to where she would go if the king granted her petition. She swallowed the lump forming in her throat. She must see to Philip first without worrying about what would become of her.

Philip jumped up, his eyes shining with excitement. "Mayhap we could ask Lord Richard to be my protector!"

Naturally, Philip would think first of Richard of Wilmont, the only lord he knew, one who'd been kind to him.

"Nay, Philip. Not Richard."

Philip mustered his courage to argue, "But why not? Is not Richard a noble lord?"

She took her confused son's hands in hers. "He is, indeed, a noble lord, and was kind to us when we needed his aid," she said, giving Richard his due. "He is not, however, a suitable protector for you."

Philip pulled his hands away. He pouted. "I like him and I think he likes me. I do not see the harm in asking."

How to explain? She took a deep breath, hoping her words would be the right ones.

"Long ago, before you were born, your father made an enemy of Everart of Wilmont, Richard's father. Both Everart and your father are dead now, but I doubt Richard will ever forget the hatred that existed between the two families, or forgive your father for his treachery. Once Richard knows who your father was, I fear he will not like you anymore."

"My father fought with Lord Richard?"

Basil had damn near caused Richard's death. She nodded.

Philip was silent for a moment, then asked, "If I promised not to fight with Richard, would he like me then?"

So simple. So childlike. So impossible a solution.

"You must understand, Philip, your father was not a nice man. He inflicted great suffering on the family of Wilmont, and as fine a man as Richard is, we cannot expect him to ignore that you are his enemy's son."

Or that I was his enemy's wife.

"Never have you told me anything of my father. I do not even know his name," Philip accused.

"His name was Basil of Northbryre. I did not tell you of him because..." She faltered. She'd been about to tell her son a lie. She hadn't spoken to Philip about Basil, not to spare her son pain, but to spare herself. "...because I wished to forget that he existed. That was wrong of me. I should have told you of him, and I will. You have my promise."

Brother Ambrose returned. "You will be pleased to hear that private lodgings are available. The abbot sends his thanks for your kind gift. He will keep you in his prayers."

A fine sentiment. Likely she would need all of the divine intervention she could get over the next few days.

"Philip, see to your pack," she said, picking up her own bundle that contained her one unstained gown and a few coins.

The monk turned to lead them out of the room. Lucinda stopped him.

"Brother Ambrose, I have but one more request. I should like to have a message sent to the palace."

The monk's eyes widened. "A message?"

She ignored his incredulity. "To King Henry."

His eyes widened farther. "What is the message?"

"Lucinda of Northbryre wishes an audience with His Majesty."

The monk's jaw dropped. "Indeed."

"Can the message be delivered within the hour?"

He regained his poise. "Aye, my lady, I will see it done. Now, if you will follow me, I will show you to your lodgings."

Taking Philip's hand, Lucinda followed as bid, wondering if she'd given away the mule too soon. All of her plans depended upon the king's willingness to hear her petition, and upon how much, after three years, Henry still detested Basil.

If the king refused to see her or denied her petition, within two days she and Philip would again be searching for a hiding place, a refuge to call home.

Chapter Four

Richard leaned against one of the many marble pillars that supported the great arches of Westminster Hall. A large crowd had gathered with the vast room; voices and footsteps echoed off the vaulted ceiling.

He'd chosen this spot to best watch the comings and goings of nobles and peasants alike, noting in particular which men of power had arrived. Most notably absent was Emperor Henry V, to whom Princess Matilda would soon be betrothed. The emperor's delegation would seal the bargain and fetch the princess who, at the age of seven, was having a grand time flaunting her impending title of empress.

If King Henry of England took offense at the emperor's absence, Richard had no notion. He just hoped the king didn't take offense that Gerard had sent his own delegation—him and Stephen—in his stead.

Richard looked toward the dais where the king presided from his throne, searching for Stephen, who was supposed to be listening to the petitions presented to Henry. With so many people crowding the hall, however, 'twas impossible to detect Stephen's position.

Boredom had set in long ago. He'd seen those nobles whom he expected to see and exchanged greetings with the most staunch of Wilmont's allies. Likely, tongues were wagging among England's and Normandy's nobility about Gerard's absence—a situation Richard had already explained far too often this morning for comfort. He had yet to give Gerard's greetings and regrets to the king—a task he was hoping Stephen would fulfill.

While he observed the crowd, Richard's thoughts wandered to Lucinda and Philip, wondering how they fared at the abbey and if Lucinda could now walk without pain. He almost hoped not, for then she wouldn't leave the abbey before he spoke to her about settling at Collinwood.

But before he asked Lucinda to become a part of his world, for his own protection, and that of his people he needed to know the secret she harbored behind her startling violet eyes. He needed to know why a Norman noblewoman trekked the road garbed as an English peasant. Surely, she answered to some male relative—a father or brother, or other male head of her family or her dead husband's. Every woman did.

Was she running away? Had she been exiled? And why?

Richard was about to bolt the hall in favor of the abbey when he saw Stephen coming toward him, perturbed.

"'Tis not a good day to ask the king for favor," Stephen declared. "He hears petition after petition and grants few."

"Not a good day, then, to ask for the hand of a fair heiress. Have you decided on one?"

"I have three I would consider. You?"

Richard shrugged a shoulder. Though he knew he

should probably court at least one woman on Stephen's list of heiresses, not one name struck the mildest note of interest.

Stephen chided. "Richard, if you wish to better your holdings, you had best make yourself known to at least a few of the heiresses. Mayhap one will take a liking to your ugly face and ask for you!"

Richard smiled. "Mayhap I should let you choose for me. Judging from your notes on the list, you have studied all of their qualities, from fairness of face to the coin they bring."

"Ha! And have you blame me if her temperament is sour? Nay, brother, choose for yourself."

Richard chuckled, then asked, "Did you happen to tell Henry of Gerard's absence."

"Aye." Stephen sighed. "Another reason to delay asking for favors today. Henry accepted my explanation with little grace. He says he understands, but 'twas quite clear he is displeased."

An unhappy Henry was also a dangerous Henry. Today was not the day to begin an attempt to heal the rift between Gerard and the king, a cause near to Richard's heart. He disliked seeing the two men at odds with each other when they had been such great companions. For now, 'twas best to stay out of the king's sight and beyond his reach until his spirits lightened.

Richard decided he'd had enough of noble-watching for the day. "I am off for the abbey. Do try to stay out of trouble."

Stephen raised an eyebrow. "The abbey? Whatever for?"

"Mayhap I wish to confess my sins," Richard suggested.

"Hardly likely." Stephen knew him too well.

"I go to visit the woman and boy who traveled with us. I wish to see if they are well cared for."

Stephen crossed his arms. "How can they be less than well cared for in Westminster Abbey? This is the third time you have mentioned this woman since you arrived yesterday. I begin to suspect that something happened between the two of you during your journey."

"Nothing happened."

'Twas a small lie he told. In truth, nothing had happened beyond her riding in the wagon and a few, brief moments of conversation. That something *might* have happened if he'd given in to the attraction that simmered whenever he looked at Lucinda was none of Stephen's affair.

Stephen studied Richard for several moments before saying, "If you wish to bring the woman to Wilmont's chambers to warm your bed while we are here, I have no objection."

Richard felt a twinge of ire rise. "Not that I intend to do so, Stephen, but should I invite a woman to share my furs, I will not seek your permission!"

Stephen didn't comment. Someone or something near the door had captured his attention.

A woman. She stood inside the door, glancing about the hall as if confused, almost frightened of entering. Lucinda.

Her simple gown of green wool hugged her curves as softly and becomingly as silk. Under a sheer white veil, held in place by a silver circlet, her raven hair shimmered almost blue in the light of a nearby torch.

She held herself erect and poised. One had to look into her eyes to see her anxiety. She might be noble, but perhaps not accustomed to attending court. Mayhap he could ease her anxiety. Perhaps he could explain the protocol or help her find whatever or whomever she looked for.

Stephen said angrily, "Mayhap you should stay awhile, Richard. I fear we are about to witness some excitement. 'Tis good that Gerard is not here. He would roar the arches down."

"Why is that?"

"The woman in the green gown, coming into the hall. Do you recognize her?"

He'd just spent the past two days in Lucinda's company and had thought of her far too often since. Was thinking far too much of her now. But, alerted by Stephen's tone, Richard held his counsel.

"Should I know her?"

"Aye, I believe you should. I saw her only the once, and do not remember her name, but I believe she is the widow of Basil of Northbryre."

The kick to Richard's gut threatened to send bile up his throat. Richard swallowed hard. Hellfire! Was it possible he'd been strongly attracted to the widow of Wilmont's worst enemy?

"Lucinda." He supplied her name to Stephen. This time, the sound of it didn't seem musical.

Stephen nodded. "That is it. I heard that she and her son had escaped to Basil's lands in Normandy. I wonder what brings her back after all this time?"

Richard didn't care. He was too busy wondering where he should have known her from, if they had met before. Wondering how his character could be so flawed that he'd wished to couple with a woman who'd rutted with Basil of Northbryre.

On the road, if he'd known who she was, he'd have

let the mule run off with Philip, let Lucinda cope on her own.

She took a small step forward, then another. She didn't limp. Had she faked the injury to her ankle? Had she laughed behind her hand at his offer of assistance, at his gullibility?

Did she know his identity? Possibly. 'Twould explain much of her nervousness, her wish to keep Philip so close to her side.

Hellfire, he'd been such a fool!

"Come," Stephen said. "She heads for Henry."

Lucinda's first thought upon entering Westminster Hall was to bring Philip here to see the arched ceiling, the marble pillars and the elaborate throne. He would think the hall grand.

She'd left Philip at the abbey under the care of Brother Ambrose. The monk had relented to her son's plea to once again explore the infirmary, and wouldn't be content until he learned the name of each medicinal herb, the purpose of every balm, and the use of all the tonics in the place.

Philip knew that she'd left the abbey to see the king, and why, though he didn't yet realize the full extent of how her petition, if granted, would change his life. Lucinda had decided not to explain too fully, for now.

The king's anger at Basil's treachery must have cooled somewhat or he wouldn't have granted her an audience. That didn't mean he would also grant her petition.

Lucinda glanced about the hall, recognizing few faces. Her hopes that she could go unrecognized and without comment faded when a woman's eyes widened and she turned to a companion to whisper behind her hand. 'Twas too much to hope that the woman only commented on the shabby state of Lucinda's garments when compared to the rest of the silk-clad, jewel-bedecked nobles.

Lucinda focused on Henry during her long walk from the door to the dais. She wanted to get this over with. Only Henry's opinion and mood mattered, not the rest of the court's. With the words she would say to the king tumbling around in her head, she threaded her way through the crowd.

As she neared the dais she took slow, steady breaths to calm a sudden tremor, which she hoped no one noticed. For as much as she feared facing Henry, she also dreaded running into Richard.

Was he here in the hall? He would be angry when he learned her identity, of that she was sure. What form would his anger take?

She would deal with him when the time came. Now she must present herself to the king and hope his anger at her late husband's betrayal didn't overflow onto her son.

The crowd thickened as she neared the throne. Her nose wrinkled at the stench of too many bodies in too little space. Were these all petitioners, or merely listeners?

"We will grant your request, Gaylord," the king was saying. "You may hunt the woodland to the east of Hawkland for small game. You may not, however, take the king's deer. In return for the privilege, you will keep the forest free of poachers."

"My thanks, Sire," a man answered, bending into a low bow. "I will enforce the Forest Law with vigor."

As Gaylord turned to leave, a man approached the king and leaned down to whisper into Henry's ear. Henry nodded, then turned to motion to someone in the crowd.

"John," the king said. "Kester informs us that you wish judgment on a land dispute."

Kester. Though Lucinda had never met the man, she knew his place at court—advisor to the king. He held a sheet of parchment, which he consulted, then glanced about the room. Seeking the next petitioner?

She watched as the procedure was repeated, then, sure of her conjecture, approached Kester. He looked up from his list.

"I am Lucinda of...Northbryre," she said. "The king granted my request for an audience today."

Kester frowned. She could almost feel his spine stiffen. "The king has many to see today. Stand aside and wait your turn."

Lucinda bristled at his obvious disdain. But, watching him add her name to his list, she moved away, toward one of the hall's many supporting pillars. At the edge of her awareness she realized some people stared at her, some pointed fingers. She ignored them. She had a higher purpose than providing entertainment for the court.

Was Richard among those assembled? Would he come forward and make a spectacle of them both? She prayed not, and resisted looking for him. 'Twould be tempting fate.

She concentrated on the proceedings. As petitioner after petitioner presented his grievance or request to Henry, she noticed that several people had been placed ahead of her, and Henry was granting fewer and fewer requests.

Lucinda was about to remind Kester that she'd been waiting overlong when he moved to the king's side, whispered in Henry's ear, then looked straight at her. She took a deep breath, prayed for the strength to remain calm, and presented herself to King Henry before he could call out her name.

The king studied her with an unreadable expression on his face. She endured it, waiting for him to speak, as protocol demanded.

"Lucinda of Northbryre," he finally said, his voice flat. "We thought you had fled to Normandy."

A natural assumption for him to make. Most women in her situation—short of funds and with her husband in disgrace—would have fled to family.

"Nay, Majesty," she said, surprised at the steadiness in her voice. "I had no desire to return to either my family or Basil's. For my son's sake, I never left England."

"Who sheltered you?"

She heard a faint hint of anger in the king's voice, and was suddenly glad that Oscar and Hetty were beyond Henry's reach.

"An old peasant couple, who have recently gone to their heavenly reward," she answered.

"You ask us to believe that you have lived as a peasant these past three years?" His incredulity rang clear. The rest of the court doubted, too, judging from the twitter she heard around her.

"Aye, Majesty, I have."

He leaned back in his throne, obviously contemplating her revelation. "We must say we are displeased that you waited so long to come before us and beg our forgiveness."

Lucinda tamped down a flash of anger. Neither she

nor Philip had done anything wrong. Basil had plotted treason, not she. Saying so to Henry, however, would do her no good. She swallowed her pride—somewhat.

"Basil's disloyalty to his king was a difficult burden for me to bear. Given his treasonous actions, I realize you make a magnanimous gesture by allowing me into your royal presence to hear my petition. I humbly and gratefully thank you for your kindness, Majesty."

She hadn't begged forgiveness, but the king seemed pleased with her flattery. How odd that she had Basil to thank for telling her of the king's susceptibility.

"What petition?"

A bit more sure of how to go about asking favor from Henry, she chose her words with care.

"I seek a protector for Philip. I would have him raised in a noble house whose loyalty to the crown is unquestioned, that he might learn the ways of the court and earn his knighthood. Someday, God willing, Philip might then serve his king as a loyal and true subject."

"Ah, but will he, Sire?" came a male voice. "Basil's tainted blood flows in the boy, and surely blood will tell."

Lucinda glanced in the speaker's direction. A raven-haired man broke through the crowd. Immediately behind him strode Richard. Beyond all reason, she wanted to reach out to Richard, to give him some explanation of her actions on the road. To him she would have apologized for what he and his family had suffered at Basil's hand.

The raven-haired speaker was likely Stephen of Wilmont, the youngest of the three brothers. Now, not only must she convince the king of her plan's validity, but do so over Wilmont's objection.

"We do not recall asking your opinion," the king admonished Stephen.

Stephen bowed to Henry. "I beg your indulgence if I overstep, Sire, but I feel obligated to speak out. Wilmont endured much due to Basil's treachery. Richard is fortunate to have survived Basil's attempt to do murder. And even now, three years after their kidnapping, Gerard's wife and son suffer nightmares of their mistreatment at Basil's hands. Surely, Sire, you can understand my concern."

What kidnapping? What other horrors had Basil inflicted on those of Wilmont which she knew nothing about? What obscenities had he committed upon an innocent woman he deemed an enemy?

Was Stephen right? Would blood tell? Would Philip grow up to be just like his father, viciously cruel, simply because Basil had fathered him?

She refused to believe it.

"Majesty," she said, drawing the king's attention. "I know that those of Wilmont have sound reasons to hate Basil. Philip, however, was but three summers old when his father died, too young for Basil to have had a lasting influence on the boy. And my son also carries my blood, both noble and untainted. Would not the proper counsel of a stalwart protector prove the stronger influence on how Philip grows to manhood? Majesty," she continued, hating the plea in her voice but unable to help it, "must the sins of the father be held against the son?"

"Trust a woman to think so unsoundly," Stephen said. "Bad seed is bad seed, passed through the male line. Sire, if you will allow, I will arrange for Basil's widow and son to sail to Normandy. If she has not the coin to pay, I will."

Lucinda strongly objected. "If I return to my family, my father will send Philip to Basil's family to be raised. Philip will but learn the same lessons as Basil learned, those of cruelty and deceit. Majesty, I beg you not to sentence my son to the fate of his father."

"My offer stands, Sire," Stephen said.

Silence reigned. Henry hadn't said a word during her argument with Stephen. She had no idea to which side he leaned. The king looked hard at Stephen and Richard, then turned to Lucinda.

"If our memory serves us," the king said, "we recall that Basil had lands in Normandy, which should rightfully now belong to your son. Who would now control those lands?"

"I assume Basil's cousin, George."

"Ah...another noble of questionable loyalty and judgment. You did well to keep the boy from his influence." The king shifted on his throne. "So whoever we name protector must have the means to fight George, if necessary, to collect the rents due from the boy's lands, and thus the protector's reward for accepting Philip until the boy is of age."

She nodded, her hopes for a favorable judgment rising. The king seemed to understand her position and was leaning in her favor.

"We know of several men capable," the king continued. "Our concern is that given the added wealth, those men might also challenge Wilmont for control of Basil's former English lands, on the child's behalf. We want peace among our nobles, not petty wars. To our mind, the perfect protector would be Gerard of Wilmont."

The king *couldn't* give Philip over to Gerard of Wilmont! Before she could protest, Stephen spoke.

"Sire," he said softly. "'Twould be most unfair to inflict the boy on Gerard's family. Have they not suffered enough at the hands of Northbryre?"

The king leaned forward. "Who better to ensure that no war is waged against Wilmont than those of Wilmont? Frankly, Stephen, our next choice would be to give the pair to you! We will not, however, because you would likely abandon them."

The pair? Merciful heaven. The king meant to make *both* her and her son wards of Wilmont.

"Majesty," she said, "would you deliver us into the hands of a man whose hatred for Basil runs so very deep?"

"You brought your petition before us, Lucinda, and will now trust us to do what is best for not only you and your son, but for the kingdom."

Henry then turned to Richard. "You and this boy are both the victims of Basil's treachery. Through no fault of yours, you nearly lost your life. Through no fault of his, Philip is deprived of a great portion of his inheritance and is in need of guidance. He requires a protector, Richard. What say you?"

Richard stood as impenetrable and cold-faced as a stone wall. Richard, the bastard of Wilmont. She could think of few men less suitable—except Gerard.

"Sire," Richard said, his tone even, "I would suggest that you do the child a disservice, not because I am of Wilmont, but because of my mixed heritage and bastard birth."

The king frowned. "Come now, Richard. Surely you do not imply that a man of bastard birth is less worthy. Look to my own offspring. Do you deem them inferior due to their birth?''

"Of course not, Sire. Although I am sure that when the lady requested a protector, she had in mind a man of at least equal rank and birth as her son, if not higher."

The king stood, a sure sign that his patience was at an end. "The fate of this child rests with your decision, Richard of Wilmont. Either the boy and mother go with you, or they go to Gerard. I will have your answer in the morn." He turned to Kester. "Dismiss the other petitioners until after nooning on the morrow."

With a sweep of his royal robe, King Henry left the hall.

In complete shock, Lucinda voiced her thought aloud. "There must be another solution."

"Aye, there must," Richard said, his fists clenched at his sides, disdain etched onto his face. "When you return to the abbey, you might pray that we find one before morn!"

Chapter Five

"I am sorry, Richard," Stephen apologized again, as he had all during the long walk from the hall up to Wilmont's chambers in the palace. As well he should apologize. If only Stephen had kept his peace, and not drawn the king's attention to them.... Now they were in a sorry mess.

The long walk had shaved the sharpness from Richard's anger, but it hadn't yet cooled completely. He poured himself a goblet of wine and sank down in a chair.

"Stop apologizing for getting us into this fix and think of how to get us out," he told Stephen. "There must be some way to convince Henry of the folly he commits."

Richard glanced about the sitting room of Wilmont's chambers, remembering the turmoil during the last time he'd occupied these palace rooms. So much had happened in the three years since. They had thought themselves done with Basil and his ilk. Now the widow and boy were throwing his life into upheaval once more—as if Basil were reaching back from the grave to do further mischief.

Just as the king had forced Gerard into a strange betrothal with Ardith, now Henry wanted to toss Richard into an unholy relationship with Lucinda. The difference was Gerard had wanted Ardith; Richard did *not* want Lucinda.

He no longer struggled with desire for the woman. It had vanished the moment Stephen had revealed her identity.

"Mayhap we could find another noble to take the boy as his ward," Stephen suggested. "Someone acceptable to both the king and Gerard."

"Pray tell, who?" Richard asked, thinking of the king's strongest reason for giving Philip to one of Wilmont. "To which noble do we entrust the boy without fear of strife when the boy comes of age? Alliances change from day to day in this kingdom. Years hence, the protector might use the excuse of reclaiming Philip's heritage to come after *our* lands!"

Stephen sighed. "Mayhap we should send to Gerard for counsel."

Richard took a long swig of wine from his goblet. "There is not a horse in this kingdom with the speed and stamina necessary to travel from Westminster to Wilmont and back again before the morn. I fear, Stephen, we are on our own."

At the moment, he saw no other choice but to accept Philip's wardship. Compelling Gerard to take the boy would be like putting a knife in his brother's gullet and twisting it.

Gerard would be furious if forced to submit to the king's edict, to the point where his relationship with Henry might suffer permanent severance. Gerard wouldn't be pleased if Richard submitted either, but it would be the more palatable arrangement, especially if Henry truly intended to include the mother in the bargain.

Hellfire. What would he do with the pair? He'd once planned to take them home to Collinwood. Unfortunately, Collinwood had once belonged to Basil and the people vividly remembered their former lord's heavy oppression. They wouldn't look kindly on their new lord for bringing Basil's widow and child among them.

His tenants' trust had been hard earned. Many were still wary, as if waiting for the day when he would become as harsh and cruel as Basil. Bringing Lucinda and Philip to Collinwood might jeopardize their budding loyalty.

Mayhap he could take them to another of his holdings and just leave them there, visit occasionally to see how they fared. But then, could he fulfill his obligations to the boy from a distance?

"Mayhap not all is as bad as it now seems," Stephen said. "Depending upon how much in fees and rents the boy's lands in Normandy bring you, this wardship could be a boon."

Richard almost laughed. "And how do you suggest I go about collecting the fees from Basil's family without taking an army to Normandy?"

Stephen shrugged a shoulder. "If Henry signs an order instructing this George to pay the rents to you, the man really has little choice. Henry is also the Duke of Normandy, George's liege lord."

"His very absent, very faraway liege lord."

Stephen tossed his hands in the air. "Very well, Richard. I gave you the benefit of my counsel and you reject all of my ideas. 'Tis your turn to suggest an option."

Richard wished he could.

"I suppose I should seek out Lucinda, see if she has any ideas. I am sure she is thinking hard on the matter, too. She likes this edict no more than you or I."

Lucinda tossed her good gown into the sack, drew the rope and tied the knot.

"Are you ready, Philip?"

"I do not want to leave," he complained, again. "Brother Ambrose promised me a tour of the stables on the morn. Please, Mother, can we not stay until then?"

She would like to indulge the boy, and if she could think of a way to sway the king from his edict, she would. She'd asked for a protector and Henry had granted one, but he'd ignored Philip's best interests, or hers, in favor of his own.

"Nay, we cannot stay. Now hurry."

"Do we go to my protector's castle, with the horses?"

"The noble whom the king would give you to is not suitable, so we must continue our search for a nice village in which to settle."

How Henry could justify making Gerard of Wilmont Philip's protector astonished her. Gerard would surely hate the very idea of caring for the son of the man who'd kidnapped and abused his wife and son. As for Richard, the expression on his face upon hearing the king's edict had left no doubt of his feelings.

Abiding by Henry's decision was the least palatable of her options, especially if Henry truly intended to give Philip's protector authority over her, too. Running away might be the coward's way out, but rather a free coward than Wilmont's prisoner.

Philip groaned and pulled a long face, but he picked up his pack. "You gave away Oscar's mule. How will we carry everything? Where are we going?"

She had no notion of where they would go. For now, beyond the city limits and into the countryside would suffice. By the time anyone realized they were gone, she and Philip would be well out of reach.

"We will find somewhere to stay the night, mayhap another abbey," she said, then pulled, pushed, and cajoled Philip through the abbey's passageways.

She broke into the sunshine of the yard, turned the corner of the building nearest the road—and came chest-to-chest with Richard of Wilmont.

Lucinda stumbled and almost dropped her pack. Richard grabbed her upper arms to steady her.

His hands were large and warm, his grip firm but not hurtful. Even as she cursed her ill luck, her body heated to Richard's touch as it had on the road. 'Twas disconcerting, this thrill along her spine at the touch of a man, especially a man as large and powerful as Richard. She should be repulsed, as she'd been every time Basil had touched her. She should tremble with fear, not attraction!

He glanced down at her pack, then over at Philip. He didn't say anything, just raised a questioning eyebrow.

"I thought it best if Philip and I left," she said, hoping he would understand. She expected him to let her go and allow them to leave. He didn't.

"Where would you go?" he asked.

"Away. Far away."

"'Twould do no good to leave. Henry would order me to find you and bring you back."

"You could say you could not find us," she offered.

"Henry would know better."

She couldn't think while this close to Richard. She took a step back; he released his grip.

"Certes, you do not want us," she said, her thoughts becoming clearer. "I should think you would be relieved that we go our separate ways."

He crossed his arms. "You are correct, Lucinda. I do not like Henry's edict, but neither can I let you leave."

Lucinda felt a tug on her skirt. "Mother?"

She was certainly making a mess of her escape. Of course, if Richard hadn't happened along to waylay her, she and Philip would be well away by now. Or had he just happened along? Had he been coming to see her?

Richard bent down and grabbed Philip's pack. "Come," he said, placing a hand at her elbow. He gave a slight push in the direction of the palace. She stood firmly in place.

"Where do we go?"

"To Wilmont chambers. 'Tis private there so we can talk. There must be some way to solve this dilemma without putting any of us at risk."

"Such as?"

"I do not know yet, but putting you and the boy in jeopardy is not an answer."

Richard watched Lucinda's ire melt into resignation. If forced to, he'd have dragged her kicking and screaming to the palace. He couldn't let her flee, no matter how much she wanted to leave and he wanted to let her go. Henry would be furious, and Wilmont's standing at court couldn't sustain another blow without suffering severe damage.

When next Richard pushed at her elbow, Lucinda turned and started toward the palace. Philip silently followed in their wake.

Richard really couldn't blame Lucinda for attempting an escape. In her position, about to be placed under control of one whom she considered an enemy, he might have tried the same thing. Then why was he angry that she tried to leave? It made no sense, but then all his reactions to Lucinda made no sense.

He'd thought all desire for her dead—until the moment he touched her again, until he'd stared into the depths of her violet eyes and found determination mixed with fear.

Richard ushered them into Wilmont's chambers and tossed Philip's pack in the corner near the brazier. Stephen had left for who knew where. Lucinda and Philip stood in the doorway, but neither seemed sure of what to do next.

"Sit," he ordered, indicating a chair with a wave of his hand. Lucinda obeyed, if slowly, then put down her pack and lifted Philip onto her lap.

Her apprehension was palpable and probably natural, given the situation. Still, it fueled his anger. What the devil did she think he would do to her? Or to the boy? He wasn't some ogre who would physically harm either of them. Surely, during the days they'd already spent together she'd learned something of his nature.

He might yell, occasionally, and had been known to throw a cup or two across the room, at times. But he wouldn't hit Lucinda.

Nay, he wouldn't hit her, because every time his hand came in contact with any part of her body he wished to stroke, not strike. Wished to caress, not bruise. What the woman did to his innards was unsettling. And must come to a halt, for both of their sakes.

"Do you want to explain to Philip what is going on, or should I?" he asked.

With a flash of annoyance, she undertook the task. Philip sat silent, his gaze flickering from Richard to his mother to his hands as the story unfolded. She did so with halting, carefully chosen words, in simple terms that Philip could understand.

Richard noted that she didn't relate Stephen's angry words or the king's displeasure with Gerard, or her fear for Philip's life should he be returned to Basil's family in Normandy. She spared him most of the details that would cause fear, or even discomfort. Richard wondered if it was wise to protect the boy. Philip would need to know the whole of it, eventually. Mayhap, however, she was wise to let him absorb the situation a little at a time.

"Neither Richard nor I am pleased with the king's decision," she told her son. "I dare say Gerard would not be pleased either. That is why we were about to leave, to spare us all unpleasantness."

"They do not want us, do they, because my father fought with them."

Lucinda smiled wanly as she stroked her son's hair. "'Twas more than a simple fight, Philip. Your father tried to destroy Wilmont. He sought to have Gerard murdered, and Richard nearly died of wounds inflicted by your father's men."

"That is unlawful," Philip stated. "Did not the king punish him?"

"The king thought to, but your father escaped. Then he tried to get others to join a rebellion against Henry. That's when Basil sent me a message to remove you from the castle at Northbryre, because he knew you might be in danger."

Richard noted that she didn't include herself within Basil's concern, which shouldn't be surprising. Men of noble rank rarely cared for their wives, would be more concerned for the safety of a son, an heir.

Richard knew it foolish to add "lack of feeling for his wife" to the list of Basil's many sins, but he did. Basil was dead and, undoubtedly, burning in hell. For his multitude of sins, Basil now suffered mightily at the hands of a far harsher master than could be found on earth. Richard found the thought comforting.

"So we went to live with Oscar and Hetty, so we would be safe," Philip said.

Lucinda nodded.

Philip glanced again at Richard, then turned back to his mother. "Could we go home? Back to Northbryre?"

"Nay, Philip. Northbryre no longer exists. Remember when I told you that your father died in a fire? That fire was at Northbryre."

Richard wondered how much of the true story she knew. Aye, technically, Basil had died in the flames. Both Ardith and Gerard had contributed deeply to his death—Ardith had stabbed Basil when he'd tried to rape her, and Gerard hadn't made any attempt to rescue the wounded man from the flames. Few people knew the whole story, but there had been speculation.

Lucinda looked up at Richard. "I also heard that

the land on which Northbryre stood now belongs to Wilmont. True?''

''The king confiscated all of Basil's lands in England, then divided them between himself and Gerard. Of Gerard's portion, he kept Northbryre and gave the rest to Stephen and me.''

Her raised eyebrow revealed her surprise. Indeed, his brother's generosity surprised many.

Then she frowned. ''If we were to go with you, would we be living on Basil's former lands?''

''Aye, at Collinwood.''

She paled. The woman obviously knew of her husband's defilement of Collinwood, his cruelty toward the tenants. Richard almost felt sorry for her. Almost. She'd done nothing to thwart Basil's ruthlessness.

Richard would forever remember the day he first set eyes on Collinwood. He'd known that the manor was in a sorry state, but he hadn't been prepared for the haunted eyes of the people. Half-starved children. Men with no pride. Women without hope.

''The royal betrothal ceremony takes place in two days,'' he said. ''Be prepared to travel on the third.''

''You will accept Philip as your ward,'' she stated.

''You would rather go to Gerard?''

''Nay, but—''

''Henry gives us few options, Lucinda. The choice is between me and Gerard—unless we can contrive a miracle.''

Lucinda was about to say something when Philip yawned hugely. The boy laid his head on her shoulder, his eyes drooping with fatigue.

Richard ducked under the arch that led to the two bedchambers beyond the sitting room. He went into the master chamber and fetched a wolf pelt from the scarlet-draped bed. 'Twas really Gerard's bed, but available for his use when at the palace.

The bed, piled high with furs of wolf and bear, was the most comfortable he'd ever slept on. He'd even shared it a few times with a wench from the palace kitchens who'd taken a fancy to him—or to the down mattress. Not that it mattered which she truly preferred. She assuaged his needs and he asked nothing more.

'Twas far too easy to envision Lucinda snuggled down on the mattress, surrounded by fur. Her violet eyes shining with desire, her lips parted and wet and—

Hellfire. His lust was damn inconvenient, not to mention unwarranted and unwanted. He must somehow reassure both mother and son they would come to no harm while in his care. Yet here he stood, picturing Lucinda on her back with her legs spread and arms open. Beckoning him to her.

She would be horrified to know how his thoughts ran. Or would she? Of course she would!

Just as he was horrified. The woman was the widow of the man who'd ordered Gerard's murder, who'd run the people of Collinwood so far into despair and hunger that even after three years of his lordship they were wary.

And he was of Wilmont, the family who'd brought Basil to his downfall, and death. Who'd made it necessary for Lucinda to flee Northbryre with little more than the garments on her back and a babe in her arms.

Hatred would always exist between Wilmont and Northbryre—unless the boy could be swayed.

No miracle would happen to release him from this duty, though he intended to ask Henry to amend the edict. He would accept the boy as his ward, but not the mother. Surely, Henry would see the sense of his request.

Richard spun around and went back into the sitting room. He tossed the wolf pelt in a corner for Philip to use as a pallet to nap.

The child was but six, an amendable age. And truly, a cute little tyke. Perhaps, with education, persistence and discipline, the boy could be saved despite his lineage.

"Come forward, Philip."

Lucinda tightened her hold on her son.

As he'd feared—the mother sought to interfere. Philip's obedience to his lord was crucial to a proper wardship.

"Come forward, Philip," he repeated, more firmly.

Philip slipped from Lucinda's lap and came to stand before him. The child's eyes reflected no fear. Richard put his hand on Philip's shoulder.

"You understand I am now your protector, and you my ward?"

Philip nodded.

"As your lord, I will expect obedience and fealty. Do you know what those words mean?"

"I must do what you tell me to do, and..." He shrugged his small shoulders.

"You will promise to serve and be loyal to me, to not betray me, no matter the temptation."

Philip turned slightly, as if to look back at his mother for permission to make such a promise.

Richard held the boy still. "'Tis a matter between us, as lord and vassal. In return for your pledge, I will feed, clothe and shelter you until you reach your majority. I am an exacting master, but not a harsh one. What say you, Philip? Have I your oath?''

The boy stared at him hard for a moment, then asked, ''We would live with you, at Collinwood?''

We.

''If that is the king's will.'' 'Twasn't a lie. He hadn't yet asked Henry for release from that portion of the edict.

''And I can have a destrier, like Odin?''

Richard sighed inwardly. A boy Philip's age would likely sell his soul to the devil for a destrier. All Richard would have had to do was promise the boy a ride on Odin to gain his cooperation. Still, someday, Philip would learn the importance of an oath, and Richard wanted to seal the bond early.

''When you are grown, and if you earn the honor.''

Philip smiled. ''I promise.''

Richard pointed to the wolf pelt he'd fetched earlier. ''My first command as your new lord is for you to take a nap. While you sleep, I will see the king to seal this bargain.''

Philip needed no more urging to curl up on the fur.

Richard walked over to the chair where Lucinda sat. In nearly a whisper, he asked, ''If Henry had not included your wardship in the bargain, where would you have gone?''

''I had not decided. We were looking for a suitable town or village when you found us on the road.''

''Give the matter thought. I intend to ask Henry to amend the edict to abolish your wardship.''

''Generous of you, my lord.''

Her tone said she didn't truly think him generous, but at the moment, he didn't care. His greatest concern was that she not run off with Philip.

"I expect you to be here when I return. Be aware, madam, that if I must chase after you and the boy, I will not be as understanding and gentle as before."

Lucinda glanced at her son. "You cannot hold Philip to such an oath. He is too young to understand its meaning."

"Mayhap," Richard conceded. "However, you are not. So you decided. Do you teach him honor or treachery? 'Tis your choice, Lucinda."

Chapter Six

Barely an hour had passed when Richard, followed by Stephen, returned to the chamber. Lucinda didn't need to ask the outcome of the audience.

Richard, with discernible disgust, headed straight for the flagon and poured a goblet of wine. He spared a glance for Philip—still asleep on the fur Richard had provided—then sank into a chair and into a sulk.

Stephen's fury couldn't be mistaken. He stormed across the sitting room, entered the main bedchamber and slammed the door behind him.

Not many moments passed before Richard spoke.

"Henry is adamant that either Gerard or I accept Philip's wardship, which I accepted. You may or may not be pleased to know that Henry retains the legal right to your fate. He does, however, insist that you accompany Philip and remain with him for two years because of his tender age and the hardships he has already suffered."

Lucinda nearly blew a relieved breath, until she realized that after the two years passed, the king could order her to marry where he wished. But then, she was a widow—admittedly an out-of-favor and impoverished widow. The king had had the right to marry her off ever since Basil's death. If she hadn't kept her whereabouts secret for these past three years, he might have done so already.

Henry's decision not only took her fate out of Richard's hands, but also granted her a reprieve.

"I am pleased," she said. "Two years gives me time to somehow amass funds to pay the fine should I choose not to marry again. And I do not wish to marry again, ever. Once was quite enough."

Richard shrugged a shoulder, indicating his disinterest in her views on marriage. "Have you no dower lands from which to draw funds?"

"Nay," she said, hoping he would ask no more questions on that embarrassing subject. Basil had bought her from her father for a paltry sum.

"Then the only fees we need try to collect are those due from Philip's lands in Normandy."

"Aye."

"Stephen has offered to make the trip to Normandy. To whom does he go for an honest accounting? George?"

"He will get no honesty from any of that family. I assume, however, that Basil's cousin George collects those rents now due Philip."

Richard gave an aggrieved sigh. "'Tis the one time I wish Northbryre had not burned to the ground. I would give a hefty sum right now to have Basil's ledger of those lands and rents."

Lucinda pursed her lips. Dare she try to bargain with Richard? 'Twould be extortion, if one looked closely, but the trade she had in mind would solve one of her problems nicely, as well as one of his. He

would think ill of her, but he already held her in such
low esteem that it mattered naught.

Would he hold Philip accountable? She didn't think
so. Though Philip's oath of fealty to Richard wasn't
binding, Richard's oath to Philip carried the weight
of an overlord to his vassal. Too, Richard's treatment
of Philip indicated his intent to keep his relationship
with Philip separate from his dealings with her.

At least, she hoped she read his intentions correctly.

She gathered her courage and asked, "How hefty
a sum?"

His eyes narrowed. "You know from whom I can
get the information?"

"Aye, for a price."

He crossed his arms on the table and leaned forward. She squelched the urge to lean back. Under his
intense scrutiny, she fought to remain intent on the
conversation, not an easy task when staring into his
clear, green eyes. Those eyes could lead a weaker
woman astray. She'd once been a weaker woman. No
longer. She could ill afford to succumb.

"Would the information be accurate?"

She nodded.

"From whom?"

"Me."

"You jest!"

She shook her head. "'Twas I who kept Basil's
ledgers. He never bothered learning to read or cipher
and mistrusted clerics. I know what was due from
every holding, both in Normandy and England."

He leaned back in his chair, astonished. After a
long silence, he asked, "For what fee?"

"My bride's price," she stated. At his further surprise, she explained, "In two years' time I will again be vulnerable to Henry's whims. Should he decide to wed me off, you will pay the fine so I need not marry."

"I must feed and shelter you for two years. At the end of that time, I would prefer you marry so I can be rid of you."

Lucinda expected his objection, yet his bluntness stung. She held back the sharp retort about to slip from her tongue. During her years with Basil, she'd learned to choose words carefully when contesting a man's wishes.

"I like the king's edict no more than you. I can affirm that the rents from Philip's lands will more than cover your expenses for his keep. Nor do I plan to let you hold me hostage to your whims. I can earn my own keep."

"How?"

"I possess the same household skills as any other noblewoman. My knowledge of the healing arts is noteworthy. I can read and write both Latin and Norman French. I can cipher. I kept Basil's ledgers because he trusted no cleric. Surely, I must possess some skill of enough use to you to earn my meals and sleeping space."

He looked her over in a slow, assessing manner, from head to toe and back again, lewdly suggesting another method by which she might serve him.

Her face warmed with embarrassment. How dare he infer that she might earn her keep on her back? Why did her woman's places tingle at the thought of lying naked beneath Richard's powerful, well-formed body? 'Twas folly to wonder if coupling with Richard would be different from her horrible experience with her husband.

Men were men. They wanted one thing from a woman—a convenient body upon which to vent their lust, a warm place in which to thrust to appease a base urge.

Richard might be younger, more handsome and vigorous than Basil. But he was merely a man with a man's cravings, which she did not intend to satiate.

"My husband often remarked on my failings as a bedmate," she said in as stoic a voice as she could manage. "You will be highly disappointed, my lord, should you choose to test my skills as a whore."

"Your comely face and shape might lead some other man to overlook that you have rutted with Basil of Northbryre, or that you lack skill in the bedchamber. I assure you, however, that I am not such a man. Have no fear that I will ever be so desperate for companionship that I would take my most hated enemy's widow to my bed."

As she was telling herself that Richard's words were reassuring, Stephen came out of the bedchamber. He'd changed his sherte and dalmatica. The tuniclike garment of brilliant scarlet, trimmed with embroidery of gold thread, blared his noble rank.

"I am off to evening meal," he told Richard, never acknowledging her presence. "Are you coming?"

Richard nodded at his brother. "I will join you shortly."

Stephen hurried out, as if he couldn't bear to breathe the same air as she. Richard downed the last of his wine before he rose from his chair.

"I will have food sent up for you and the boy."

"That is not necessary, my lord. Philip and I can eat at the abbey upon our return."

"I sent word to the abbey that you will not be returning. You and Philip will stay here in Wilmont chambers." He waved a hand at the arch. "Beyond and to the rear is my bedchamber. Take from my bed whatever pelts are necessary to make a pallet out here."

Lucinda fought panic. Noblewomen didn't reside within a man's chambers without a chaperon present. Her reputation—what little she had left—would be utterly destroyed!

"Surely you jest! Philip may stay, but you must allow me to return to the ladies' court in the abbey, as is proper."

"What I must do is ensure that the king's edict is obeyed. Therefore, I have placed a guard outside the door with orders that neither you nor the boy is allowed to leave."

Stunned, realizing that he intended to keep her confined as if she were his prisoner, she couldn't find the words to object as he continued.

"You will find parchment, quill and ink on the table in my chamber. Making a list of Philip's holdings should keep you busy until I return."

Then he was out the door.

Richard's coldness and utter dismissal of her concerns and wishes sent a chill down Lucinda's spine. Neither, she noted, had he agreed to her price in return for the list.

Lucinda opened the door, and true to Richard's word, a guard stood without. A large man with an unwavering stance and expression, he didn't seem vulnerable to any plea she might make for release.

Too, she'd seen how Richard's men obeyed his orders without question. She suspected that not one of them would disobey him no matter how prettily she begged.

She closed the door and leaned against it, taking a deep breath to calm her scattered thoughts and racing heart. She'd felt trapped before and dealt with it. Until now, she'd always managed to make the best of a bad situation. First during childhood with uncaring parents, then with a mean and unscrupulous husband. She could do so again while under Richard's care.

Briefly, her anger flared and she considered telling Richard that he could bloody well get his information elsewhere. Instead, she went to fetch the writing supplies.

His bedchamber proved austere. A bed, with a thick mat piled generously with pelts, surrounded by heavy draperies, stood against the far wall. No fire burned in the hearth. One chair, a small table, and a trunk—which she assumed contained his garments—completed the furnishings.

She fetched a pelt from the bed. Bear. Black and shiny and warm to the touch. 'Twould make a soft, comfortable pallet. She hugged it close, hoping its softness would soothe her trepidation. But the fur smelled of Richard, of the man who held her son's future in his hands. Who could break her in two if he wished. To whom she couldn't deny a strong physical attraction and still be truthful with herself.

She'd witnessed Richard's softer and nobler side while on the road. He could be gruff, but he could also smile. A cuff of his hand would send her flying across the room, but he had yet to touch her in anger.

So far, each time he'd laid hands on her, she'd felt not only his strength but his gentleness and warmth.

He valued honor and duty, and so would value honesty. If she gave it to him, would he return it in kind? Mayhap, when she gave him a full account of Philip's lands, he would see that eventually paying her bride's price wouldn't be a sacrifice when compared to what he was gaining. And mayhap, if he learned to trust her, or at least not hate her, the next two years might not be harsh.

And after that?

Lucinda returned to the sitting room and placed the writing supplies on the table before spreading the bear pelt near the hearth next to Philip. Her son slept the sleep of the innocent, without worry or nightmares. She pushed back the lock of his hair that always fell forward when he slept.

For now, she would see Philip settled, then worry about her own future.

Richard tried to force Lucinda out of his musings. But no matter how engaging the people around him at table, or how tasty the food, or how entertaining the jongleur, his thoughts wandered back to the woman he'd imprisoned in Wilmont chambers.

He'd placed a guard at the door, true, but not only to keep her from whisking her son away. Too many people had suffered under Basil of Northbryre and wouldn't hesitate to harm his widow and son in retribution. Lucinda might not be able to get out, but no one could get to her, either.

Stephen slid onto the empty bench on the opposite side of the trestle table. "I have learned much about this George. Indeed, he controls Basil's former lands in Normandy. He will be greatly surprised to learn that Lucinda and Philip are still alive. It seems Basil's family assumed that the pair died along with Basil. When do you wish me to leave for Normandy?''

Richard pushed aside a trencher of food he'd barely touched. ''The royal betrothal ceremony takes place on the morrow. Any time after that is fine.'' He locked his eyes on his impetuous brother's. ''Stephen, I thank you for taking on this task, but I want you to take great care. Do not rush into an encounter with George. If you find it prudent to inform the man of my claim on Philip's holdings by messenger, do so. Have you chosen the men you will take with you?''

Stephen waved a hand, brushing Richard's concerns aside. ''Aye, I have. You worry too much. I do not intend to incite a potentially lethal confrontation with George.'' Stephen grinned. ''In truth, I have the easier duty. 'Tis you who must inform Gerard. Will you send a messenger?''

In answer, Richard simply grunted, sending Stephen into gales of laughter.

Informing Gerard just might be the more onerous task. Gerard would *not* be pleased, but given the alternative, couldn't complain overmuch.

''When you leave for Normandy, I will head for Wilmont,'' Richard said. ''Gerard will rant and rave, but in the end, will be relieved he is spared Philip's wardship.''

And mayhap, Richard added silently, by accepting the duty with grace, King Henry's ire toward Gerard would ease. Not that Gerard would admit that he cared one way or the other.

Stephen's gaze drifted away, to somewhere over Richard's shoulder. His hand lightly touched Richard's arm. "There," Stephen said so softly that Richard strained to hear. "Look. The woman in the blue gown. Is she not a vision?"

Richard turned to look. "Aye," he said, noting her shining auburn hair and wide brown eyes. Her shape, lithe and supple, was clearly defined beneath shimmering, sky blue silk. She was beautiful, but his idea of a vision had changed lately. To his chagrin, he'd come to prefer raven black hair—and violet eyes—over all other colors. "Who is she?"

"Carolyn de Grasse," Stephen said, entranced. "Not only is she beautiful, she possess the voice of a lark."

One of the heiresses on Stephen's list. He knew his brother better than to think that only the woman's beauty attracted Stephen.

"And well landed," Richard said, realizing who her father was. "You aim high, Stephen."

Stephen nodded slightly, his eyes still on Carolyn. "She is her father's only heir. 'Tis rumored she seeks a husband who can protect her lands and give her strong, healthy sons to continue her family line. And I think she favors me."

"What about the father? Who does he favor?"

"He lies on his deathbed. Carolyn comes to court in his stead." Stephen tore his eyes from the object of his fascination. "The best part is that she is no simpering virgin. She has already buried two husbands."

"Two? How old is this woman?"

"Eight and twenty."

"Ancient."

"Well seasoned."

Suddenly remembering a snippet of gossip he'd

overheard, Richard leaned forward. "Is this also the woman who is suspected of poisoning her last husband?"

"Aye. 'Tis said she rid herself of him because he could not pleasure her. While I think her much too sweet a person to do away with anyone, if she did away with the man for such a reason, I have nothing to worry over. And I intend to prove it to her. Mark my words, Richard. I will bed her before I leave, and will pleasure her so thoroughly that she will weep for me until I return."

Stephen's utter audacity never failed to shock Richard, and warning Stephen to have a care would do absolutely no good. The most he could do to protect Stephen was to warn Gerard of their brother's intentions and let Gerard do some checking on the woman while Stephen was in Normandy.

Richard got up. "Before you become so entangled with this woman that you forget your duty, come up to our chambers. Mayhap Lucinda has written out the list of Basil's holdings by now."

"Go on ahead. After I arrange a tryst with the Lady Carolyn, I will join you. By the by, you should look at the list of available women again. This affair over Philip has brought you to the attention of several of the heiresses, and many look upon your actions with favor. You should not let the prospect of advancing your fortune lapse."

Richard strode toward Wilmont chambers, shaking his head. He knew of no one except Stephen who possessed the gall to simply inform a woman that he was taking her to bed and get away with it. Certainly not Richard.

Certainly not with the woman who he had once

considered bedding. *Lucinda.* Before he knew her identity. Before her request of the king had ruined his plans. Despite Stephen's beliefs, Richard doubted that any heiress would look far beyond his bastardy no matter how much they admired the stance he'd taken on his brother Gerard's behalf.

Likely, Stephen would bed his Carolyn, and aye, she would probably weep when he left her bower. Though Richard had shared a pallet with a few willing wenches—never so many as Stephen had—not one of them had wept. Not one would be bereft if she never coupled with him again.

Lack of practice led to lack of skill, both in the training yard and the bedchamber. He preferred the training yard where he was confident of his well-honed skills.

The guard stood at the door to the chamber, alert for trouble, as Richard expected.

"She is inside?" Richard asked.

"Aye, my lord," the man answered. "She peeked out once, saw me, then ducked back in again. Ain't seen or heard a peep from her since."

"Visitors?"

"Except for the servant who brought food, nary a one."

"Good. Go have your meal. I plan to remain here for the rest of the evening. You won't be needed again until nightfall. Edric will relieve you at midnight."

The guard bowed, then strode down the hall.

Richard opened the door to find Lucinda and Philip seated at the table, their trenchers before them. Both rose as he entered the room.

Lucinda looked the same as when he'd left. She'd

neither changed her gown nor fussed with her hair. Yet, somehow, she seemed more beautiful, more tempting. More the vision, the siren.

Desire flared hotter than ever before. His physical reaction to Lucinda was neither welcome nor logical. But he wanted her badly. To the point of pained loins.

Mayhap, if he had her just once…

In that thought lay disaster. Never, ever, would he couple with Basil of Northbryre's widow. Remembering who she was helped cool his ardor.

"Philip, take your trencher over to the hearth. I wish to speak with your mother," Richard told the boy.

It irked him that Philip looked to Lucinda, who nodded her permission. The boy needed to learn that his mother's opinions and wishes no longer mattered, only Richard's. The boy would learn, eventually, but for now all Richard required was the list of Basil's lands to give to Stephen and a good night's rest.

She waited to sit until after he took the chair Philip had vacated.

"Your list," she said simply, sliding two pieces of parchment across the table. "I made two, one for you to keep and one for you to send with Stephen."

Richard could barely believe what he was reading. Did King Henry have any notion of the fortune he'd placed in Richard's hands? Richard doubted Henry knew, or the king would have diverted some—probably most—into the royal treasury.

No longer did Richard need an heiress to expand his holdings. If the list proved true, marble from Caen's quarry would soon grace Collinwood's floors. His wine cellar would rival Gerard's. Grain and spices would flow to his doorstep.

But for all of the goods and services listed, 'twas the amounts of coin due that nearly made his hands shake. His coffers would fill to the point of bulging. Enough to purchase hide upon hide of land. Enough to equip his tenants with new plows and the oxen with which to pull them, and the arms necessary to defend his growing empire.

Enough to easily put a little aside to meet Lucinda's price.

All depended, of course, on George's cooperation. Even if he didn't comply, Richard reasoned, for this amount of wealth Gerard would provide an army to force George into submission, and Richard could pay back his brother out of the wealth won.

So calmly, as though she hadn't just handed him the keys to his future, she continued to eat. Her dainty fingers dipped into the trencher for a piece of meat slathered with heavy, molasses-laden gravy. She bit the morsel in half with pearl white teeth between rose-lush lips. He struggled to hold himself in place when she licked the gravy from her fingers.

"Does it meet with your expectations?" she asked, glancing at the parchment he held in a too tightly clenched hand.

"If reliable, aye," he answered, his voice too husky for his liking.

"'Tis a true accounting," she said. "You should warn Stephen that George might argue its validity, but I assure you that this is what is due."

"Why did you not go back to Normandy and claim this in your son's name?" he asked the question that had niggled at him from the beginning.

"I have no army with which to claim it," she said. Then her violet eyes clouded over. "Basil's relatives are not pleasant people. I feared for both my life and Philip's. A woman and small boy would have little chance against them.''

If George shared any of Basil's character—rather, lack of character—she'd been wise to hide from them.

''Stephen leaves for Normandy on the day after the morrow. We will leave then, too. Have you any belongings that need fetching from the abbey?''

''Nay. We have our packs.''

''The mule?''

''I gave the mule to the monks in payment for our shelter. I wish them joy of the beast.''

Philip sat near the hearth on his wolf pelt, greedily consuming the bread that had served as his trencher, as if it were his last meal. Richard noted the bear pelt. Lucinda was resigned, it seemed, to staying. Still, he would leave the guard in place.

He rose and headed for his bedchamber.

''My lord,'' she said, halting his steps. ''Do we have a bargain?''

For her bride's price.

''We do, if your accounting is honest.''

'''Tis complete. I would not cheat my son of his full inheritance when he comes of age.''

Which was probably why she'd made two copies of what made up Philip's inheritance. One for Stephen to give to George, and one to warn Richard that she would know if he cheated her son out of so much as a sou when Philip reached his majority.

''Then 'twould appear, Lucinda, that we have a bargain.''

Chapter Seven

The brothers looked splendid, Lucinda admitted. On this morning of the royal betrothal, Stephen again wore scarlet and gold. Richard wore black and silver—less pretentious but just as rich. The dark garments perfectly accented his blond hair and fair features, and drew attention to his green eyes.

After breaking fast, both would ride in the procession that would wind through the city's streets to give everyone a last look at the Princess Matilda.

Stephen was in a rush to be off. Richard lagged behind, giving Lucinda the impression that he wouldn't be overly upset if he missed the procession.

"I will have food and ale brought up," he said. "If you need aught else, inform the guard."

"Could we go down and watch the procession, my lord?" Philip asked, his excitement barely held in check.

Richard shook his head. "Nay. 'Tis far too dangerous down there for one so little." At Philip's fallen expression, he added, "If you wish to watch, pull my trunk to my bedchamber window. In truth, you will see more of the procession and the entertainments in the courtyard from far above the crowd.''

Philip's smile for Richard was adoring, as though Richard had arranged a special perch for Philip to watch. Lucinda wondered if Richard simply didn't want them down among the crowd because he still feared she would abscond with her son.

Stephen opened the door. Edric, the crusty old captain of the guard who'd shown such kindness to her and Philip on the road, stood without. It seemed unfair that Edric would miss all of the pomp because he was stuck inside the palace passageway.

''My lord, might Edric guard us from within the chambers?'' Lucinda asked.

''To what purpose?''

She brushed aside his misgivings, knowing it would take a fair amount of time, and many acts of honesty on her part, to earn his trust. ''I merely thought that Edric might also enjoy watching the procession.''

After a moment's hesitation, Richard turned to his guard. ''What say you, Edric?''

Edric bowed. ''I do as you command, my lord.''

''You may do as you wish, if you have a care. Should you decide to guard from within, do not let Lucinda talk you into anything foolish.''

Edric looked offended. ''They are not to leave the chamber, and none are allowed to enter but you and Lord Stephen. I would follow those orders from either within or without.''

Lucinda couldn't help but smile at Edric's impertinence.

Richard crossed his arms. ''Do you want to watch the procession or no?''

"I wouldn't mind seein' it, my lord. 'Tis said the princess will ride a cloud white horse, and wear a cloak of spun gold. These old eyes have never seen the like."

"Richard, we will be late," Stephen admonished.

Richard glanced from Philip, to her, then back to Edric. "Do as you wish, then. I will return after nooning."

Edric closed the door after the brothers and slid the bolt.

"My thanks for your kindness," Edric said stiffly.

She noticed the absence of an honorific. 'Twas her due to be addressed properly, but just as she must have patience with Richard, she must tolerate—within bounds—slights from his men. Being the widow of a traitor, she wouldn't be easily accepted by anyone, especially those in service to Wilmont.

"How long before the procession begins?" she asked.

"Some time yet. Have you seen the entertainers in the courtyard? I hear there is to be a dancing bear."

"Truly?" Philip exclaimed, his eyes going wide.

Edric looked down at Philip with an expression akin to pity. "So I hear."

Philip dashed for the bedchamber and managed to push the trunk several inches without aid. Then Edric put his muscle behind it and shoved it beneath the window. Philip scrambled atop the trunk, leaning too far out of the window for a mother's comfort.

She put her hands on Philip's waist just as he lurched forward, his arm fully outstretched, pointing down and to the left. "Oh, look! There *is* a bear in the courtyard! And he dances on his hind legs!"

Richard may have kept them here for his own reasons, but Lucinda admitted he'd been right about their vantage point. She could see the entire courtyard, as well as the street in front of Westminster Hall, without hindrance.

With fascination nearly matching Philip's excitement she watched the bear whose black fur matched the pelt she'd slept on last night—on which she'd dreamed of Richard. No doubt because the pelt no longer smelled of bear but held Richard's scent. Human male.

She remembered little of the dream now. Just that Richard stood before her, desire in his eyes, and gently stroked her cheek. She woke aching in places where a widow should not ache, for a man she couldn't have and shouldn't want.

"Acrobats!" Philip cried, drawing her attention back to the courtyard.

Men walked on their hands and flipped their bodies in midair. They tumbled over and around each other in precisely coordinated patterns.

She sensed Edric move in behind her. She shifted slightly to give him a better view.

Musicians followed the acrobats. Then a scantily clad woman who walked on a rope strung high off the yard between two poles. Philip clapped and cheered for each in turn.

A knock sounded at the outer door. Edric drew his short sword from his belt.

"'Tis likely only servants come with our meal," she told her guard.

"Likely," he said, but didn't put his sword away as he left to answer the door. He returned moments later, bearing a platter of bread, cheese and cups of ale, which he put on the table.

He then grabbed a fistful of the back of Philip's tunic. "I will hold whilst you eat."

Lucinda felt a brief flash of panic, then chided herself. Edric's duty was to care for Philip. Richard's man would guard the child with his life, if necessary. She let go of Philip's waist and went over to the table.

She broke off a piece of cheese, shoved it into a chunk of bread and gave the food to Philip. He ate absently. She doubted that he knew who gave him the food or what he ate.

"Would you care to share our meal?" she asked Edric.

"I ate."

"Ale, then?"

His eyes narrowed with suspicion, as if she were offering poison. "Not whilst on duty."

She went back to the table and broke her fast, struggling with frustration. Dealing with these men of Wilmont would test her fortitude sorely. Edric's kindness easily succumbed to suspicion. Stephen refused to acknowledge her very existence. Richard looked for hidden motives behind her every word or action.

'Twould be a very long two years if she must watch her every word or action. But then, she'd been in their constant company for a mere day. She silently confessed her guilt of behaving in a similar manner, not trusting them much either.

Trumpets sounded.

"Mother, come look! The princess approaches!"

Lucinda moved to the window and looked down at the little girl atop a brilliant white horse. A cloak of shimmering gold draped her shoulders and flowed down to beyond her feet.

Matilda was but a year older than Philip. Her royal

bearing, however, contradicted her age. Here was not a little girl, but a princess bound for the Roman Empire to become its empress. And she knew it.

Behind Matilda rode three men. The emperor's delegation, Lucinda guessed. Then came the nobles of England and Normandy. Richard and Stephen rode in the third row—high placement in the procession, indeed.

"He is truly wondrous," Philip sighed.

"Sired and foaled of the finest of Wilmont stock," Edric said proudly.

They spoke of Odin. Lucinda stared at Richard. He rode straight-backed, his chin raised high and expression stoic. Truly wondrous. Odd that she felt a tingle of pride.

Richard looked up and acknowledged Philip's wild waving with a slight nod. His gaze locked with hers for an unsettling instant, then he turned his eyes forward again, a grim set to his mouth. He passed on, headed for Westminster Hall, where feasting and entertainment would go on far into the night, interrupted only by the betrothal ceremony this afternoon.

"His lordship does not care for pomp," she uttered the observation aloud.

"Nay, he does not. But he does what he must for the benefit of Wilmont," Edric said with an edge to his voice.

"I did not mean to insult him, Edric. I merely notice that he looks uncomfortable."

"Humph. He should not. For a bastard he has done right well. Richard can stand his ground with any of them without shame."

Philip spun around to ask Edric, "What's a bastard?"

"A child born out of wedlock," Edric answered.

"Is that a bad thing?"

Edric thought a moment before answering. "Depends on what the person does to rise above it."

"Am I a bastard?"

Philip's question took Lucinda by such surprise she sputtered, "N-nay."

"Oh," Philip said, disappointed.

A hint of a smile touched the corner of Edric's mouth. "You may not be a bastard, Philip, but you have another shortcoming to rise above. You could do worse than to model your life after Richard of Wilmont's. Now go eat."

Philip jumped down off the trunk to do Edric's bidding. Edric left the bedchamber. She heard the bolt slide and the door close behind him.

"What shortcoming?" Philip asked, spitting crumbs from talking with his mouth full of bread.

She sat down on Richard's bed, suddenly weary. "The shortcoming is not yours, but your father's. I have told you what a hateful man he was. Many will hold his faults against you."

"So I must rise above them, like Richard."

It seemed a daunting task for one so young. "Aye."

"Aught else?"

She ruffled his hair and smiled. "You must learn not to talk with your mouth full of bread. Look, you make a mess. Out to the sitting room with you."

Philip was napping when Richard returned to the chamber, looking overwarm and out of sorts.

"Are you all right?" escaped Lucinda's mouth before she thought better of asking. 'Twas not her place, nor should she care.

"I will be as soon as I get out of this garb. A servant is fetching ale for me. Let her in."

He disappeared into his bedchamber. No sooner had he done so than Lucinda opened the door to a serving wench bearing a large flagon and cups.

No guard stood outside the door. Surely, there must be one. She poked her head out into the passageway, looking right, then left. No guard? Was Richard finally coming to realize that she didn't intend to run?

She closed the door.

"I see no need for a guard while I am in the chamber," he said from the archway.

"I see," she said, her lightened spirit fading.

He'd traded his black silk for unadorned brown linen.

She poured ale into his cup. He drank it down like a man dying of thirst, then held it out for her to refill.

"I assume the betrothal ceremony is over," she said.

"'Tis not yet started. I left the hall when the closeness of the crowd became overbearing. No one will miss me."

Lucinda didn't agree. A man who'd ridden in the third tier of nobles in a royal procession would certainly be missed, and his lack of attendance commented upon.

"You should return to the hall for the ceremony, if naught else," she told him. "Should someone wish you ill, and whisper into the king's ear, you will suffer the consequences."

He groaned and laid his head back on his shoulders,

then stretched his neck from side to side. She knew how to ease his pain.

"Sit in the chair," she ordered, and to her amazement he gave no argument.

The moment she touched him, he tensed. So did she. Quicksilver heat rushed through her limbs and flared in her nether regions. Putting her hands on a man's neck should not affect her so. No matter how warm, how thick, how muscled.

She determinedly regained her composure. "I have not the hand's span or strength to strangle you. Be at ease."

Richard tried, but the feel of her fingers kneading at the knots in his neck was nearly too much to bear. Aye, the pain in his neck succumbed to her manipulations, but another pain seized him. He highly doubted she would be willing to massage that pain, too.

He'd left the hall when the crowd had closed in around him and the air grew stale and unbreathable. Coming back here had seemed such a good idea, but he'd not counted on Lucinda having her sweet way with his neck.

Her thumb pushed into the worst of the knots. His groan of undiluted pleasure made her laugh lightly. A dainty, musical sound. She worked without comment, and he allowed her to continue far beyond necessary.

Lucinda was right. He should go back to the hall, for more reason than the one she'd stated.

He'd dismissed the guard. If he went back, he must take his charges with him. He couldn't leave them vulnerable, especially not after the comments he'd heard today from some of Basil's victims. He doubted that any of them would dare take action while Lucinda and Philip were under Wilmont's care, but he wouldn't take the chance.

Richard removed Lucinda's hands from his neck. "Would you and Philip care to see the betrothal ceremony?"

Lucinda wasn't interested in the ceremony, but she would love the chance to escape the confines of Wilmont's chambers.

"You would take us?" she asked, incredulous that Richard offered, considering his insistence on keeping her and Philip confined and guarded.

"I would not ask had I not meant to."

She looked down at her gown. "Neither Philip nor I have garments suitable for so grand an occasion."

"We will keep to the shadows. The crowd's attention will be on the king and princess, not on us."

Lucinda wasn't so sure, but that wouldn't stop her from going. She woke Philip and made them both as presentable as possible.

They made slow progress during the walk from the palace to the hall. Many of the entertainers she'd seen from the bedchamber window still lingered to ply their trade for the city folk not allowed inside the hall with the nobles. When Philip complained that he couldn't see around the gathered crowd, Richard hoisted the boy onto his shoulders.

They entered Westminster Hall just as King Henry called for silence so the ceremony could begin. With his hand on her elbow, Richard guided her to a spot along the wall that offered a fairly unobstructed view of the raised dais at the far end of the hall.

The nobles had spared no expense for their court finery. Highly decorative embroidery, worked in gold or silver or bright hues, in patterns she'd never seen before, trimmed dalmaticas and gowns of silk or tightly woven linen. Some smiled in obvious delight with the king's political move, others frowned in deep disapproval.

The betrothal of Princess Matilda to Emperor Henry V of the Roman Empire took little time. Papers were signed. Gifts were exchanged. Promises were made. Upon such actions were two mighty kingdoms joined.

She looked up at Richard to comment, but he wasn't paying heed to the events taking place on the raised dais. His gaze flickered about the hall, as if looking for someone.

Or looking for danger.

A prickling sensation skittered across the back of her neck, turning her from Richard to observe the crowd. No one seemed to be watching her, yet her senses had come alive at a perceived threat.

She might be making something out of nothing, but she suddenly longed to return to the shelter of Wilmont's chambers.

"Seen enough?" Richard said.

"Aye, my lord," she answered, probably betraying her discomfort, but at the moment she didn't care.

Lucinda followed Richard out of Westminster Hall, staying very close in his wake.

Very early the following morning, Lucinda stood outside of Westminster Palace near the supply wagon in which she was to ride. Philip was so anxious to leave that he'd already climbed into the wagon and taken a high seat on a crate.

The assembled company consisted of the same men

who'd accompanied Richard to Westminster, with the exception of two, who were now mounted and ready to leave with Stephen. The brothers were nearby, saying farewells.

"Have you sufficient funds?" Richard asked his brother.

From atop his destrier, Stephen answered, "Of course. I also have the list." With a widening grin, he continued. "If this proves accurate, Richard, I shall expect a healthy reward upon my return."

"We will discuss a reward if you return with your head still atop your shoulders," Richard countered his brother's teasing. "Have a care. We know not how George will react to the news, and may be forewarned."

The prickling on the back of her neck returned. She'd known all along that someone who knew Basil's relatives might be here at court, might inform them of what she'd done. 'Twas only since the betrothal ceremony, however, that the threat of harm seemed so immediate.

For the first time since their initial meeting at court, Stephen looked at her. "'Tis you who should have a care, Richard. Watch your back," he warned, then wheeled his horse and galloped off.

Stephen's warning didn't surprise her, yet his words roiled in her gut like a rotted piece of meat. Thankfully, she need not deal with Stephen, but with Richard, whose rancor didn't run so deep.

Richard gave a hand signal. His men-at-arms fell into formation, half in front of the supply wagon, half behind. Just as she was about to climb into the wagon, she felt his hands at her waist. He lifted her, turning her body around, with little effort.

As always, the warmth of his hands and shock of his touch reverberated through her body. Not trusting her voice, she let the sensation ebb before she said, "My thanks."

He nodded, his gaze flickering around the insides of the wagon. "You and Philip should do well enough in here."

Lucinda knew how uncomfortable bouncing around in the wagon could be, having done so for three days with an injured ankle. "How many days until we reach Collinwood?"

"If we traveled straight to Collinwood, it would take four days. However, you will have a break in the middle because I must stop at Wilmont first."

Lucinda felt every drop of blood drain from her face.

"Wilmont?" she whispered, unable to say the name louder. Only in her most horrible nightmares had she dreamed of entering the fortified castle at Wilmont, or of facing Baron Gerard within his lair.

"You need have no fear," Richard said. "I will not allow you within Wilmont's walls."

Chapter Eight

Richard kept his distance from his charges for the two days required to reach Wilmont. He knew how they fared, for Edric took his duty seriously and reported on the state of Lucinda and Philip's health. For some reason, Edric also thought it important to relate each cute or funny story of Philip's antics in the wagon.

The boy, at least, was enjoying a delightful journey.

Lucinda, according to Edric, became more fretful with each passing league. Richard saw no reason. He'd assured her that she wouldn't step within Wilmont's walls, which meant she needn't face Gerard or Ardith.

She should believe him, and thank him. Instead, she'd made it easy for him to keep his distance by nearly snubbing him. As if he were to blame for her uncommon situation. As if he were about to give her over to Gerard and some unimaginable horror.

Hellfire, Gerard would want as little to do with Lucinda as she did with Gerard.

In the waning hours of the day, he pushed the company hard to within a short distance of Wilmont. He guided the company off the road to a sheltered glade near a fast-running stream.

He tossed Odin's reins to a man-at-arms. "Take him to water and rub him down with grass, but do not take the saddle off. I will be leaving shortly."

After he saw his charges settled, he would head for Wilmont, where he could sleep in a comfortable bed and enjoy Ardith's tasty meals. Away from Lucinda.

Lucinda eased out of the wagon, Philip jumping down after her. She brushed the dirt from the boy's tunic, as was her habit.

Richard beckoned to Edric. "Choose three men to camp here with you tonight," Richard ordered the one man in his guard whom he knew possessed a tender spot for Philip. Edric would let no harm come to the boy or the mother. Too, Lucinda had developed some trust in Edric. 'Twas to this old, crusty soldier she gave her smiles or a few words around the nightly campfire. The smiles and conversation Richard neither wanted nor encouraged. "I am leaving Lucinda and Philip in your care while I go on to Wilmont."

"Aye, my lord. Will you be back on the morn?"

"Pitch three tents and take enough food from the wagon for two days. If I will be away longer, I will send supplies from the castle."

Edric turned and went about the task of setting up camp. He also stopped for a word with Lucinda, apparently informing her of Richard's orders.

Lucinda glanced his way, but showed no sign of her feelings about the arrangement. She tucked Philip's hand in hers and headed for the stream. A soldier followed the pair.

She would be safe here while he concluded his business with Gerard.

The sound of two horses, coming on fast, didn't surprise Richard. He'd expected one of the patrols that roamed Wilmont lands to find him, but he didn't expect to spy his brother, Gerard, atop one of the horses.

"Hail, Richard!" Gerard called out, reining in his horse, a huge grin on his face. "I did not anticipate seeing you for some days yet."

"Gerard," Richard said flatly, wishing his destrier was within reach.

Gerard's gaze took in the activity around him, his smile fading. "Where is Stephen? Why do you set up camp?"

"Stephen is well. A few of my men will stay here this night," he said, then tried to smile. "Return to your hall, Gerard, and order a fresh keg of ale made ready. I will join you shortly and tell you all."

Gerard leaned forward in the saddle. "You act oddly, Richard. What has happened?"

Richard crossed his arms. Knowing he was courting his brother's flash-fire temper, but willing to do so to send Gerard away, he said, "More than I care to relate in an open glade where everyone can overhear us."

"All did not go well at court."

"Nay, it did not. I will fetch my horse and—"

Hoping that the rustling behind him signaled Odin's return, Richard looked over his shoulder.

Lucinda and Philip were cresting the incline that led up from the stream. She stopped short and went deathly pale as she recognized Gerard. Her hand darted out to grab Philip's tunic and haul him in close.

Gerard became livid, apparently identifying Lucinda on sight, as Stephen had. "What in the devil's name is *she* doing here?" Gerard shouted, setting his horse to skittering.

Richard prayed for patience and the right words. "'Tis part of what happened at court, Gerard." He laid a hand on his brother's knee. "I swear, you need have naught to do with her or the boy. This is not the place for explanations. Let us get to a private place, first."

Gerard stared at Lucinda a moment longer, then looked down at Richard. "I will *not* have the bitch and her pup in my hall!"

Richard fully understood Gerard's feelings. However, his patience with his brother was beginning to fray. Gerard should know that Richard would do nothing to hurt or insult either Gerard or his wife.

"I did not intend to bring them within your walls. They stay here this night, under guard."

"As far as I am concerned, you can leave them for the wolves!"

Richard ignored his brother's ignoble statement, taking it for what it was: Gerard's resentment that, again, Basil of Northbryre was to affect his life.

"You will say nothing of her to Ardith," Gerard continued, his fury ebbing somewhat. "I do not want my wife distressed."

Richard shook his head. He wouldn't, though he wondered how Gerard would avoid telling Ardith. She would know the moment Gerard entered the hall that something was amiss, and had a way of extracting explanations from Gerard even when he didn't want to give them.

"Go, Gerard. When I am able, I will follow."

"Be quick," Gerard ordered, then wheeled his horse and tore up great divots of grass in his haste to be gone.

Richard turned. Lucinda stood as frozen in place as a statue, and wore a shade of sickly gray. He thought for a moment to ease her fear, to tell her that Gerard's anger was often loud and spear-point sharp, but rarely prolonged or lethal. Gerard's infamous battle roar had earned him the title Lion of Wilmont, but only at extreme provocation did he bare his teeth and pounce.

Better to let her fear, he decided. Lucinda would receive no warmer welcome at Collinwood. There, her fear would serve her well, keeping her alert for any danger.

"Edric, have you all you require from the wagon?" he called out, anxious to follow Gerard.

"Aye, my lord," Edric answered.

"Then have the men form up. We will be away as soon as I fetch Odin."

Richard passed Lucinda and Philip on his way to the stream, stopping only long enough to issue a warning. "Stay close to camp and Edric. Wolves are not the only dangerous animals that roam this forest."

Lucinda allowed herself to breathe. The immediate danger had passed. Gerard was gone and Richard was leaving.

She loosened her grip on Philip's tunic, her knuckles having turned white and stiff from holding on so tightly.

"Mother, that man on the horse looked just like Lord Richard. Is he Gerard, the baron?"

"Aye," she said.

They looked so alike as to be twins! But there the

similarity ended abruptly. She highly preferred Richard's calm demeanor to Gerard's volatile manner.

The shock of seeing Gerard had rooted her to the forest floor, nearly scaring her witless. She'd had only enough sense about her to grab hold of Philip.

She couldn't allow that to happen again. A man like Gerard would sense her fear, use it to his advantage. Thank the Lord, she needn't enter the castle, might not face him a second time.

"Are there bears in the forest?" Philip asked, picking up on Richard's warning of dangerous animals.

"Mayhap," she said. "You should ask Edric, he will know."

As Philip ran to Edric, Lucinda looked about her. There might be wolves and bears roaming about, but the fiercest prowler of this forest was the lion who reigned supreme over Wilmont.

Richard perched on the foot of the bed he would occupy tonight, his elbows on the knees of his splayed legs. A few feet in front of him, Gerard straddled a wooden chair, arms crossed on the back's top, a jewel-encrusted goblet dangling from his fingers.

Between them sat a near-empty keg of ale.

Richard gave Gerard every tidbit of information or gossip he'd garnered at court. Which petitions were granted and which denied. Who rose in Henry's favor and who slipped downward.

Not enough land had passed hands, or into the wrong hands, to threaten Wilmont. Many heiresses remained heiresses, still up for grabs, including the Lady Carolyn whom Stephen had vowed to bed.

"Did he?" Gerard asked.

"I have no notion. He did not say and I did not ask."

Gerard sat very still and quiet while Richard told of how he'd become Philip's protector. While concerned when told of Stephen's journey to Normandy, Gerard eventually agreed that Richard's decision to send Stephen had been wisest, under the circumstances.

"So," Richard concluded his tale, "I will take Lucinda and Philip to Collinwood. I stopped at Wilmont only to let you know how things stood."

Gerard's ire rose. "I regret that Henry chose to inflict punishment on Wilmont through you. On the morrow, I will send a message to Henry, tell him to rescind this ridiculous edict. Surely he can place the child in another's care."

"Leave it be," Richard heard himself say.

"Leave it be? Surely you jest. Had I been there, I would have told our interfering king exactly what he could do with—"

Miffed, Richard interrupted. "Gerard, Henry insisted that either you or I accept Philip. If you protest, he will only become angered and demand you take the boy. Do you want that? Or would you prefer a permanent rift between Wilmont and the monarchy?"

"You *know* I want neither! But to have Henry shove this galling wardship down our throats is not to be borne."

"You need not bear it. I will, for all of our sakes."

"And the woman?"

"I must tolerate her presence for two years. 'Twill be a test of endurance, I assure you."

Gerard had no notion of how hard a test of Richard's fortitude lay ahead. Having Lucinda about, day after day, month after month, would test his mettle to a high degree.

Even now, he wished she were here, massaging away the knots of tension in his neck. 'Twas a mistake to have let her minister to his pain. To learn of the magic in her fingertips. To enjoy each manipulating stroke.

Richard pulled the list of Philip's holdings from inside his tunic and handed it to Gerard. "Besides, the wardship does bring rewards."

Gerard looked it over, then let out a long, low-pitched whistle. "Rewards, indeed. Worth fighting for, if necessary."

With a wry smile, Richard said, "Stephen already claims recompense for going to Normandy to look them over. Should I require your help to secure them, I suppose you will want a share, too."

"Naturally. Do you think my help necessary?"

Richard told Gerard all he knew of George, and of Lucinda's warning that George might not give up the tributes easily, even by order of the Duke of Normandy—Henry, King of England.

Richard got up, intending to dip his cup into the ale keg. The lightness of his head—and the sight of the bottom of the keg—stopped him.

"I need food, Gerard."

"Evening meal is some time off, but I am sure Ardith can provide something to put in your stomach."

Richard followed Gerard down the passageway and stairs that led from the bedchambers down to the great hall. Boyhood memories sprang up, prompted, he supposed, by the changes he noted along the way.

Ardith was now chatelaine of Wilmont. She'd

made small changes, here and there, to the interior of the castle. Added candles in more ornate stands. Tapestries—which depicted peaceful pursuits instead of glorious battles—now blocked drafts. Banners in bright colors graced the rafters, hung beside the ancient weapons of Wilmont forefathers.

The place seemed warmer and more friendly, more tolerant. Even Gerard's mother, Lady Ursula, had lost some of her old bitterness, which might be the greatest change of all. She sat near the huge hearth, working spindle and distaff, and managed to acknowledge his presence with a slight nod of her head when he and Gerard approached her.

"Mother, have you seen Ardith of late?" Gerard asked. "Richard's stomach grumbles."

Without missing a beat in her spinning, she smiled wryly and said, "Your sons, Gerard, have a fondness for rummaging about in the stable. Shortly after you and Richard went up the stairs, they came in fairly reeking of horse droppings. Ardith decided to cleanse both the boys and their clothes by taking them down to the stream."

Roaring a string of blistering oaths, Gerard turned heel and ran out of the hall, Richard close behind.

Lucinda sat on a log, her bare feet soaking in the stream. She wished she could shuck more than her hose and shoes and wallow in the crystal-clear water. Mayhap later, if Edric allowed her the privacy, she would. For now, she kept watch over Philip, who'd waded out to his knees, the hem of his tunic getting wet.

She harbored no illusions about her status. Somewhere in the woods behind her lurked a guard, watch-

ing her and Philip to ensure they remained safe, and
safely within reach. She surely wasn't welcome at
Wilmont; Gerard had made that quite clear. Not that
she wished to enter the man's lair. Nor, she knew,
would the people of Collinwood be pleased to see her.
That, too, she could accept.

In less than a fortnight, since leaving the village
where she'd found a measure of contentment, her entire life had turned upside down and sideways. The
king had granted her petition for a protector, and she
had to admit that though hardship lay ahead, Philip's
future looked brighter. And though she had reserva-
tions about placing Philip in Wilmont's care, she conceded that, of all the brothers, Richard was the best
choice. He'd already taken measures to see Philip's
inheritance secured, and would likely raise Philip the
best he knew how.

'Twas her feelings for Richard she wrestled with
now.

She'd thought her marriage had soured her for all
men for all time. Basil's brutality should have purged
her of kindly thoughts for any male. She'd truly
thought it had, until getting to know Richard.

Lucinda drew up her legs and hugged her knees, in
a vain attempt to still the yearnings that simmered
within at the thought of the man who'd awakened
them. She burned with deep desire for the strong,
handsome, intelligent man who'd, too quickly and
thoroughly, besieged her senses.

She would never let him know, of course. He
would be horrified to learn that she longed to slip into
the shelter of his powerful embrace. Shocked to hear
that the widow of the man who'd nearly caused his
death yearned for a kind word and tender caress. Ap-

palled at the knowledge that if he crooked a finger in invitation to his bed, she would go to him.

Richard was aware of her, as a man to a woman. She'd known it the day he'd looked her over, and she'd retorted that she would make a poor bedmate. Damn, 'twas galling to admit that she desperately wanted to prove her statement wrong. With Richard.

She shook her head at her foolishness. 'Twas sheer folly to hope for more than Richard's tolerance of her presence.

Behind her, she heard voices. A man's, a woman's and...children's giggles?

"Be sensible, Edric," the woman said. "You cannot bar me from the stream. Look at the boys. *Smell* them!"

"My lady, you should return to the hall. Consider your...condition. Lord Gerard will *not* approve of—"

"Bah! I am merely with child. One would think me on my deathbed the way Gerard hovers. While the boys wash, you can explain to me why you and these men camp here while Richard and the others enjoy the comfort of the hall. Daymon! Everart! Get into the water."

Several yards downstream, two boys—one blond and as tall as Philip, the other auburn-haired and smaller—broke through the brush and ran for the stream. They stopped short of the water to shed their shoes, then plunged in, garments and all.

Daymon and Everart. Gerard's children. Which meant the lady who Edric so earnestly tried to dissuade from coming down to the stream must be Ardith. Lucinda guessed at Gerard's reaction to a chance meeting, and started to call Philip out, intending to leave before being noticed.

Then wondered why the devil she should. No one had given a care for her feelings—not the king, or Richard, especially Gerard. Still, the woman was with child and innocent of any wrongdoing. Lucinda rose from the log, but it was now too late to escape.

Ardith of Wilmont stood at the edge of the brush, gowned in fine yellow linen, clutching dry tunics for her boys against the swell of her belly. She stared at Lucinda for several heartbeats, then noticed Philip. Quite beautiful, with auburn hair and startling blue eyes, she appeared fragile. The look she turned on Edric, however, was anything but frail.

"Edric, explain," Ardith said, in a unyielding tone.

Lucinda couldn't hear Edric's words, but she could guess at what he said from Ardith's reactions. Poor Edric shouldn't be the one revealing her and Philip's identity, of how they'd come to be camped so near Ardith's home. Her heart went out to Ardith, who shouldn't have to suffer a reminder of what must have been the most horrifying days of her life.

Squelching the urge to approach Ardith and apologize for whatever harm Basil had inflicted on the woman, Lucinda resumed her seat on the log. Somehow, she had to get over wanting to make amends for every nasty, vile thing Basil had done in his life. It couldn't be done, not in a lifetime. Nor had she been responsible for, or able to control, Basil's actions. She and her son were blameless. 'Twould take time and patience, unfortunately, to convince the rest of the kingdom.

Philip stared at the boys, who busily scrubbed at their tunics. He then turned to her, a plea in his eyes. She shook her head and mouthed the words, "Stay where you are."

Her son's disappointment broke her heart, but 'twas for the best if he didn't try to become a playmate to Gerard's sons. Or she an acquaintance of Gerard's wife.

However, Gerard's wife had other ideas. Ardith's steps were slow but purposeful. Lucinda braced for the woman's outpouring of outrage. To her surprise, she saw no hatred in Ardith's eyes. They'd gone carefully devoid of emotion.

"I did not know you or the boy existed," Ardith said. "No one spoke of a wife or son, at least not to me."

The statement didn't require comment, so Lucinda simply acknowledged it with a slight nod.

"Edric says that Richard is to be Philip's... protector. If that is so, then we should get to know the boy. 'Tis inevitable that we will be in each other's company from time to time and—" She turned away, unable to hide a sudden tear. "Sweet Mother, I had not thought this would be so hard!"

Lucinda pursed her lips, unsure of whether to be outraged or sympathize. One thing she knew. If she reached out, Ardith would either back away in revulsion or begin sobbing, and Ardith was trying so damned hard to be civil.

"Then be easy on yourself, Ardith. I have no wish to cause you further hurt."

Daymon and Everart came running up for their dry tunics. Heedless of Ardith's upset, they stripped. Everart needed a bit of help from Daymon in getting the clean tunic over his head.

Ardith seemed to rally. "Now find sticks to scrape your shoes clean," she said in a tone used by mothers when expecting a protest.

Everart didn't disappoint. "But they are...rank!"

"And whose fault is that, I ask you?" his mother rejoined. "If you had not seen fit to jump into the manure, Daymon would not have gone in to pull you out. By right, you should clean Daymon's shoes, too."

Everart stuck out his lower lip.

"I will help him," Daymon said.

"You have your own shoes to clean. Everart needs to learn that he cannot depend on you to pull him out of every scrape he gets into and clean up his messes."

Daymon shrugged a shoulder. "He is little yet."

Ardith smiled, transforming her face. She wasn't lovely; she was exquisite. And the warmth in that smile revealed her true character.

"Little, aye. But not too little to learn."

"Might I help him, my lady?" Philip asked.

He'd come out of the stream, unable to resist the pull of companionship any longer, even if it meant cleaning manure from a littler boy's shoes.

To Lucinda's relief, Ardith's smile faded but didn't disappear. "If you wish," she said softly.

Everart looked at Philip with open admiration and thanks.

"Who are you?" Daymon asked, in protective older brother fashion.

"My name is Philip."

They studied each other for a moment, then Daymon declared that he knew where to find sticks and all three raced off.

Ardith took a long breath. "As I was about to say, I would like you and Philip to come to Wilmont for evening meal."

Lucinda cringed. "Gerard will most surely object."

Before Ardith could say more, a roar echoed through the woods. "Arr-dith!"

Ardith sighed. "That would be Gerard. Richard is likely right behind him. I promise you, no harm will come to you or your son from Gerard or Wilmont's people. Will you come?"

Lucinda looked downstream to where the three boys bent over two pair of shoes, then into Ardith's utterly guileless eyes. The thought of entering Wilmont terrified her, but she sensed that if anyone could aid Philip's acceptance within Richard's family circle, it would be Ardith.

"If your husband and Richard agree, Philip and I would be pleased to share your meal."

Chapter Nine

At Gerard's insistence, Richard sat with his family at the table on the raised dais, though he would rather be at the far end of the trestle tables with Lucinda and Philip.

Richard had always felt uncomfortable up on the dais, could never get over the feeling of being on display. He'd agreed to the placement tonight only to keep Gerard calm. So he sat beside Daymon, sharing his nephew's trencher, waiting for the meal to be over so he could relax.

Richard could have spared them all the unease of this meal by forbidding his charges to leave camp. But Ardith had insisted that she would be upset if not allowed to extend some form of basic hospitality. Gerard's agreement hadn't come easily, but when it did, Richard deferred to Gerard's judgment.

Philip ate as if the food were manna from heaven, and looked about him in awe at the splendor of Wilmont's great hall. He seemed not to notice that nobody except his mother sat near him or talked to him.

Lucinda was a Norman noblewoman, her rank higher than any other woman's in the hall save for

Ardith and Ursula. Yet she sat at the far end of the tables—Gerard's doing—pretending not to notice the insult. With a stiff spine and uptilted chin, she shared a trencher with Philip with the same dignity and grace as if she sat among her true peers.

"Father says Philip is the son of Basil of Northbryre, the man who kidnapped me and Ardith when I was little," Daymon said.

"Aye, that he is," Richard confirmed, smiling at Daymon's opinion that he was now all grown-up. In some ways, he was. His position here at Wilmont, as the lord's acknowledged but bastard son, had matured the boy beyond his physical age. Richard well knew how Daymon felt.

Even now, some of Wilmont's people thought it fitting that the two bastards shared a trencher so no one else would suffer their taint. Others didn't understand why their lord allowed the bastards at the high table. A few were horrified at how lavishly Gerard had gifted Richard with land, raising him high above what should be his proper station, as Gerard would one day also do for Daymon.

The people tolerated Daymon and gave their loyalty and love to Everart, the heir.

"I do not remember much of the kidnapping, just being frightened—and the dogs," Daymon stated. "Father says I need not remember all of it, but to never forget that 'twas Basil who meant to take my life, and Ardith's."

Richard wasn't surprised that Daymon's memory of the kidnapping had faded. The boy had been only three at the time. Richard, however, well remembered Basil's vile nature. While he hadn't witnessed the kidnapping, Richard participated in the rescue. If they hadn't stormed Northbryre when they did, neither Ardith nor Daymon would be alive.

"One must always 'ware one's enemies."

"Is Philip like his father? Is he my enemy?"

Northbryre had been Wilmont's enemy for decades, going back to before Richard's father had been born, fighting over land that Wilmont held and Northbryre wanted. No one of Northbryre, except Philip, now remained to contest ownership.

"You met him, Daymon. What think you?"

"Philip seemed nice enough. He scraped Everart's mucked up shoes, and he did not have to."

Basil would turn over in his grave if he knew.

"Not the actions of an enemy," Richard said, wondering when he'd come to see Philip as merely a little boy and not so much the son of Basil.

Stephen maintained that blood would tell. Gerard probably held the same opinion. Once, Richard would have spouted the same sentiment, but something about the boy made him doubt. Did Lucinda have the right of it? Would upbringing win out?

"He looks lonely down there," Daymon said. "Mayhap Father will allow him to stay and play after meal."

Richard felt a familiar pang. Both he and Daymon knew what it was like to feel the outcast. Philip and Lucinda must, too.

"Best not push your father too hard, Daymon. Leave it be, for now. Mayhap another time."

Gerard rose, signaling the serving wenches to begin clearing away the remains of the meal, and the lads to start folding up the trestle tables. He then walked down to greet his knights, would give them each the attention due from their lord, then ensure that Wilmont's guards were properly assigned for the night.

Ardith and Ursula headed for chairs near the brightly glowing hearth, where they would spend the evening hours spinning or doing needlework, attended by the castle's womenfolk.

The hunting dogs snuffled about in the rushes, hoping for scraps. Daymon and Everart joined a group of children, and would likely find some loud, exuberant activity to engage in.

Richard headed for Lucinda and Philip, who stood alone and apprehensive in the middle of the hall.

Gerard stopped him. "I do not want them back in my hall, Richard," he said quietly. "Take them away before Ardith becomes more involved with them."

Briefly, Richard felt as if he were being sent away as punishment for having the temerity to do his duty. But he understood the reason behind Gerard's order. Gerard protected those he loved most dearly in the best way he knew how.

Richard smiled, unable to resist teasing. "You could always say no to your wife, Gerard."

Gerard rolled his eyes. "Some day I may learn how, but until then…"

"When I take them back to camp, I will order Edric to be ready at first light. Do not give away my bed. I intend to enjoy it tonight."

"When you return, we should talk more."

About Lucinda and Philip. About the lands in Normandy. About the king. All subjects Richard wished to forget about for a while.

Richard shook his head. "Why not wait until Stephen returns? We truly will not know how things stand until then."

Gerard smiled wryly. "If you do not wish to talk, then mayhap we could have a practice bout."

That appealed. "'Twill be dark soon. We will have to ring the yard with torches and wear hauberks."

"Which will please Ardith to no end."

"Then prepare to sweat, Gerard."

Lucinda and Philip hadn't moved. They waited for him in the middle of the hall, Lucinda's hands resting on Philip's shoulders.

"My lord," Philip said, "might I say farewell to Daymon?"

Before Richard could answer, Lucinda said, "Nay, Philip. Daymon is busy with—"

"I have no objection. Do so quickly," Richard said, overriding her denial.

Lucinda glared her displeasure. Richard stared back, willing her to let the boy go. Reluctantly, she let Philip loose. She watched her son go, anxious.

"We leave for Collinwood at first light," he said.

"As you wish," she said flatly.

Richard cupped her elbow and gently pushed her toward the door. "Come. Philip will be along."

The now familiar shock when touching her raced up his arm. The sweet scent of her engulfed his senses. He hung on despite the effect of her nearness, knowing that if he let her go she would stop. As it was, she walked slowly, waiting for Philip.

Nor did her steps quicken until she heard her son's youthful footsteps racing to catch her.

"Philip, come down from that crate. Another hard bump will toss you right out of the cart," Lucinda warned.

"Lord Richard would let me ride up here," the boy said from his unstable perch.

"That might very well be, but Richard is not here, and I say come down!"

Reluctantly, Philip obeyed, grumbling. Lucinda rejoiced that Richard rode at the head of the company so he hadn't overheard her. 'Twould have been just like the man to counter her order.

These days it seemed that no matter what she told Philip he could or couldn't do, Richard took an opposing stance. 'Twas irritating to the extreme. She'd managed to raise Philip to his sixth year all on her own. What did Richard know of when to allow a child's wishes and when to say nay? Just being Philip's protector did not make him an expert on how to raise a child.

Adding to her vexation, Philip had declared yesterday that he wished to grow up to be just like Richard. While Richard might be a decent model, the man *did* have faults.

The trouble was, she had a hard time recalling those faults whenever he stood close enough for her to take him to task. Damn the man, with just a smile he could muddle her thoughts, with a look he could tie up her tongue. With a few smooth words he could sway her into agreeing that his way might be best.

For the past two days, Philip had ridden either in the cart with her or on Odin with Richard—both dangerous places for a small child. Thankfully, they were near journey's end and she need no longer worry about Philip falling off one or the other and breaking open his head.

According to Edric, Collinwood was but another

hour's march away. As much as she wanted this journey over, she dreaded the final destination.

She knew of Collinwood from Basil's ledgers and the steward's reports. The holding was land-rich, capable of producing hundreds of bushels of grain. Basil had claimed the bulk of the harvest, leaving little for his vassals for their own use or to trade at market for other goods.

The reports from Collinwood's steward had always been bleak. Indeed, each spring report had contained an overlong list of those who had died over the winter. She'd always suspected that most of those had either starved or frozen to death.

Basil hadn't cared. So long as he received his due, he saw no reason to feed people more than necessary, or ensure that they were adequately sheltered.

Philip scooted down to where he could just see over the top of the cart's side. "Look, Mother, pigs!" he cried, pointing toward the woods.

Two sows, ripe to give birth, dug their snouts into the earth, foraging for whatever acorns might be left over from last fall's droppings. Not far off a young boy, a bit older than Philip, watched over them.

A grin washed over the boy's face. He waved vigorously, and one of the soldiers near the end of the company raised an answering arm.

From that brief signal, Lucinda knew they must now be on Richard's land. Curiosity piqued, she began to take note of other signs of how the holding fared.

Wattle and daub huts dotted the countryside. Most seemed in good repair, a few boasted freshly thatched roofs. Oxen and cows grazed near the huts. Most were bony about the haunches, but that was to be expected after the winter months.

The tenant farmers, too, looked healthy—and happy. Most of the people smiled and waved at the company. Not one of them appeared disheartened or fearful at Richard's return.

Lucinda slipped out of the wagon to walk alongside, the better to see what lay ahead.

She nearly gasped when Collinwood came into view. Richard had raised a palisade out of tall, stout trees to surround the manor, a defensive measure Basil had deemed an unnecessary expense. A moat ringed the palisade. She couldn't tell where the water came from or where it went to, but the water *flowed* like a stream.

Anticipation heightened as they crossed the plank bridge that spanned the moat. She was eager to see if Richard had made as many improvements within the palisade as without.

Huts lined the inner palisade, one a smithy's that stood next to the stables. From another hut she caught the pungent smell of dyes, and from yet another, the aroma of leather.

The manor stood at the far end of the bailey, and while it wasn't about to fall down, it showed the least improvement. He hadn't added space to what she knew was a one-room hall, where Richard would eat, sleep, hold court and rule his fief, attended by whatever soldiers and servants he deemed necessary. The thatched roof needed repair and, in places, drafts would whistle through the timbers where they needed mortaring.

Richard had taken care of his people, placing their needs over his comforts.

The entourage came to a halt near the manor's door. Richard dismounted. A man came running from the stable to fetch Odin and lead the destrier off to the stable. The rest of the men began to drift off.

"This is not a castle, like Wilmont," Philip said, dismayed.

She took his hand to help him jump out of the cart. "Not a castle, but a fair manor, and our home now."

Home. A lump formed in her throat. 'Twas not truly her home, but Philip's, since he would remain here until coming of age. Her future was far less certain.

A gray-haired, frail-bodied man came out of the manor, followed by two dogs who loped over to Richard, tails wagging fiercely, begging for the petting that Richard gladly gave them.

It struck her as odd, then, that only the dogs greeted Richard with any enthusiasm. Save for smiles and the wave of a few hands—amid many curious looks at her and Philip—no one paid much heed to his arrival.

'Twas dreadfully wrong. After all Richard had done to improve their lot, these people should greet him with waving banners and full cheers.

"Hail, Connor," Richard said to the man, who smiled and answered too softly for Lucinda to understand the words.

She recognized the name from the reports from Collinwood to Northbryre. Connor the steward, who'd served the holding since long before she'd married Basil. He'd been old even then, and she hadn't expected him to have survived.

The two men talked, their voices low. Then Richard looked over his shoulder at her and Philip. She knew the moment when Richard told Connor who

they were. Connor gave a sharp gasp. The face he
turned toward her reflected his horror.

Richard waved her forward. She held tight to
Philip's hand, feeling like the biblical Daniel entering
the lion's den.

"Lucinda, this is Connor, steward of Collinwood,"
he said.

She nodded at Connor. "I remember you, from
your reports. 'Tis nice to put a face to a name."

Connor's mouth twisted into a sneer. "'Twas no
pleasure of mine to write them, Lady Northbryre."
He glanced down at Philip. "And this would be the
devil's whelp."

Lucinda's hand tightened on Philip's.

"His name is Philip," Richard said, the hint of a
reprimand in his tone.

"What would you be wantin' me to do with them,
my lord?"

Lucinda shivered. If Richard told Connor to take
them behind the manor and slit their throats, the steward would have done so, gladly.

"For now, they will reside in the manor."

"O'course. We must keep a close watch on them."
Then Connor turned heel and stamped off toward the
manor.

"Give him time and patience," Richard said. "He
is old and sore used, and will be the last to come
around."

Time and patience. The phrase rang empty. She
might as well hope for a miracle.

The last soul in the manor still awake, Richard sat
on a stool near the banked central fire pit, a mug of
ale in hand and a keg not far off.

A loud snap from the pit brought one of the dogs' heads up, and from on a beam above, the flap of his falcon's wings. Connor snored on his pallet. Edric, not yet ready to give up his duty as their personal guard, slept within reach of Lucinda and Philip.

The boy had curled up on the wolf pelt he now considered his. Lucinda slept near him, stretched out on a bear pelt.

The day could have been worse. So far, no one had thrown anything at Lucinda and Philip, or threatened to do them bodily harm. For the most part, his vassals had simply steered clear of Collinwood's newest residents.

Philip's normal exuberance had lasted throughout the tour of the bailey, and flared bright in the stables. Richard now knew what to do if the boy's spirits ever needed a lift—sit him on a horse. Any horse.

Lucinda. The woman was a fighter, he would give her that. The spark in her eyes had faded, but she would rally, and he hoped she would do it soon. He didn't think he could bear to watch her for too many days, hide behind the indifferent, aloof mask she'd donned after her first meeting with Connor.

As if his thoughts had called out to her, she stirred. Her delicate hand pushed aside the wool coverlet. Slowly, she rose on her elbow, looking around, disoriented.

Sleep-sheened eyes spotted him.

He thought she would lie back down and go back to sleep. She wrapped the coverlet around herself and gingerly rose, then padded toward him, her night rail brushing the tops of her bare feet.

'Twas more beauty and sensual grace than a man should have to look upon late at night after drinking too much ale—unless the woman was his and available for the taking.

Lucinda belonged to no man, and more and more, Richard was beginning to forget to whom she had once belonged. It didn't seem right that a woman of Lucinda's beauty should not belong to someone, or that a man who'd been dead for three years should affect his feelings now.

Hellfire. He'd met her less than a fortnight ago, and she'd already managed to turn his mind upside down and sideways.

"May I?" she asked, waving a hand at the ale keg.

"You need not ask for food or drink. Whatever is here is yours for the taking."

She took hold of the dipper and pulled it upward, then sipped from the bowl. "Even your ale has a fine taste, Richard. After all I saw today, I wonder if anything or anyone at Collinwood is not exemplary."

Collinwood's lord was far from perfect.

"You approve of what I have done here?"

"I had never seen Collinwood, but I know what life must have been like for these people. You have lifted them up out of hell. How could I not approve?"

Richard remembered the first time he'd seen the holding, the buildings in shambles, the people near skeletons. "This is one of the finest fiefs in the kingdom. I never understood how Basil could let it—bah, I have no wish to dredge up the past tonight."

She let the dipper sink back into the keg. "The holding flourishes because its present lord has scruples, which its former lord did not possess. You should be very proud that your vassals are both healthy and happy."

"All but one or two."

She raised a surprised eyebrow. "Truly?"

"You and Philip. Life will not be easy for you here."

"We will survive."

She would, but that wasn't satisfactory. Richard put his mug down on the rush-covered floor, disturbing the rosemary sprinkled within to keep the rushes sweet-smelling. The aroma of the herb, however, couldn't overcome the heady scent of the woman who stood sleepily before him.

He got up, fully aware that he might regret his actions on the morn. Mayhap she'd cast a spell over him, or more likely he'd drunk just enough ale to muddle his mind. But he could no more keep his hands off Lucinda than he could stop breathing.

Richard cupped her face in his hands. To his amazement, she didn't pull back, just looked confused.

"Smile, Lucinda."

"Smile? Whatever for?"

"Because I have not seen you smile today and I wish to see it again."

"'Tis the ale speaking."

"Mayhap, but 'tis still my wish."

The corners of her mouth tilted upward, slightly.

"You can do better," he said.

Her full, lush mouth widened. She might even be laughing at him, but damn, he didn't care. Kissing Lucinda was a compulsion he chose not to fight.

His lips met hers gently, urging a response he didn't think he would get. Her hands came up to clutch his wrists, but not to push him away.

Then she was in his arms, pressed fully against him, fire burning in her deepening, demanding kiss.

The desire he'd doused with calm reason since the day they'd met flared into an inferno that burned hot and bright.

Too hot, too long, for a woman whom he sensed would tumble down onto the rushes with him with little urging.

Too fast. Too soon.

He broke the kiss, breathing heavily, his thoughts still muddled but becoming clearer.

"Mayhap the ale speaks too loudly," he said. "'Twould be wise if we refrained."

Her violet eyes glittered. And for just a moment, he thought he saw regret.

"Mayhap," she said softly, and padded back to her pallet.

Chapter Ten

Lucinda bent down and tugged at Philip's coverlet. "Up with you or we will be late, and you know how Connor blusters when anyone is late for meals."

Philip groaned but stirred, rustling the straw mat beneath his wolf pelt.

Satisfied that he woke, Lucinda looked around what must be the tidiest hut in the kingdom; she'd cleaned it often enough for lack of other chores to fill her days. Timber framing supported walls of wattle and daub, covered by a thatched roof. The hut had been her home for the past four days.

Between her and Philip's pallets stood a chest, old but sturdy, which now held their garments. A small table and stool took up much of the remaining space. The hut was small but, according to Connor, the largest that could be built with materials currently on hand.

Connor, who'd become the bane of her existence, had balked at building her hut, had even voiced the opinion that she and Philip could find sleeping space in the stable. Thankfully, Richard hadn't felt the same way. Aye, Richard wanted her out of the manor at night, but not so badly that he would make her bed down with the horses.

She still flushed whenever she remembered how wantonly she'd kissed Richard, which no doubt led to his ordering her hut built. He'd initiated the kiss, a gentle touching of lips. Engulfed in bliss so foreign to her experience, she'd lost her head and pressed for more. If Richard hadn't come to his senses, she'd have given herself to him right there on the manor floor.

Lord help her, she wished Richard possessed less sense. For all the problems between them, she wished to know Richard as a woman knows a man. Unfortunately, their kiss must have told him so, because now he avoided her.

As it was, they still saw each other several times a day, mostly at meals. Everyone who dwelled within the palisade took their meals in the manor, for Richard allowed no fires other than the manor's pit, except for the blacksmith's forge. A wise move. A stray spark could burn the whole place down.

Philip crawled out of his pallet and donned a new tunic—a gift from Richard.

"The sun is barely up," Philip grumbled.

"'Twill be a fine spring day," she said, pushing aside useless romantic thoughts about Richard to concentrate on the task at hand. She possessed two strong arms, deft hands, and an agile brain. Today she would demand that Connor assign her some chore, to help earn her keep—and to keep from going witless.

Philip hadn't known a moment's boredom. He spent his days with Edric, or with Richard, learning about soldiering and the proper running of a manor. Her inactivity, however, would shortly drive her to distraction. But trying to convince Connor was like arguing with a dead tree. Once more, she would try, but if Connor turned his back on her again, she would take the problem to Richard.

She hurried her sleepy-eyed son out of the hut and across the bailey. In the manor, she took her place at the high end of the row of trestle tables where everyone ate together, including Richard. No dais graced the hall at Collinwood. Richard sat on a stool at the end of the table, with everyone else, in order of rank, on benches stretched down the sides.

Lucinda sat immediately to his left hand, across from Connor at Richard's right. Richard's acknowledgement of her Norman heritage and noble rank irked Connor to no end.

The placement sometimes irked her, too. Far too often her food went neglected while she noticed little things about Richard. Like the way his fingers wrapped around a goblet. Or when he licked gravy from a corner of his mouth. Or watching his lips move as he spoke, and longing for another kiss.

The subject of her musings took his seat and broke a large chunk of bread from the loaf sitting in front of him. Lucinda waited for Connor to take his portion before breaking the rest in half for herself and Philip. No priest resided at Collinwood, and no one seemed inclined to say grace, so they ate without a blessing.

As usual, Connor launched into a list of the happenings about the manor that day. The rushes needed changing. The squeaking hinge on the door would be replaced. Edric intended to begin teaching Philip the art of polishing chain mail. The noon's main course—fish.

"We are also in need of firewood, my lord," Connor said. "I assigned a few of the soldiers the task of gathering it from the forest to the south."

Richard took a sip of ale from his cup, washing down the bread. "I thought we had an ample supply last I looked."

"We did, but we are now short. We used some of the bigger logs to build the frame for Lady North-bryre's hut."

Lucinda hated the name Connor had branded her with upon her arrival. Not only was it improper, but served to remind everyone of her past. As Connor well knew.

She'd planned to challenge Connor today, not quite this way, but took the opportunity presented.

"I am not Lady Northbryre, Connor," she said, causing his head to turn sharply to look at her. "Since Gerard of Wilmont now holds the property, only his wife may use the title, if she chooses. Properly, you should call me 'my lady' or, since I give my consent, you may use my name. Lucinda."

He nearly choked on his rising anger, and she carefully masked any reaction. She'd coped with the explosive temper of a man far more dangerous than Connor. Inside she might quake, but she refused to show Connor any sign of anxiety.

She turned her attention from Connor to Richard. Seeing no anger, only mild surprise that she took Connor to task, she forged ahead.

"Since Connor seems to feel that building my hut has caused a lack of firewood, I offer to help gather more."

"Impossible." Connor spit out the word.

"Why impossible, Connor?" Richard asked.

"The men will be out there to work, not guard a...a

lady who should not be allowed out in the forest alone with a group of men!''

''Then let them work,'' she countered, encouraged by Richard's lack of outright refusal. ''I need no guarding. Nor do I fear being alone with Richard's soldiers. They are well disciplined and will do me no harm,'' she added, realizing that she believed it.

Connor leaned forward. '''Tis not your safety that concerns me, *my lady,* but the men's!''

''Connor, enough,'' Richard admonished in a low, deceptively calm tone.

Connor leaned back at the rebuke. ''The woman is not trustworthy, my lord. 'Tis why she must be confined to her hut, kept away from Collinwood's people. So long as she stays in her place, we may yet survive the years until we can be rid of her.''

Confined to the hut? 'Twas the first she'd heard of such, but apparently not the first time Connor had proposed the plan to Richard.

''It makes no sense to confine either Lucinda or Philip,'' Richard said. ''So long as they cause no problems, hurt no one, they are allowed the freedom of the bailey.''

''Surely,'' Connor countered, aghast, ''you will not let her roam about beyond the palisade, my lord.''

Richard shrugged a shoulder. ''If Lucinda wishes to gather wood, I see no harm in it. And if it eases your mind, I will go along to watch her. I had planned to check the state of the game in the southern wood anyway.''

He said it so casually, igniting a fresh look of horror on Connor's face and causing an unsettling flutter around her heart. The thought of tramping about the southern wood with Richard's soldiers hadn't caused her a twinge of disquiet. The possibility that she might find herself alone in the southern wood with Richard caused a thrill she had no right or reason to feel.

Yet finally, she had a worthwhile task to perform— even if it was only gathering firewood. So did Richard—checking on the availability of game. Certes, they would do so separately.

Richard set his men to felling two large dead trees along the side of the road, then wandered back into the wood in the direction Lucinda had taken—with a basket in hand to search for kindling. Easily followed, easily found.

She looked up when she heard him, then went back to her task as if he weren't there.

He gave up pretending that he was looking for hares, or birds, or any other small game, admitting that his quarry the entire time was right before his eyes—picking up small chunks of wood, putting them in her basket.

Lucinda.

He sat on a log and allowed himself the pleasure of watching her lithe, supple form perform a dance of sorts, as she bent over and reached for kindling from the forest floor.

She'd performed another dance earlier, one of words, with Connor. The woman had gall and courage, he'd give her that. She'd challenged Connor with the spark of self-assurance that had been missing in her behavior lately.

He'd begun to worry about her state of mind. She'd held to her hut, coming out only for meals. He'd known all along that if she were to find a place for herself at Collinwood, she would have to fight for it.

Oh, he could have ordered his vassals to cooperate, to give Lucinda the deference due her. But they would have resented her all the more for his telling them to accept a woman they had no wish to accept. He could only help her in small ways, by giving her a high seat at table, acting as a buffer against Connor.

Lucinda needed to gain the people's respect on her own. And she had it within her power to do so, if she only would.

With a hand to the small of her back, she raised up and stretched backward, adding a new pose to the many images of her that kept him awake at night.

Not that he needed more than the memory of their one kiss to keep him awake, longing for another. He wanted Lucinda. Fighting his lust had become a hopeless battle, especially now that he was almost certain she would welcome his advances.

Too, he'd wrestled with Basil's ghost. The specter hadn't vanished, but grew weaker with each bout. Lucinda had been a victim of her marriage, just as he'd been a victim of his birth. Neither of them had control over events not of their doing. In truth, if Lucinda were the widow of almost any other man, she might be far beyond his reach.

Yet she stood in his forest, with a few steps between them, his for the taking if one of them took those steps.

Lucinda bent over again. Two layers of fabric, a gown of gray wool and a chemise of cream linen, were all that barred his manroot from the core of her. His own knee-length tunic didn't count. 'Twas easily pushed aside. No breeches bound him, for he wore only short hose criss-crossed with leather straps.

"Ouch!" Lucinda bolted upright, sticking a forefinger in her mouth.

He didn't dare stand up and go over to her with his arousal full-blown. She would see in an instant what he'd been thinking about. Seduction. Tangling his fingers in her long raven black hair, drowning in her exotic violet eyes. Finding a patch of long grass, laying her down, easing himself into her body. Claiming her as his lover.

"A sliver?" he asked, his voice rough.

She put the basket down, then turned her hand to examine her injured finger. "Mayhap."

"Come here and let me look."

Lucinda didn't hesitate to obey Richard's command. She walked toward him, slowly, giving her pounding heart a chance to quiet.

She'd thought, at first, that Richard had wandered her way and would move on. Then he'd plunked down on a log and stared at her with a breath-stealing intensity that thrilled her right down to her toes. Her body flared to instant arousal and she ceased thinking rationally.

She wanted a kiss, and more, if Richard was willing.

Perhaps she should feel shame for the brazen way she'd flaunted her body to tempt him. To both her dismay and relief, she felt no remorse, only a burning passion for the man who'd awakened her desire.

No sliver pierced her finger. A mere scratch, done apurpose, drew little blood. If Richard hadn't asked to look at the wound, she'd have asked him to. A base ploy, but hopefully not a futile one.

She stopped in front of him and held out her hand. He took it, gently, and examined the scratch.

"I see no sliver," Richard said, his voice as ragged as her knees were wobbly.

"Good," she said, the word more breathed than spoken.

"Aye, good," he agreed, then turned her hand and kissed her palm.

He caught her around the waist and pulled her into the V of his outspread legs. She stepped toward him and sought his shoulder for balance. The flicker of his tongue on her palm, moist and rough, set her shuddering. The low moan she heard came from her own throat.

And through it she heard the crack and rumble of a falling tree.

Richard felt Lucinda tremble just as the tree crashed to the ground. They had little time before the men felled the second tree and would come looking for them. Not that he needed much time to gain his release.

But a woman needed more, those strokes and caresses in sensitive places that ensured her full pleasure.

He shouldn't be thinking like this, not when he wasn't sure that Lucinda was willing. But if she was, and even half as aroused as he...

Richard pushed himself to his feet and found his answer in glittering pools of violet, alight with smoldering passion. For him.

He pulled her in close and molded his lips to hers, trying to hold back and be gentle. Lucinda didn't allow it. She kissed him back as fiercely as she had before.

His body burned for the woman in his arms, who pressed so close that she couldn't harbor any illusions about what would happen between them. Now. In an outdoor bower.

If he could find a patch of grass to lay her down on.

Richard broke the kiss and held her tight, her cheek pressed against his chest. His heart thudded hard against his ribs as he surveyed the surrounding wood.

"Richard?" Her voice was high, a bit thready. Her hands clenched around fistfuls of his tunic, as if afraid he would let her go.

She had nothing to fear, not on that score.

"A moment, Lucinda. I merely look—" He found a spot where the grass reached knee-high, where the sun beamed down to the ground unhindered by the trees. "There. All right?"

Lucinda didn't look. "I don't give a fig about where!"

"Then put your arms around my neck, woman."

She obeyed immediately. He picked her up and carried her to the pallet that nature had so thoughtfully provided. Within moments, Lucinda lay right where he wanted her—stretched out beside him.

They didn't have time to remove garments, to caress and linger over each other's bodies. Only time to appease the driving hunger that gnawed at them both.

Yet he couldn't bring himself to push Lucinda's skirts up and rut like a beast. Her face, her neck, were soft and smooth beneath his lips. Her hair felt like silk, her lips tasted like warm honey. He found and explored her woman's curves, wishing he could gaze upon and touch her naked breasts instead of her wool gown. Her nipples hardened as if they were uncovered, responding to the stroke of his fingers.

When he could stand no more, he reached for her hems, pushing the garments toward her waist, his hand skimming the inside of her leg. Her knees came up when he reached the apex. She gasped when he petted her private hair, and arched into his hand as his fingers found and caressed the moist, hot entrance to her female berth.

One more time he kissed her, hard and long, until her breath came in short, sharp bursts. Satisfied that she was fully prepared for him, he knelt between her spread legs and uncovered that which he'd touched but not yet seen. And gazed upon perfection.

His lover possessed the shapeliest, creamy white legs he'd ever had the pleasure to gaze upon. Her firm thighs were made to clamp a man to her through the fiercest coupling.

Lucinda squirmed under this most intimate gaze. She knew he would be tender and giving, unlike anything she'd ever experienced.

Richard lowered his mouth to hers, kissing her gently, moving to her earlobe, her neck.... He lavished her with kisses and caresses, sweet and yet demanding. She reached for Richard. Her fingers in his hair, she pulled him away before she shattered into nonexistence. A deep breath helped calm her raging ache, eased her yearning to be filled and possessed. He would possess her when he entered her. She would be his, whether he wanted it so or not, because for the first time in her life she wanted to be filled, to take a man into her.

He shifted, then rose above her slightly. She knew

what the movement meant. She put a hand on his broad shoulder.

"Wait," she said.

He gave her an incredulous look.

"I want...I should..." She shook her head. She lacked the courage to express her wishes out loud. These feelings were too new, the emotions too heady. She might be dazed, but not so far gone as to neglect her part in this.

She pushed on that solid shoulder. "Up. On your knees."

Slowly, he obeyed, his tunic falling down to cover him. 'Twas that under the tunic which had gone neglected.

Richard watched Lucinda scoot forward slightly, then reach for his tunic, her stare directed at the place where his manroot prodded the garment outward.

Bold minx. He didn't stop her from satisfying her curiosity, from uncovering what she wished to see, or from tucking the hem into the girdle at his waist, exposing him to the soft spring breeze and her gaze.

"Oh, my," she whispered, her eyes wide.

He hadn't thought his loins could feel heavier or more coiled. Hadn't realized how difficult it would be to keep from howling like a wolf at the moon, delighted with her obvious admiration and approval.

Then she touched him, just one finger on the tip. He hissed at the shock, but held statue still as her hand moved around and down to between his legs, then up his shaft.

"Lucinda?"

"Hmm?"

She didn't even look up, still mesmerized. And while a part of him reveled in her enthrallment, another part urged him to use the part of his body that fascinated her before it disappointed her.

"Must we still wait?"

"Nay," she said, easing back down onto the grass. "I see there is no need."

She raised her hands, inviting him back down. He needed no further urging to join her and slip inside her warmth, so deep, so tight. Those shapely legs curled around his, and the thighs he'd judged firm pressed him further into her snug berth.

Hellfire, she was tight around him, driving him to near release at her slightest move. He strained to hold himself back to give her time.

"Wait," he breathed.

She arched upward.

"Hellfire."

He gave her all he had, stroke after penetrating stroke. Her face twisted with near pain, her breathing labored. And then, on an upstroke, her head went back and her legs tightened around him. She came apart, taking him with her into a bliss he hadn't known existed.

On the very edge of his awareness, Richard heard the second tree fall.

"Hellfire," she said.

He agreed.

Sweet heaven, with a bit more time, on a mattress or pile of furs, and naked—oh, aye, definitely naked—what utter delight might they find in each other.

"Next time we will do this right, on a comfortable pallet with no one around to disturb us," he vowed, then realized he'd said it aloud.

Lucinda didn't look upset at the prospect. She cupped his cheek with her hand.

"Aye, my lord, next time."

Chapter Eleven

Richard slowly opened the door to Lucinda's hut. Though he needed to rouse Lucinda, he hoped to let Philip sleep. 'Twas barely dawn, the sun's rays providing a soft light so he could see them on their pallets.

Lucinda rose up to almost sitting the moment he stepped over the threshold. Alarmed, she stared at him until she identified the intruder, then relaxed.

Richard nearly forgot what he'd come for. The woman was a beauty when mussed. Her unplaited black hair swept around her shoulders like a cloud of dark smoke, framing her face of creamy white. She blinked several times, clearing her mind of sleep. Those eyes narrowed, questioning his presence.

He whispered. "Edric is hurt. Come."

She nodded, but didn't get up. He knew she waited for him to leave the hut, so she could rise and change from night rail to gown. He forced his feet to move.

Richard stood outside the hut, imagining her removing the night rail, baring her body. As yet, he'd seen only half of what promised to be a glorious sight in whole—Lucinda, naked and sprawled on a pallet awaiting him. For the past two days, since their coupling in the forest, he'd watched for the chance for another such coupling. It hadn't come as he'd hoped. Their first had been an impulsive coming together. The next would require planning, an arranged tryst.

The thought didn't sit well. He could more easily excuse giving in to a moment's fancy than a devised joining with a woman he shouldn't want, but lusted after as he'd never lusted after a woman before.

She came out of the hut, covered with her rough-weave gown, her hair hastily plaited and unveiled. "What ails Edric?"

"His knee. One of my soldiers came to fetch me, saying Edric had tried to walk but the knee buckled under him."

Her head tilted. "Why come for me?"

"Philip once commented that you had some skill in the healing arts."

"You test me?"

"Nay. I simply thought you the most suited to tend the captain of my guard."

He hadn't really thought out his motives that far. But 'twas true. The moment he'd heard of Edric's ailment, he'd also thought to fetch Lucinda.

"Did Edric injure his knee?"

"I have no notion. I have not spoken to him yet. Will Philip be alarmed if he wakes to find you gone?"

She shook her head. "He will be fine. He knows I would not go far."

They walked to the armory in silence.

Edric sat on his cot, clad in only a tunic, the affected leg stretched out. Two men-at-arms stood nearby, chatting with him. Richard waved them out of the armory.

Edric glanced at Lucinda, a slight frown on his face.

"What did you do to your knee, Edric?" Richard asked, drawing the old soldier's attention.

"Nothing. 'Tis fine. I will walk out the pain—"

"I hear you already tried to put weight on it and could not. I brought Lucinda to have a look."

Edric gave an aggrieved sigh. "If you insist, my lord."

Lucinda brought a hand up to cover the hint of a smile that hovered at the corners of her mouth. Richard wished she would let the smile break through, though Edric might not appreciate it.

"I insist. Lucinda?"

She bent to grasp Edric's bare, bony knee, then ran her hands along the sides. Lucky Edric. Richard could almost feel the gentle massage of her thumbs on his own leg as she searched for the source and cause of Edric's pain.

"Well?" Richard asked.

"'Tis fine," Edric stated again.

"'Tis not fine, but could be worse," Lucinda said. "Nothing is broken, or knotted, so far as I can tell. A stiffness of the joint, I would say. A treated hot compress should ease the discomfort. After a few days' rest—"

"Days?" Edric exclaimed, incredulous.

This time her smile burst forth, directed full force at Edric. "Days. Remember when you insisted that I not use my twisted ankle? Well, Edric, I now prescribe that you not use your knee."

"'Twill not take days. I am not a fragile woman."

"Nor am I. Pain, however, takes its own sweet time

to subside, whether in a woman or a gruff soldier. Once wrapped, you can walk on it, but sparingly.''

"I have duties to perform. I cannot be lying about—"

Richard interrupted. "Aye, you can, and will," he told Edric, then turned to Lucinda. "Get whatever you need from the manor. You know where the herbs and bandages are kept?"

"I have seen the basket."

Collinwood boasted no healer. Women tended to their own family's hurts. A large basket, filled with linen strips for bandages, dried herbs, jars of salves and healing oils, sat in a corner of the manor for everyone's use.

"If there is something you need that you cannot find, ask Connor or one of the serving women."

She nodded, but looked unhappy at the prospect. She'd no more than left the room when she came back in. "Do not let him off that cot," she said, then left again.

"That sounded suspiciously like an order, my lord. Never thought I would see the day when one of Northbryre would be giving orders around here again," Edric said without rancor. 'Twas simply an observation, not a condemnation.

Richard had chosen Edric for the captain of his guard from among Gerard's highly trained men-at-arms. The old soldier had helped whip into fighting shape the capable, if not matchless, small garrison of local men who took pride in their status as soldiers in service to Richard of Wilmont.

Without being ordered, or even asked, Edric had also taken on the task of beginning Philip's training. Wherever Edric could be found, there would be Philip trailing close behind. Richard knew he needed to become more involved with the boy's training and education. He'd given the matter some thought, but hadn't yet acted on it.

"How does Philip?" Richard asked.

Edric thought a moment, then answered, "Not badly. Smart little tyke, that one. And a charmer. If it were not for who sired him..." Edric shrugged. "The men seem to accept him among them."

Edric's doing, by example. Now, if only Connor were a better example for the rest of the people...

"The rest of the people will take a while longer," Richard observed.

"Aye, and they will accept the boy before the woman. 'Tis easier to like a charming child than a haughty noblewoman."

Richard thought "haughty" too harsh a term, but could see where her self-protective aloofness could be seen as such.

"Lucinda should smile more."

"She might, if she had something to smile about. Mayhap you should send her out to gather kindling again," Edric suggested. "She enjoyed the outing, judging from the look on her face when the party returned."

Richard didn't comment on what else she'd done in the forest that she enjoyed. Thoroughly. As had he. He'd made her his lover, and part of her look upon returning had been the result of being well pleasured.

Edric did have a point, however. Lucinda's delight at having some chore to do had been obvious.

As it was this morn. Tending Edric had made her smile.

She wasn't smiling when she returned to the armory, empty-handed. "The women will not allow me near the herbs. Connor told them that I am not to touch anything within the manor unless he was there to watch me. He is not about."

Richard sighed inwardly. Of all the people at Collinwood, Connor was Lucinda's biggest challenge. The man hated too much, too hard, to come around to accepting her any time soon. If ever.

Richard put a hand out to Edric. "Come, lean on me. We will go into the manor. Lucinda can wrap your knee there."

"My lord, you cannot expect me to cross the bailey using your lordship as a crutch!"

"Would you rather be seen draped over my shoulder? Your choice, Edric."

Edric grumbled during the whole, slow walk to the manor. Richard eased him onto a bench, then fetched the basket and handed it to Lucinda. He didn't reprimand the worried-looking servants, they'd been obeying Connor's orders. Orders he would tell Connor to rescind.

The servants returned to the task of preparing the tables where the manor folk would soon break fast. Lucinda dug out what she wanted from the basket and set about making a compress. People straggled into the manor, among them Philip, who followed his natural inclination to seek out Edric.

"I have a chore for you this day, Philip," Richard said. "Edric has watched over you for many days and done a good job of it. 'Tis now your day to watch over Edric."

The boy's eyes went wide. "Me?"

"Aye, you."

Lucinda bent down in front of Edric, an herb-coated bandage in her hands. Edric hissed when it hit his knee.

"'Tis best hot," Lucinda said. "The heat will ease the soreness and speed the healing power of the herbs."

With deft hands she wrapped the knee, tight, and tied off the bandage.

"What did you do to your knee?" Philip asked Edric.

"Nothing."

"Then why does Mother wrap it?"

"Because Lord Richard insisted."

"Can you walk?"

"Nay, he cannot," Richard injected. "Your duty today, Philip, is to keep Edric from using his leg unless necessary. Should he try to ignore my order to rest, you are to come and tell me. Understood?"

Philip's expression turned somber. "Aye, my lord."

"Good. Now, let us break fast."

Edric tried to get up. Philip put his hand on Edric's chest and pushed him back down—not hard for the boy to do because of Edric's unbalance.

"Stay where you are," Philip said with a good deal of command in his voice for one so young. "I will bring the food to you."

Philip scampered off.

Edric looked up at Richard with narrowed eyes. "'Tis a sorry day, indeed, when I must answer to a whelp of six."

"You answer to me. The boy is my enforcer. Give him grief and I will find a way to make you suffer."

Edric cussed as Philip walked up, a cup of ale in

one hand, a piece of cheese balanced on a chunk of bread in the other.

Philip handed over the food to Edric. "Mayhap, when we finish, we could play a game or two."

"Aye, mayhap," Edric grumbled and tucked into his cheese.

Richard left the two to their own devices. Lucinda followed him to the table. Connor still hadn't returned from wherever he'd gone off to.

"I hope Edric knows other games than how to toss dice. Philip need not learn too many vices before he is grown," Lucinda said, with a hint of suggestion that Richard should talk to Edric about it.

"One cannot be around a group of soldiers without learning to toss dice. Besides, my father felt the game a good way to practice ciphering and the handling of coins."

"There are better ways to learn one's numbers than by gambling."

Aye. Dull ways. Richard remembered one tutor who thought it fun to place columns of numbers on a slate and watch young boys struggle to add them up. He'd disliked it then, and didn't care for it now, though he must to keep his accounts in order.

The discussion with Edric about Lucinda's lack of duties rolled around in Richard's head. She'd once been the chatelaine of a large household, and kept Basil's accounts. Those damn ledgers filled with all of those numbers.

He grinned to himself. If Lucinda wanted a chore, he knew just which one to give her.

Connor appeared and lowered onto his seat. "Forgive my tardiness, my lord. One of the mares is due to foal and I wished to check on her progress."

"How does she?"

"Nicely. In a few more days we should have a foal to add to your list of possessions." He looked down the table. "I see the servants carried on without me so no one suffered unduly."

"Only Edric," Richard said, nodding Edric's way. "His knee pains him. When I sent Lucinda for bandages the servants turned her away. 'Twas an unnecessary annoyance, Connor. Lucinda is to have the same access to the manor's resources as everyone else. You will make that known."

Connor shifted on the bench. "My lord, some of those herbs could prove deadly in the wrong hands."

Lucinda let out a small gasp at Connor's insinuation.

Richard folded his arms on the table and leaned toward his steward. "If Lucinda intended to poison anyone, I suspect it would be you. And if that were her intent, I also suspect she would have found a way to do so long before now. Since you still live, I feel we are all safe. Lucinda is not a prisoner here, Connor. You will cease treating her as one."

Connor replied in the only manner he could. "As you wish, my lord."

Feeling the matter settled, Richard got up and retrieved several rolled pieces of parchment from a chest near his pallet.

"Bring the remains of your meal to your hut, Lucinda. I have a chore in mind for you and wish to discuss it in private."

On the small table in her hut, Richard spread out the accounts of his holdings. All but two of the holdings had once belonged to Basil.

Richard stood behind her, looking over her shoulder, almost touching her, but not quite.

"I see you know these holdings," Richard said, his warm breath teasing her ear.

"Aye," she said, struggling to concentrate on the parchment in front of her and not the man behind her. "I see many of Basil's former English holdings. You wish me to verify these for you?" she asked, thinking it the only reason why he would expose the extent of his wealth.

"Aye, but I also wish you to take over the recording. Soon the spring rents and goods will arrive. I like receiving them, but dislike recording them."

Delight warred with disbelief. "You would trust me with your ledgers?"

"You know exactly what to expect from each holding. I have no doubt you can keep the ledgers in order."

She turned slightly to study his face, now very close to hers. With little movement on her part, she could wrap her arms around him, kiss him, draw his attention from the ledgers. But 'twas the ledgers they'd come to her hut to discuss, and the man was actually serious about his offer.

"You do not fear I would steal funds from you?"

He shook his head. "I also know exactly what to expect from each holding, and will check the recording once completed. Should you try some scheme, I would know of it."

Richard didn't trust her completely, but that didn't bother her. A smart lord checked his underling's work, particularly when it involved large sums of coin. She took it as a compliment that he would even show her the ledgers.

These ledgers were beautifully done, neatly lined, the words and numbers scripted in a bold hand. Richard's hand.

"I would find great pleasure in helping you with these accounts. My thanks."

He reached around her to pull one of the papers forward, brushing against her arm, sending a delicious tingle racing through her limbs.

In the woods, he'd promised an unhurried "next time." She'd waited for two days for him to come to her again. This morn, when she'd wakened to find him in her hut, she hoped he'd come for such a reason.

Could he have more on his mind now than these ledgers? She dearly hoped so. She certainly did. Her body burned for want of his touch, more so than it had in the woods. Now she no longer only wondered about shared pleasure, she knew what Richard could make her feel—and craved more.

His mouth moved in the most provocative manner. "You will find I have made changes. Durwood no longer supplies chickens, but pigs. And Southton's... Lucinda, do you hear a word I say?"

"Aye. You like chicken."

The corner of his mouth twitched. "I prefer piglet."

"How nice, then, that you can get them from Southton."

"Your mind has wandered. To what place does it stray?"

To beyond heaven. To wondering at how brazen she'd become in so short a time.

"Not far, merely down to the list of goods due from Norgate." She ran her finger over an item on that list. "I see you still receive bear pelts. Bear pelts make for softer pallets than long grass."

Richard glanced at the bear fur he'd long ago given Lucinda to use as her pallet. A woolen coverlet lay rumpled atop the fur, turned back from when she'd crawled out of it this morn. Where, if not for Philip's nearness and Edric's knee to attend, he might have crawled in to join her.

Was her comparison of fur to grass accidental, or was she truly inviting him to share the fur with him now?

He put his hands on her shoulders, turned her around, and found his answer in sultry pools of violet.

"You prefer soft fur to coarse grass to lay upon?"

"I prefer your skin against mine, whether on fur or grass."

Her door bore no bolt to slide to ensure privacy but, hopefully, they wouldn't suffer interruption—Philip was watching Edric, and unless some urgent matter came up, none of the manor folk would come looking for him.

Richard hoped no urgent matter beyond his own urgent need arose, for he was quickly losing interest in any activity except taking Lucinda to her pallet and having his fill of her.

He bent to kiss her mouth, and reveled in her heated, eager response. She grabbed hold of his tunic as he slowly backed toward the fur. When he stopped, she didn't, taking the extra step necessary to press her body fully against his.

Locked in an embrace, he sought other skin to taste. She shivered when he nuzzled her neck just below her ear.

Go slowly, he told himself, unraveling her heavy

braid. The twists of silken black gave way easily to his busy fingers.

Her fingers, too, were busy, undoing the leather girdle about his waist. She wore no girdle. Indeed, his exploring hands soon learned that in her hurry to dress she hadn't donned a chemise, only her gown. Just as he'd simply tossed on a tunic, which her exploring hands discovered—and slipped under. The heat of her hands on his outer thighs spread inward, tormenting him. If she touched him now, they might not make it down to the fur.

He pulled away and quickly slipped the boots from her feet and her gown over her head, unveiling her to his hungry eyes. He feasted on what he'd only dreamed of. Of dusky-tipped breasts that begged him to touch. Of a body beautifully curved from the long, sleek lines of her neck to the high, graceful arch of her feet. A siren's body, singing a beckoning melody.

Entranced, he answered, tumbling into her spell and onto the fur. Lucinda received his weight with a satisfied sigh. He turned that sigh to soft moans as he kissed, and tasted, and petted until he knew every inch of her lovely form and found each of her sensitive places.

Suckling her nipples made them pucker. Stroking her inner thigh brought her knee up. Deep kisses drove her wild. She arched at the mere stroke of a finger through her moist heat.

"Have you been thinking about coupling all morn, as I have?" he asked.

"When you came into my hut to fetch me, 'twas not to tend Edric that I hoped you came," she said, breathless.

"Then tend me now, Lucinda. Ease my ache."

To his amazement, she chuckled low in her throat and teased. "Do you ache, my lord? Your knee, perhaps? Shall I begin there?"

"Begin any place you wish, minx."

Lucinda began by tugging off his boots, wanting him as naked as she.

Kneeling between his legs, she gave his calves and thighs her attention, with long strokes, purposely avoiding the source of his ache. She uncovered him to the waist and paused to admire that part of his body that made him male—a very virile and solid male. But she didn't linger there, more intent on removing his tunic. He helped her by sitting up so she could pull the tunic up over his head.

Almost immediately he latched onto one nipple, then the other, all the while stroking her back and bottom. She tried to foster patience, to let him fondle and kiss where he would, until patience yielded to the burning passion fanned by his skilled caresses.

Lucinda leaned forward, pushing him back, falling with him gently to the fur.

Her hands skimmed along the breadth of his shoulders, so wide they nearly spread the width of the pelt. She moved lower, to kiss and caress the smooth contours of his chest, that rose and fell with his deepening breaths. And lower, to his rapidly beating heart.

And lower yet—where she stopped, and couldn't go on.

Across Richard's lower ribs a jagged scar slashed across his body, as if someone had tried to cleave him in two.

Someone had. One of Basil's mercenaries.

She stared at the scar, tremors of hate for Basil and compassion for Richard scurrying through her trembling limbs. How could Richard bear to lie with the widow of the man who'd been responsible for this horrible, life-leeching wound?

Desire fled, pushed out by a strong, deep ache in her heart. She laid her cheek across the rough flesh of the wound that could have ended his life, fighting the overwhelming urge to cry a stream full of tears and spit venomous curses.

"Lucinda?"

"I knew—" Her voice broke and she had to begin again. "I knew you had been wounded, but I did not know…merciful heaven, how you must have suffered!"

He rolled to his side and pulled her up. She threw her arms around his neck and held tight, unable to look him in the face, fearful of what she might see.

"'Tis over," he said roughly.

"But not forgotten. Evil such as Basil's can *never* be forgotten, nor far from your memory when you bear such a mark."

He was quiet for a long time, then said, "The scar I wear reminds me of him, aye. But had I died, 'twould have been a swift and honorable death. Others suffered greater agonies for a longer time before they perished. Now the scar serves to remind me that Basil's loss was my gain, and helps me be a better lord to those Basil once abused."

She loosened her grip and backed far enough to see his face. She doubted that his vassals saw him as their savior. Most likely, they'd seen only one lord replacing another lord and he'd faced their hostility and mistrust. But little by little, in his quiet, steadfast way, he'd won them over.

"Do they see the honor of your heart, I wonder?"

she mused, brushing back his blond hair. "Or do they only know that you ended their suffering?"

He claimed her hand, kissed her palm, then moved it down, ever downward to between his legs. "Make me into no more than a mere man, Lucinda. Only a man whose current suffering is in need of relief."

Her hand wrapped around him in an intimate caress, feeling his power, feeding his pleasure. With a tenderness so foreign and appealing, he rekindled her flame until she burned hotter than ever. When he could endure no more, he covered her and claimed her with long, firm strokes. So deep as to touch her where no man had touched before. Lucinda tumbled into that special world where only Richard could take her, taking him with her. And in the aura of its light, saw her danger.

Basil had abused her body and done his best to muddle her mind. More times than she could count he'd ripped out her heart. But he'd never touched her soul.

Richard did. He broke through every shield she raised, penetrating deep to the core of her very being. Leaving her vulnerable and unprotected against him.

She held him tightly, still joined with him, breathing hard. Grasping for the shards of her shattered defenses, Lucinda feared the pieces would never again fit tightly.

Chapter Twelve

"Are you ready, Lucinda?"

"Whenever you are, my lord."

By the gleam in his eyes, Lucinda knew Richard referred to an activity other than comparing the contents of the cart to the list of tributes due. His indiscretion flouted all decorum and ignited a flush that probably colored her cheeks.

Yet, truth to tell, she would rather be rolling around on her pallet with Richard than counting geese and kegs of ale, too. If she read his mind aright—a skill she was getting very good at—sometime this afternoon he would come to her hut and make love to her, and everyone at Collinwood would know.

In the two months since they'd become lovers, Richard had never taken any steps to hide their liaison. He openly visited her hut whenever the whim struck him, taking the one precaution of ensuring that Philip was occupied elsewhere.

She'd taken one precaution as well—the packet of herbs she secreted deep within her body to block his seed. Richard knew, and approved.

Sometimes he took her with mind-numbing tenderness, at other times with ravaging urgency. No matter how he joined with her, Richard took care to send her reeling beyond the heavens.

Always, whenever his lust blossomed, she was ready and eager for him. And damn the man, he knew it. Even now he wore a smug smile. He'd become adept at reading her thoughts, too.

"Three geese," she read from the list.

He chuckled and turned to his task. He put his hand on a crate at the back of the cart, then drew back sharply when one of the creatures hissed and snapped.

"Three geese, but soon to be two," he declared, pointing at the offending fowl. "I will have this one for evening meal."

Lucinda noted which goose vexed Richard and thereby sentenced himself to the soup kettle.

"I will inform Connor. Next is a sack of unmilled oats."

"Here, sitting beside two kegs of ale. I dearly hope this is better than the last batch."

And so it went, on down the list and the contents of the cart that came from one of Richard's far-flung holdings, one that had once belonged to Basil.

As steward of Collinwood, Connor kept the records of the holding's revenue, of the fees and goods due to Richard from Collinwood's vassals. At each of Richard's holdings a steward performed the same duty.

Richard, however, had kept the accounting of his stewards' reports and ensured that Gerard, his liege lord, received a portion. Lucinda didn't question Richard's reason for giving over this duty to her; she was too glad to have some duty to perform. It made sense, however, since she'd known what to expect

from each of Basil's holdings once she learned which
ones Richard now oversaw.

This cart represented the last of the spring tributes.
In a few days' time, some of these goods would be
sent to Wilmont.

"Three large pieces of leather," she read the last
item.

"Nay, no leather. I asked the steward to barter the
leather in exchange for this." He pulled a large sack
to a clear spot at the back of the cart. "If he got this
right, I might forgive him the inferior ale and that
beastly goose."

Curious, Lucinda walked over to see what he'd
bought. He unwrapped two lengths of finely woven
linen, one of ruby red, the other of pale green. Exquisite.

"Summer comes. You would swelter in your wool
gowns," he said.

He'd ordered the linen for her. She ran her fingertips over the fabric. So smooth. So beautifully dyed.

"You can sew, can you not?" he teased.

"Aye. Of course. Naturally," she blubbered, and
looked up to see how very pleased he was, with both
the gift and her delight. "'Tis beautiful, Richard. My
thanks."

"I will order the cart unloaded while you record
the goods received. Tell Connor to have the goose
feathers set aside for a feather-stuffed mat. Gerard has
one, and I intend to have one, too. Think how very
cozy that will be."

He walked off with a swagger. Incorrigible man.

Lucinda rewrapped the fabric and picked up the
sack to take it to her hut so nothing untoward would

happen to it, already planning how she would cut, sew and decorate new gowns.

She turned, and came face to face with Connor, and the familiar and still disturbing menace directed her way. She quickly brushed it aside and pointed at the crate of geese.

"Richard wishes the dark gray goose cooked for his evening meal—"

"And its feathers set aside for a cozy mat. I heard."

Had he, then? How long had he been standing near, listening? Spying, more like.

"Then I will leave you to set about it," she said, and moved to go around him.

He blocked her way and reached up to tug at the rope that secured the sack she carried. "A fine gift for one so undeserving. Though mayhap I misjudge. Noble men often reward a leman with fancy gifts for a good tumble, and unlike the rest of his lordship's possessions, you do look a bit ragged."

She bristled but held her temper. She would *not* become involved in a public argument of this nature with Connor! His very suggestion that Richard considered her a possession was preposterous.

"Connor, if you would stand aside, I have duties to perform."

"Of course," he said with a mocking bow. "I am sure you will wish to appropriately thank his lordship for his gracious gift. I must say, I find it vulgar that he chooses to rut with a woman of so sordid a past, but then, mayhap that is what he finds so appealing. How better to honor Basil's memory than to use the vermin's wife as a whore?"

Inwardly, she flinched, but allowed Connor to see

only an uptilted chin and icy look as she brushed past him.

Connor was wrong. Had to be wrong. But what if he had the truth of it? *Nay*, her heart screamed, but her head reeled with uncertainty.

She entered her hut and dropped the sack of fabric down on the table.

Had Richard simply used her as a means of vengeance on Northbryre? Every time he joined with her, was he secretly despoiling the woman who had once belonged to his most hated enemy? Had she blindly cooperated in her own defilement?

Nay. If Richard meant to despoil, he wouldn't take the time to give her pleasure.

And despite Connor's allusion, she wasn't Richard's possession, mere chattel to do with as he pleased. If anything, she belonged to King Henry— an unpleasant thought altogether. She might be dependent on Richard for food and shelter for as long as she must remain within his care, but he owned no rights to her body. She'd given herself to him by her own will, out of her own needs.

Needs she'd never perceived within herself until meeting Richard. If anyone had told her, up until a bit over two months ago, that she could enjoy intimacy with a man, she would have called the person daft.

Truly, if Richard used her, she had no right to complain, for did she not use him, too?

A boisterous ruckus in the bailey drew her out of the hut. Three men had ridden in, stirring the dust and ruining her day.

Stephen had returned from Normandy.

* * *

Richard strolled out of the manor just as Stephen reined in his mount, scattering dirt. Behind Stephen rode the two guards who had accompanied him to Normandy. The guards and horses looked road-weary, but not Stephen.

Apparently, Stephen considered riding into Collinwood an occasion of some import. He wore no hauberk or helm, but a fine-linen black dalmatica trimmed in scarlet over a bloodred sherte. Not a speck of road dust marred his garments. 'Twas irksome how the man could appear fresh and impeccably attired when all others drooped.

"Hail, Richard!" Stephen cried out through a sparkling grin. He fairly sprang out of the saddle and dropped lightly to his feet. "I bring good tidings."

Richard couldn't help but return his half brother's smile. "I see as much. If you brought bad news, you would have ridden in here wearing a hefty scowl. Your trip went well?"

"Aye, *very* well. Offer me a goblet of wine to wash the dust from my throat and I will tell you all."

Once in the manor, Richard ordered a serving wench to fetch goblets and a flagon of wine. Stephen removed his riding gauntlets and tossed them onto the trestle table.

"'Tis good to be back on English soil," Stephen declared. "I may be Norman, but Normandy is so foreign. Each time I go, I am surprised anew that I feel no connection to the land of my heritage."

"Why should you? Granted, both of your parents were Norman, but your upbringing embraced both Norman and English ways, more so than most. How many nobles do you know who have learned the English language?"

Stephen slid onto a bench. "Aye, well, I had no need of English while in Normandy, I can tell you. The Latin that Father insisted we learn served me well, though. Hellfire, Richard, you should have seen the tangle of documents and records and ledgers that George keeps on his holdings. One would need to be a cleric to understand it all."

A serving wench set goblets and a flagon of wine on the table. Richard waved her off and poured out the beverage himself.

"George cooperated with you, then?"

"Not at first. He refused to see me. So I called upon some of the holdings and told each steward to no longer send rents to George, but to you." With a smug look, Stephen added, "Some of those stewards sent word to George about my visit, for he soon sent for me. He apologized for his earlier rudeness, saying he thought I was a charlatan because he believed Lucinda and Philip had died along with Basil. 'Twas only when the nobles who'd attended the royal betrothal returned to Normandy and told him of Lucinda's court appearance that he believed I was who I said I was and that I may have some claim on him."

"And you believed that?"

"'Tis possible, I suppose. George tells a tale of traveling to England shortly after hearing of Basil's death, to learn what he could of his cousin's holdings. 'Twasn't long before he learned that King Henry had confiscated everything Basil held in England. So, George claims, he set out to see what became of Basil's heir. No one remembered seeing Lucinda or Philip after Basil's downfall. When the search proved futile, and he did not receive any word from them after several months, he assumed they no longer lived.

He returned to Normandy, and as Basil's closest relative, took possession of the remaining holdings.''

"Did he dispute Philip's right to those holdings?"

"Nay, but he was shocked that I knew exactly which holdings were Philip's and what rents they paid. If not for the list I carried, I doubt I would have received an honest accounting. However, George is willing to do right by you, Richard. Indeed, under the circumstances, he is prepared to be very generous.''

Philip ran into the manor, a helmet clutched in his little hands. *Not quite so little anymore,* Richard acknowledged with an odd pang in his chest. The boy had grown since coming to Collinwood, requiring new tunics and shoes.

The boy's headlong rush to the table halted abruptly when Philip saw Stephen. His look of joy faded to uncertainty.

"You may approach, Philip.''

Philip did so, at a more sedate pace. He placed the helmet on the table for Richard's inspection.

"Edric said I should show you your helm, my lord. I polished it by myself this time," he said with a note of youthful pride.

Richard ignored Stephen's frown and picked up the leather helmet. Philip had done a fair job of polishing the silver studs and noseguard. Only one stud showed a small smudge of tarnish.

Richard pointed to the stud. "Apply a harder cloth to this one, then I will inspect again.''

Philip studied the imperfectly polished stud, then used the sleeve of his tunic to finish the job. He turned hope-filled eyes on Richard.

"Well done," Richard told him. "You may tell

Edric that I give you sole charge of polishing my helm. How goes the work on the chain mail?''

Philip screwed up his nose. ''Slow. All those rings!''

Richard held back a chuckle. Polishing a full suit of chain mail was indeed a tedious job. But not one beyond Philip's ability or patience level.

''A warrior's mail is both a mark of his status and his protection in battle,'' Richard said. ''Take care to make the rings gleam, and mark any that need repair. My life could depend upon your diligence.''

Philip picked up the helm with a somber nod. ''So Edric says.'' The boy glanced at Stephen, whose frown had deepened. The child's face twisted into several expressions that Richard now recognized as an attempt to summon courage.

The boy had had ample opportunities to practice the skill over the past months. Philip faced the same censure and snubbing as Lucinda. And just like his mother, Philip faced adversity with dignity and forbearance.

Finally, Philip asked, ''Shall we still ride this noon?''

'Twas a question Philip shouldn't have felt the need to ask. Richard let a bit of ire show. ''I promised you we would, did I not?''

''Aye, but since Lord Stephen has arrived, you might rather spend the time with him.''

''Have I ever broken my word to you, Philip?''

''Nay, but—''

''Nor will I. My promise to you stands firm. A good lord always keeps faith with his vassals, Philip. Remember that.''

Philip directed another solemn nod Richard's way. Then he turned to leave.

"Philip, your manners."

The boy turned back. "My apologies, Lord Richard," he said in a manner too tight and mature for a child of six. Philip then executed a bow to Stephen, and a deeper bow to Richard. "By your leave, my lord."

Richard nodded his permission. Philip then strode out with all the bearing of a soldier.

"You coddle that boy, Richard," Stephen said.

"The boy is far from coddled. If anything, he works far harder to gain my approval than any other boy at Collinwood."

"'Twould seem he works hard because the rewards are greater. What other boy would earn a ride for polishing a helmet?"

"'Tis not so much a reward as another lesson," Richard defended his decision. "He needs to learn to sit a horse in accordance with his rank. Philip *is* Norman, a noble. My duty as his protector demands I ensure Philip knows all he needs to know before he comes of age and assumes control of his lands. I intend to raise the boy as our father raised us, by giving him the best tutoring available and by good example."

Stephen's eyes narrowed. "Richard, the boy comes from bad blood. Not only was his sire a cruel, dull-witted, greedy man, but so is this cousin of his— George. One can only assume that the bloodline is tainted. 'Tis against the rules of nature to think the child could escape the affliction."

"Then let us pray that the blood of the mother proves stronger than that of the sire. The woman shows no sign of avarice. Her blood could be the boy's salvation.''

''Surely you jest! Have you learned nothing of the woman in the past months?''

Richard had learned much about Lucinda and learned more each day. He admired not only her beauty and intelligence, but her tenacity and courage, qualities that few women of his acquaintance possessed.

And her fire. Hidden behind the aloof facade that she showed the world smoldered a passion unlike any he'd ever known. Each time he tapped into Lucinda's fire, he came away drained and warmed, body and soul.

''I know the woman,'' Richard said.

''Ah, but which woman?'' Stephen asked. ''George told me somewhat of how she came to wed Basil. He tells of a woman skilled at disguise, of a cunning and intellect so sharp that it frightened her father. 'Tis said her father gave her in marriage for the price of a broodmare, and considered himself fortunate at Basil's willingness to have her.''

Stephen leaned forward, intense in his assertion. ''The boy is doomed, Richard. Think of Basil's avarice, abiding within the same mind as a man with sharp wits. Think of the havoc and suffering such a man might inflict upon an ill-prepared victim.''

Richard shook his head. The thought that Philip, an endearing and obedient child, could become this monster Stephen described was too outlandish to fathom. And Lucinda? Stephen didn't understand that her disguise shielded her vulnerability. Neither, apparently, had her father understood. How insulted and pained she must have felt at the pittance for which she'd been sold.

"Hellfire, Stephen, you make it sound as if both should be locked away like dangerous beasts! Mayhap once you get to know them you will soften your swift and damning judgment."

"Not I. I have no desire to have more contact with either of them than I must, and as of the morn neither must you. Even now George awaits them in Dover. The more swiftly you can get them there, the more quickly they can return to Normandy."

A numbing chill ran though Richard's blood. "What are you talking about?"

"George is willing to take them both, and is prepared to pay handsomely for the trouble they have already caused you. Three wagons loaded with a year's worth of the tributes from Philip's holdings awaits delivery of the woman and boy. I thought it a generous trade."

Stephen looked very pleased with himself for making such a bargain. Richard held back the fist he was tempted to place squarely on his brother's jaw.

'Twas so typical of Stephen to rush headlong into a bargain with George without thinking the whole thing through. Stephen had seen only the chance to be rid of Lucinda and Philip, but hadn't considered the consequences.

"I see," Richard said tightly. "And did you happen to stop and get the king's approval for this trade?"

Stephen shrugged. "Why should you need Henry's approval? You are the child's protector and may do with him as you wish. The woman must go where the boy goes."

"Henry gave them to me knowing full well that Philip had family in Normandy. If Henry wanted Philip returned to Normandy, he would have given the boy to George. Now, if I send the boy to George without Henry's permission, once again Wilmont will suffer the king's displeasure. Surely, Stephen, we do not need one more royal mark against us when we have just begun to win back favor."

"Oh. Well, then you shall just have to ask Henry. I see no reason why he shouldn't approve."

Richard could, but it didn't matter, because he wasn't about to ask the king for release from this duty and risk angering Henry merely for asking. Too, he'd made a bargain with Lucinda—her bride price in exchange for the list of Philip's lands. 'Twas a debt he owed and needed the income from Philip's lands to pay.

That he would miss Philip's sunny face and Lucinda's fire played no part in his resolve to keep the pair at Collinwood. His own feelings on the matter must not influence a decision of such import.

"Nay, Stephen. This matter is settled. The boy is under my care and will remain with me."

Stephen shifted on his stool. "Then what will you tell George?"

"Not I. 'Twas you who agreed to present this bargain and you who will give him my answer. On the morn, you will get on your horse and ride south to Dover. Give George my greetings and thank him for his offer, which I must refuse. Then send the wagons of goods to me and send George back to Normandy."

Stephen sighed. "He will not be pleased."

"His feelings concern me not. Henry's royal edict will be obeyed—by me, by him."

Connor came into the manor, a grin spread across his face, and ambled slowly toward the table.

"My lord Stephen," he said with a slight bow. "How good to have you visit us! 'Tis too late to arrange a feast for today, but surely tomorrow—"

"There is no need, Connor," Richard interrupted, staring pointedly at Stephen. "My brother will be leaving for Dover at first sun."

"First sun?" Stephen complained.

Richard smiled. "Aye, the earlier the better. Take heart, Stephen. Your service to me is near an end. Afterward, you can go to Wilmont and give Gerard a report."

While Stephen groaned, Connor nodded his approval. "Aye, my lord. If you are to be the savior who removes these loathsome persons from our midst, I agree—the earlier the better. I have already told the woman to begin her packing. On the morrow, as soon as she is gone, I will have the hut torn down and the beams returned to the woodpile."

Richard didn't need to ask from whom Connor had heard the news. Stephen's guards must be spreading the tale. He could well imagine the delight running rampant in the bailey. Connor had taken his elation one step too far, however, by taking the news to Lucinda. The man's continued hostility toward Lucinda could no longer be borne.

Richard rose from his stool to his full height, feeling not a twinge of guilt for fully intending to intimidate his frail steward.

"Well, Connor, since you took it upon yourself to tell Lucinda to pack, you may now be the one to tell her she need not. You will also apologize to her for putting her to the trouble."

Crestfallen, Connor babbled, "But my lord, I heard...they are not leaving?"

"Nay, they are not!"

Connor looked to Stephen for confirmation.

Incensed by his steward's impertinence, Richard slammed the table with his fist, rattling the goblets. Connor took a step back and swallowed hard.

"Do I now have your complete attention, Connor?"

"Aye, my lord," he said, his voice small.

"Did I not just give you an order?"

Connor bowed. "I will inform the...lady."

"And you *will* apologize! And just to ensure that you do, you will do it within my presence. If I hear one belittling word or insincere tone, you will apologize over and over again until you get it right."

Connor's lips went thin. "Surely, my lord, you do not expect me to grovel before that...her."

"I expect you to show Lucinda a measure of consideration. She is as human as any other person in this manor and, by the saints, you will remember it."

Connor began his slow trek to the door. Before Richard could follow, Stephen cleared his throat and, grinning, got to his feet.

"You know, Richard, I am quite glad that you do not lose your temper often. You look and sound just like Gerard when you do, and I find that frightening."

"You do not look frightened, and well you might, for I am not terribly happy with you, either."

If anything, Stephen's smile widened. "I know, but again like Gerard, your anger flares hot and then cools. Neither of you can maintain a rage for long. Which bodes well for me, since both of you throw things while in a rage, and because I seem to have the ability to ignite you both. While I still believe you make a mistake in not handing these two over to George, 'tis your decision to make and I will abide by it. Now, while you see to Connor, I am off to chew on two guards whose mouths flap too freely.''

They walked out of the manor side by side, then Stephen veered left toward the stables. Richard noticed that Connor stood outside the door to Lucinda's hut, waiting. Indeed, most of his people stood about the bailey, staring at him, waiting for some pronouncement. None, however, seemed overly joyful at what they'd surely heard—that Lucinda and Philip would be gone on the morn. Some smiled, but most appeared indifferent.

Except Philip, whose sucked-in bottom lip and glittering eyes revealed his feelings. And Edric, whose hand rested lightly on the boy's shoulder, looking askance.

Richard took the few long strides necessary to come within arm's length of them. ''Edric, I have a chore to see to, then will take Philip riding. Prepare the pony. And tomorrow, if the sleeve of my chain mail is perfectly polished, we will do so again.''

The old soldier nodded his understanding, his expression reflecting his approval. Philip's expression remained unchanged. Richard bent down and chucked him under the chin.

''Thought you were about to get out of polishing my mail by departing for Dover, did you? Alas, boy, the chore is still yours. You are not going anywhere, except for a pony ride.''

Philip's eyes brightened. Tears threatened. He tried to say something and choked on the words.

Unable to do otherwise, Richard hefted Philip up

and held him tight through the heartrending sobs that shook the boy's body. The child could act so grownup that 'twas sometimes hard to remember that he was yet a little boy. And right now, Philip was one very upset little boy.

"Shh," Richard whispered, rubbing the child's back. "'Tis all right, Philip. Have no fear that I would send you away. Be at ease."

Richard held the boy close until, with one last sniffle, Philip's head rose. Swollen eyes squinted in a face red and wet.

"Go with Edric. I will come for you in a bit."

"You...won't be...long?"

"Nay, not long at all," he promised, hoping he spoke true.

If Lucinda was as upset as Philip, 'twould take far longer to soothe her than her son and be nowhere near as easy.

Chapter Thirteen

Six strides didn't allow for satisfactory pacing, but Lucinda paced anyway, unable to sit.

She dashed away her last tear and took a steadying breath to quell her terror and anger. Connor had relayed the details of Stephen's unholy bargain with George with such fervor that she hadn't questioned his tale, or doubted that all of Collinwood weren't now celebrating their lord's good fortune.

Richard would be sore pressed to refuse George's offering. Any man would. A year's worth of goods in exchange for a woman and boy whom he hadn't wanted responsibility for in the first place was simply too tempting to resist. And he would make numerous people happy—not only his vassals, but his family, particularly his brother Gerard.

Nothing and no one could induce her to return to Normandy, especially under George's control. Merciful heaven, if she stepped aboard the boat she was doomed. George wouldn't have qualms about tossing her and Philip overboard in the middle of the Channel. None would be the wiser for months, and if anyone questioned her demise, George would concoct some story and likely be believed.

Had Richard already agreed to the bargain Stephen struck with George? Was there yet time to talk him out of it? If she couldn't convince Richard to refuse, then what?

Escape. She'd done so before and could do so again. She would take Philip and go into hiding once more, and this time remain hidden.

She glanced at the luxurious linen that had captured her thoughts earlier. Amazing how one's concerns could drastically change in the course of an hour. At the moment, she could not care less whether or not Richard used her, not when survival took precedent.

Poor Philip. Had someone told him? He would be very upset at the prospect of leaving Collinwood. He loved his new home, along with Edric and Richard. Particularly Richard. Philip thought of his protector as a mix of mentor and father, and wouldn't understand how Richard could send him away.

In her headlong rush out the door, she didn't see Connor until she crashed into him and knocked him down. Impulse brought an apology to her lips and a hand out to help him rise. She withheld both. The man deserved a knocking on his arse.

He looked up at her. "I need to speak with you."

"Wag your malicious tongue elsewhere, Connor. I have no wish to hear whatever you intend to say."

"You must listen," he said, struggling to gain his feet.

"I must find Philip." Lucinda turned to see Richard standing in the middle of the bailey, his arms wrapped around her little boy, giving comfort.

Her heart lurched and her ire faded. Even from this

distance she could tell Philip had been crying. A dark spot marred the shoulder of Richard's tunic, where Philip shed his tears.

After a reassuring squeeze, Richard put Philip down and shooed him toward Edric.

She'd once thought Richard an unfit protector for Philip, being neither full Norman nor a highly placed noble. The man was of bastard birth and her late husband's enemy. None of those things mattered to her anymore.

Richard came toward her with long strides. A tall, muscled warrior, strong of body and purpose. His arms swung at his sides in rhythm to his footfalls, his hands clenched. Hands that could skim over her with serene tenderness or stroke her with urgent hunger. Either way, guiding her to beyond the heavens. Hands that she'd heard could wield a sword with deft skill had also comforted a small child.

A hint of anger tinged Richard's expression. All of her old defenses against a man's anger threatened to rise, then subsided. She'd never feared the back of Richard's hand as she had Basil's. This might be unwise, but Richard wasn't given to bouts of extreme fury.

She'd come to envy his inner tranquillity, admire his calm but firm treatment of his vassals, appreciate his effort to give Philip a noble's education, and cherish the time he spent with her alone.

Nay, her former doubts of his suitability no longer existed. She couldn't have selected a better man to act as protector for Philip.

Or found a better lover. Or chosen a better man to love.

The realization severely tested her already fractured

composure. But there it was. Undeniable. She loved Richard.

And he must never know.

Never had she felt more vulnerable to a man's whims. This man she loved could be about to send her away.

As he came nearer, without hesitation or effort, she eased into a pose and expression of complete apathy. To give any of her feelings away now could mean disaster later.

Richard watched her muster her defenses. She didn't yet know that he wasn't sending her away, that Connor had too hastily told her to prepare for a journey. Later, when this confrontation was done and she no longer felt threatened, she would remove the mask.

And when she did, and her emotions came to the fore, he would be right beside her, eager to comfort.

He came to a halt a few feet in front of Lucinda, but addressed Connor. "Begin."

"My lord, I regret my presumption—"

"Not to me. To Lucinda."

Connor's mouth twisted, as though the words had gone sour in his mouth. The steward clearly disliked this forced show of deference to Lucinda, but Richard didn't care, so long as the man did what he'd been ordered to do.

"Lady...Lucinda," Connor said tightly. "Lord Richard has refused the bargain between his brother and your husband's family. You need not prepare for a journey. I...I regret...any disruption to your day I may have caused."

Connor's delivery and choice of words left much to be desired, yet should have drawn a response from

Lucinda. She gave none—not joy, not satisfaction, not even relief.

"You told Philip?" she asked of him.

"I did. He seemed pleased. Even now he and Edric prepare the pony for today's ride."

"Then 'twould seem all is as it should be," she said, then turned and strode back into her hut.

Stunned, Richard merely waved Connor off when asked for permission to leave.

All was not as it should be.

Lucinda should be elated, or at the very least relieved, that he wasn't sending her off to Dover. Didn't he deserve a word of thanks or a small gesture of gratitude?

Or was he making too much out of nothing? Lucinda was a private woman, not given to public display of emotion. Indeed, to most people she showed only her cool demeanor.

Only when they were alone did her facade fade, allowing him a unique glimpse of the tender and passionate woman within. She certainly wasn't a woman to throw herself in his arms and cry on his shoulder for all to see, as Philip had done.

From outside her hut, he called her name. It took an inordinate amount of time for Lucinda to open the door, and she didn't step aside to allow his entry.

"I thought you planned to ride with Philip," she said.

"I do."

"Then you had best be about it. He will be disappointed if you are not prompt."

"Philip will wait." Richard stepped into the doorway, forcing her to take a step back. "My concern is for his mother, who seems eager to be rid of me. Why is that?''

Lucinda backed another step, allowing room to move into the hut and secure the door behind him. Shutting out the world. Closing them into the cozy confines of the shelter where she dwelled, where she—so far—showed no qualms about welcoming him onto her pallet and into her warmth.

Her scent, a mixture of innocent wildflowers and heady earthiness, saturated his senses, urging him to take her in his arms and taste her, too.

She glanced at his wet shoulder. ''Philip's welfare is always my greatest concern. He needs your reassurance now, not me,'' she said, still cool and distant.

Richard put his hands on her shoulders, felt her tension. ''Do not hide from me, Lucinda. I will not allow it.''

Her chin came up. A spark of defiance flashed in her violet eyes.

He continued. ''You may show your blank face to the rest of the world, but not to me. I *know* you were upset, mayhap frantic. Nor have your fears eased. You, too, need succor. I give you mine. Neither you nor your son go to Dover.''

'''Tis a good bargain—a year's worth of goods in trade for Philip and me. I doubt your brother understands why you do not accept, and he may press you further.''

Why couldn't the woman take him at his word? All she need do is trust him, and she should know him well enough by now...or mayhap she didn't, or mayhap Basil had broken his word far too many times for Lucinda to trust any man. And, hellfire, her father had sold her for the price of a broodmare.

"Stephen thought to free me of my responsibility as Philip's guardian. The only man who can do so is King Henry, who gave Philip to me, in part, because he does not wish the boy returned to Basil's family. So, until Henry says otherwise, Philip resides with me until his majority."

He didn't remind her that her freedom would come far sooner than her son's. In a bit under two years, Lucinda would be free to go, or stay, as she chose.

Richard tried not to think of that bleak day very often.

"If you think George will return to Normandy without some kind of satisfaction, you had best reconsider," she said.

"He has no choice." Richard cupped Lucinda's face in his hands. "George can offer me all of the riches in Normandy and my answer will be the same. I will not barter you away, Lucinda. You have my word."

He sealed the pledge with a thorough kiss. She pushed lightly against his chest—a feeble protest. He persisted, urging a response that he knew she could give. Inevitably, Lucinda's arms came around him.

A sweet victory, but one he had no time to celebrate in the way he wished. He broke the kiss gently.

"I will return," he whispered against her kiss-swollen mouth, then left before his own control slipped too far.

Lucinda poked her head into the manor before she entered, searching for Connor. To her relief, the steward wasn't inside. Actually, no one tarried within the manor except Stephen, who sat at a table, sipping on his ale. He wouldn't acknowledge her, much less speak with her, and that suited her very well.

She rummaged through the sewing supplies for a pair of shears, needle and thread. Working on her gowns would keep her hands busy during the long afternoon ahead.

Supplies in hand, she headed to the door, only to have her path blocked by Stephen. He glanced pointedly at the shears in her hand.

"Apparently, whatever whore's trick you used to seduce Richard into granting you the run of the manor worked well." He tilted his head. "I fail to see what he finds appealing. Your eyes are an unusual color, but hold no warmth. Mayhap he finds you convenient."

"Mayhap," she said stiffly, tamping down her rising anger and embarrassment. "Or mayhap Richard possesses compassion where others do not."

"Ah, found that out, did you? Very good. He tends to judge people unharshly unless given reason. 'Tis a trait of his that I worry will get him into deep trouble one day. But then, those who would do him ill eventually show their true nature, and Richard can be very ruthless. I imagine you saw his scar."

That horrible scar along his ribs. The scar she avoided looking at whenever they made love. She nodded.

"Did he tell you how he got it, or what he did to the man who gave it to him?"

Lucinda wasn't sure she wanted to hear what Stephen seemed eager to tell her. "I know that Basil's mercenary captain, Edward, mistook Richard for Gerard, and Richard was wounded in the fight."

"Humph. 'Twas Edward who dealt the final blow, but only after Richard fought off ten others."

Ten? Her shock must have showed.

"Aye, ten," he said. "They caught him alone, unarmored. He managed to kill three and wound several others before they left him for dead. His rage must have been a glorious sight."

Lucinda couldn't imagine Richard in a rage, but didn't say so. Stephen no longer looked at her, but at some spot behind her, as if he were no longer at Collinwood.

"Richard came precariously close to breathing his last that night, and damn near died again during the trip home to Wilmont. He bled so heavily that we ripped up nearly every linen aboard ship to change his bindings."

Lucinda shuddered, picturing Richard so near death's door, reminding herself that this was all in the past, that Richard had lived to regain full vigor.

Stephen gave a sharp laugh. "Then he damn near killed himself all over again to recover, because Gerard needed him at court to bring Basil to his knees. I could have gladly strangled the man for thinking he knew more than the king's surgeons and Wilmont's healer. Stubborn man."

The love in Stephen's voice brought a lump to her throat. Gerard the baron, Richard the bastard, Stephen the adventurer. All so different, yet bound by a tie so strong that each would do anything for the other. Even die.

Stephen's eyes cleared as he faced her again. Her hand closed tight on the shears, and she waited for Stephen to make his point.

"I suspect Richard lived partly to please Gerard.

He also wanted revenge, which he got. Did you know that Richard slew Edward?"

No, she hadn't, but she wasn't surprised.

"At court?" she asked.

"Nay, months later, when we rescued Ardith and Daymon from Northbryre."

Richard claimed to have let go of the old hate, claimed his scar now served as a reminder to be a better lord. But could one ever really put aside all the pain, both his own and that of those he loved dearly?

Stephen hadn't forgotten or forgiven. His anger yet smoldered. As did Gerard's.

"If there were some way I could undo..." she began, then stopped. She wasn't responsible for what Basil had done to those of Wilmont or anyone else, and he'd died for his sins. "I had no say in Basil's affairs, as most wives have no say in their husbands' affairs. Richard knows this and treats Philip and me accordingly."

"Which leaves him open to betrayal, and therein lies my concern. For you, Lucinda, were wed to a man to whom treachery came as easily as breathing, whose lies flowed from his mouth as swiftly as water down a stream. That vermin's blood flows within your son's body, and the male bloodline *will* tell. One has only to look to Richard to see the proof.

"He is a bastard, of English peasant and Norman noble. As a child, he withstood the vile curses some flung his way. He grew up knowing his life would never be easy, and he never sought the easy way out. As a man, he has built a life that many told him he could never accomplish. Beware, Lucinda, if I find that by word or deed you betray him, put him in jeopardy of losing what he has gained, I will come looking for you.''

With that, he walked away, back to the table and his ale.

Lucinda stared at him, indignant that he should think her capable of such treachery—and so blindly condemn Philip.

''Stephen.''

He looked up.

Shaking, she said, ''As a child, Philip often hears the vile curses flung his way. Growing up will not be easy for the son of a traitor. As a man, I hope he accomplishes, honorably, whatever he wishes to accomplish. Should you so much as try—by word or deed—to turn Richard against my son, I will come looking for you!''

Not until she reached her hut and saw the blood pooling in her palm did she realize the shears had cut into her hand.

Through most of the evening meal, Lucinda succeeded in ignoring Stephen—who had usurped Connor's usual seat across from her—and Connor, who scowled and picked at his food. Richard and Stephen discussed how the royal betrothal and eventual marriage of Princess Matilda and Emperor Henry might later affect England.

Lucinda didn't voice her opinion that shipping a young girl off so far from home seemed a cruel thing to do to any child, royal duty or not.

''By the by, you never did say if you...saw the Lady Carolyn before you left for Normandy,'' Richard said.

Stephen smiled like a cat who'd gotten into the

cream. "I did, and must say that our rendezvous went very well. She was quite pleased when I left her."

Richard shook his head. "I wonder at your audacity. But then, I should not be surprised. Did the two of you come to some agreement?"

"Nay, not as yet. I do have several qualities she finds irresistible, but I am sure her father will want to examine my heritage and accounts before we make a bargain. Too, the lady might wish to again sample my attributes before she makes up her mind. I am not worried."

Lucinda tried not to turn red, having caught the gist of their meaning. Merciful heaven, she'd examined Richard's qualities and attributes enough times.

"I gather you have decided to ask for Carolyn."

"Aye. As soon as I have done with this business of yours, and reported to Gerard, I will take the trip up to Northumbria to seal the bargain. Carolyn, too, has a few attributes which I would not mind seeing again. She will make a fine wife."

"Somehow, I cannot see you settling down to married life, Stephen. You will make a poor husband!"

"Ah, but that is part of the beauty of this bargain. I made it clear to Carolyn that I find staying in one spot too long stifling. She has no objection to my traveling to visit my lands, to court, to Collinwood to see you or Wilmont to see Gerard any time I please. I gain all of the benefits of holy wedlock without the boredom."

Lucinda snickered inwardly. The man was so full of himself that he couldn't see that Carolyn gained as much as he. From experience, she knew that the most pleasurable times of a marriage were when the husband was gone.

"And what of you, Richard? How goes your search for a wife? Did you…see any of the heiresses on the list?"

Lucinda's hand tightened on her goblet.

"Nay, not enough time."

"You still have the list?"

Richard gave an indifferent shrug. "'Tis probably in my packs somewhere."

"You should get it out, Richard. If you wait too long, some of the more eligible will be spoken for."

"I am in no hurry. When one crop is harvested, another crop comes into season."

"Aye, but the pickings could be slim. And you could use the funds for the many projects you have started in your various holdings. How goes the mill at Durwood?"

"Slow," Richard said, and launched into complaints of lack of skilled labor and supplies in the area.

She hadn't given a thought to Richard's search for a wife since leaving court. Apparently, neither had Richard.

At some time in the future, Richard would marry. 'Twas proper and inevitable that he should take a wife. He would likely bring her here, to the place he considered his home. The woman would take over as chatelaine, take her proper place at Richard's table— where Lucinda now sat—share his bed and bear his heirs.

Jealousy reared up and threatened her composure. Visions of Richard tumbling on a pallet with another woman rolled around in her head, bringing forth an unreasonable hatred.

She had no right to feel jealous because she had

no claim on Richard. He was free to wed where and when he pleased. He might share her meals and her pallet, but he would never take her to wife.

In his own way, Richard might care for her, but she possessed no lands to bring to him. His people considered her as dirt beneath their feet. Gerard would never sanction such a marriage, and Richard wouldn't marry where his brother didn't approve.

If married to Richard, she wouldn't mind a husband's constant presence. With Richard she could be herself without fear of reproach.

She could love him as her heart yearned to love him, without the heavy sadness that offset the bouts of joy.

'Twas foolish to wish for things that could never be, but still, the fantasy haunted her.

Chapter Fourteen

"**W**hy does she not just push the baby out?" Philip asked.

A dainty palfrey labored in the stall, and Richard thanked the fates that she'd chosen to deliver during daylight hours instead of in the middle of the night. She was doing well for her first time. Soon now, but not quite fast enough for Philip, she would be a mother.

"'Tis not that simple, Philip," Richard said, his hand on the mare's belly, feeling yet another tightening. "Certes, she will push the little one out, but not until she and the foal are full ready. She will know when to push."

Scrunching down, Philip leaned over to put his hand next to Richard's. "'Tis hard work!"

"Aye, that it is."

"And painful! And messy!"

Richard chuckled, remembering Philip's exclamation of distaste when the mare's water broke. "That, too."

"Then why do they do it? I surely would not want to."

"Nor I," Richard agreed. "But that is part of why females are female, to bring children into the world."

"Like me?"

Richard ruffled the boy's hair. "Just like you. Think on it, Philip. If your mother had not given birth to you, you would not be here now to watch the mare give birth."

Philip's face settled into a thoughtful pose. Richard knew another question would surface. The boy's curiosity brewed question after question, some of them beyond Richard's ability to answer.

Yet, he tried, at times just so he wouldn't look bad in the boy's eyes. Being a protector could sorely tax one's pride. Now that he had Philip to look after, Richard could sympathize with his father, Everart. With three curious boys to satisfy, Everart had done so with patience and humor. Richard couldn't help wonder if Everart had ever felt at a loss, as he sometimes did with Philip. As he probably would again someday, with his own sons.

The horse blew, struggling with her pains, probably wishing she was out in some clover-laden meadow rather than lying on this bed of straw.

Philip got up and walked around Richard to pat the mare's neck. "'Tis all right. Hush."

"Not too close to her head, Philip. Stay out of biting range."

The boy scooted back a little. "She likes me. Why would she bite?"

"If a pain hits her too hard, she may lash out. Best your fingers are beyond her reach."

"Oh."

A good boy, was Philip, quick and eager to please.

A bright boy with a bright smile. A boy any man would be proud to call his own.

Hellfire, but Basil had been a fool among fools, spending all of his time in the relentless pursuit of land—Wilmont land in particular—instead of enjoying Philip's company.

And Lucinda's.

Richard rarely gave a thought to the man who had been Lucinda's husband, Philip's father. When he did, 'twas usually to gloat—to himself—that what had once belonged to Basil now belonged to him. The lands. The boy. The woman.

Imagining those three as a family—well, it just didn't work. He couldn't picture Lucinda awaiting Basil's return to hearth and home with the glee and anticipation that Ardith awaited Gerard. Nor would Basil have strode through the doors to sweep his son into a grand hug as Gerard did with his sons.

The belly under his hand convulsed again, but this time he felt a shift that hadn't been there before.

Richard got up and flicked straw from his hose. "Come. 'Tis almost time. Let us give her room."

Philip gave the mare a final pat, then followed out of the stall, giving way to the stable master and a lad who would oversee the birth and help the mare if problems developed.

Richard hoped everything would go smoothly, not only for the mare and foal's sake, but for Philip's. A birthing gone bad was a dreadful thing to watch, not the miracle he wanted Philip to witness.

"Oh, look! I see the foal's hoofs!" Philip shouted, then stood openmouthed as the head and, eventually, the body appeared.

Though Richard had witnessed foals' births many

times before, each time he came away awed that a
bundle so big could reside in its mother's body. The
foal slipped out with nary a hitch, all black, slick and
gangly.

"A male, my lord," the stable master said. "A
good-sized one, with all parts where they should be."

Philip looked up, his mouth opening. Richard
quickly cut off the expected question about misplaced
parts.

"He will need a name, Philip. What do you
think?"

The boy turned to look again at the foal. "He is
all black. Mayhap Blackie?"

The foal chose that moment to try out his legs,
wobbling so badly he went down on his haunches.
Philip giggled, and from behind him, Richard heard
other laughter—light, melodious and female.

Lucinda. She'd spent the past few days in her hut,
working on her gowns, and today wore the one of
light green. A refreshing change from the old peasant-
weave of gray. Her plait of black hair hung forward,
draped over her shoulder. Beautiful. Enticing. Like a
lover should be.

She came up beside him, adding her scent to his
already deluged senses. "I heard the foal had been
born," she said. "All is well?"

"Aye," Philip answered. "He has all his parts! The
legs do not work right, though. Mayhap we could
name him Stumble!"

"Choosing a name, are you?" Lucinda asked.

"I already thought of Blackie."

"Not a bad name, but I imagine common among
black horses. What about Midnight?"

Richard heard the list of names that mother and

child continued to banter over, but paid little attention.

Lucinda and Philip were a family. Their affection for one another showed in the easy way they talked together, their smiles, their touches. Such as a family should be.

Like Gerard's family. A loving wife. Adoring sons.

Lucinda and Philip needed no one but each other for their happiness, not even the man to whom they looked for their daily bread. They both liked him, but they didn't need him.

Mayhap, someday, some woman would look upon him as Ardith looked upon Gerard. Some boy would run to him as Daymon and Everart ran to their father.

He needed to marry, as Stephen had taken such pains to remind him nearly a sennight ago. An heiress, preferably, who would bring land and coin to the marriage. Of such was made an empire.

Would his sons look up at him with the same trust and respect as Philip did? Would his heiress open her arms and warmth to him as willingly as Lucinda greeted him? Hellfire, could he go to another woman without remembering the feel and taste of Lucinda?

He captured a strand of her hair that had come loose from her plait. Silken black, like the foal. So often he'd compared it to the color of a raven's wing.

"We will name the horse Raven," he said.

"Raven?" Philip asked.

"Aye, 'tis perfect."

When Stephen returned from his errand, he didn't come alone, but had the sense to bring the wagons loaded with goods inside the circle of the palisade and leave George and his escort camped several leagues outside.

"I tried to tell George you were adamant, but he would not take my word," Stephen said as they strode into the armory. "He thinks you refuse the bargain because you want a higher fee for Philip's release."

Several soldiers milled about the armory. Edric and Philip sat tossing dice. All looked up as Richard entered.

"How many men serve as George's escort?"

"Twenty."

Richard turned to Edric, now standing. "Choose another five men to accompany us, in full battle gear, ready to ride as soon as possible. I want guards positioned both outside the palisade and along the wall-walk."

Edric barked orders. Men scrambled. Philip looked excited and fearful all at once.

"Don your mail, Stephen. You come, too."

"Ah...Richard, a show of force is hardly necessary. I doubt that George intends to attack Collinwood."

"Mayhap not, but I want him to know I am full ready to defend what I consider mine."

Stephen sighed. "Full mail it is," he said, then left the armory.

Richard strode toward where his chain mail and weapons were stored. "Come, Philip. You have polished my chain mail often enough. Now you can help me into it."

Richard donned his heavy hauberk of thick leather covered with metal rings. He settled it on his shoulders, then sat down on a stool so Philip could shut the fastenings.

When done, Richard rose and stretched, testing. Satisfied that all was secure, he grabbed his baldric, the leather holder for his broadsword.

"May I come?" Philip asked.

"Nay, you may not," he said.

"Why?"

Richard sighed inwardly. He should have expected this from Philip. Philip was much too small, too precious to be exposed to danger. The boy wouldn't like that answer, however.

"You are not yet a trained soldier. You have no armor, no helm, no sword—"

"I do! Look!" Philip ran to Edric's cot. From beneath, he pulled out a small, wooden practice sword. He slipped it into his girdle and strutted back toward Richard.

Aghast, Richard asked, "Where did you come by that?"

"Edric made it for me while his knee mended."

Richard crossed his arms. "Did he also show you how to use it?"

"Some. Want to see?"

Richard nodded.

Philip pulled the sword from his girdle, set his body into a solid stance, and took several swipes at an imaginary foe. The child possessed a natural grace and mastery of movement that astounded Richard.

"Very good," he said.

Philip tucked the sword away, a satisfied smile on his face. "Then I may come?"

"Nay."

The smile drooped to a pout.

"I have another duty for you," Richard said, slipping his sword into the baldric. "Three wagons sit in the bailey. All of those goods need be recorded, carted and stored, and the wagons sent back out to George. Help your mother with the recording. Connor can see to the unloading."

"But—"

"A good lord needs to know his Latin and numbers as well as how to wield a weapon. 'Twill be good practice for you."

Philip's nose scrunched in distaste, but he relented. "Aye, my lord."

Richard slipped his sword into the baldric, then picked up his conical leather helmet with the silver studs and gleaming noseguard. He doubted he would need it. Truly, he wanted George to see him full-faced, to see displeasure and resolve.

He plunked the helmet onto Philip's head. 'Twas too large for the little head. The boy could barely see.

"While you help with the recording, you are also to protect your mother. Should the unforeseen happen, you are to guard her with your life."

Philip's shoulders squared. His body puffed up. "A good lord protects the womenfolk and children."

Richard hid a smile. He put a hand on the boy's shoulder and steered him toward the door. "That he does."

The bailey swarmed with people. Near the palisade's gate, Stephen, Edric and his soldiers awaited him, mounted. Odin pranced at the head of the line.

Richard strode toward the wagons. Philip's little legs pumped fast to keep up.

Lucinda stood at the tail of the head wagon, parchment in hand. Connor stood nearby, directing the men who had already begun the task of unloading the crates, sacks and kegs. Near the head of each wagon stood a guard, keeping each of George's drivers in his seat. The work stopped as he approached.

Lucinda's gaze slid from his face, to his mail, on down to her oddly attired son, then back up. He thought to take a moment to utter soft words of reassurance, then decided not to. She didn't trust words. His actions would better serve his purpose.

He leaped up on the back of the head wagon. He didn't need to call for his vassals' attention. All looked to him. 'Twas his first real test as their lord. They had sworn their fealty to him in return for his protection.

Richard swept a glance though the bailey, noting his soldier's positions. All were in readiness.

He pitched his voice deep and loud so all could hear.

"The goods in these wagons represent a full year's worth of tribute from the lands of my ward. I receive them early because George harbors the mistaken belief that I can be easily swayed from my duty as protector of the boy. George is about to learn the error of his thinking. Richard of Wilmont is not swayed from duty toward *anyone* over whom he holds lordship."

He swept the crowd again, letting his promise register.

"As soon as the wagons are unloaded, send them out and shut the gate behind them. Do so quickly. I want these wagons close on my heels. Let no one leave the protection of the palisade, and let no one open the gate to any but me or ours."

Richard jumped down beside Lucinda, signaling one of the guards to come forward. "Should you find anything amiss,'' he told her, ''send Theo out with a message before you release the wagons.''

''As you wish,'' she said. He heard it, a slight waver to her voice. Worry.

He cupped her cheek. ''You are not to fear, Lucinda. I will not allow George anywhere near you or Philip.''

''Have a care, Richard,'' she said. ''George is as dangerous as Basil was.''

His chest fairly swelled. She worried not for herself or her son, but for him. If he didn't have on chain mail, he'd have pulled her into an embrace. He settled for a touch of his lips to her forehead.

''If I remember correctly, within one of these carts is a cask of wine. Draw us a flagon, for later. Be aware, woman, that I intend to sip most of it from the cup of you.''

She blushed furiously. ''How can you think of... merciful heavens, go. And Godspeed.''

Chuckling, he pushed his hands into gauntlets as he crossed the bailey. He took Odin's reins from the stable master and mounted the destrier with a flourish. A tug back, a signal of knees, brought the horse up into a rear, his front hooves flailing. The horse came down snorting, pawing at the ground, eager to be off.

''You know, Richard,'' Stephen said flatly, ''for one who hates being the center of attention, you are giving an outstanding performance.''

''I merely show off Odin's training.''

''Indeed.''

''Ready?''

''Lead on, oh mighty lord.''

With a tap to Odin's sides, he did, more sedately than he might have if his brother's words hadn't leaned toward sarcasm. Stephen had made his point, and was correct. Still, Richard rode more lightly, smiled more widely, just because Lucinda worried over him. Foolish, but there it was.

Once down the road, out of sight of Collinwood, he turned to Stephen. "Tell me about George."

"He looks like Basil. Bald. Squinty gray eyes. Big belly. Slick tongue."

Richard added, "Arrogant. Pompous. Thinks the world should bow to him simply because he is a Norman baron."

"Just like our brother Gerard."

"Ah, but Gerard merits those bows, deserves respect. Men of Basil and George's ilk demand it without earning it, and woe to the man who does not bow down quick or deep enough."

"You do not intend to bow."

"I do not intend to get off my horse."

They rode in silence for the rest of the way to where Stephen had instructed George to await word. As any good escort would, the men who served George hustled to grab shields and weapons the moment they spotted mounted men in chain mail.

From Stephen's description, George was easy to pick out. Clad in an emerald dalmatica trimmed in an ornate pattern of gold thread, the rotund little man labored to get up from the ground where he'd been sitting under the shade of a tree. 'Twas a comical, pitiful exhibition.

Richard reined in several yards in front of the forward-most of George's soldiers. He sat silently atop Odin, forcing George to waddle over to greet him. George examined Richard's men, frowned slightly, then set his features into a pleasant posture.

"Richard of Wilmont, we finally meet," he said. "Stephen has told you why I come?"

"He has."

"Good. Then come share a wine with me, and we can discuss—"

"We have naught to discuss, George. Did not Stephen tell you that I intend to carry on as Philip's protector? King Henry entrusted me with the duty until Philip reaches his majority."

George waved a hand in the air, dismissing the royal edict. "The boy is blood of my blood. His holdings rest on Norman soil. Certes, even Henry will see the wisdom of what we do once 'tis done."

"'Tis already done! You should not have bothered leaving Dover. Truly, you might have remained in Normandy. Henry is also Duke of Normandy, your sovereign. You are bound to obey his dictates the same as I."

Richard saw a flash of anger, quickly smothered.

"Henry holds the title of duke, but his influence is not so far-reaching in Normandy as here in England. We do not fear his wrath as you English-bound landowners do. Give the boy over to me and keep the goods I offer as payment for your trouble. Indeed, if you wish to bargain for more, I am willing to listen."

Richard leaned forward in the saddle. "I do not accept bribes. I do not bargain away my honor."

"Honor? Is that why you hesitate? 'Tis no obstacle. Why, should Henry ask how you came to give over the boy, tell him I took Philip from you by force and absconded with him."

Richard glanced about at the twenty men, led by a man who could barely move. He could almost hear

Henry's reaction if told such an absurd tale. "You jest."

"I do not. Richard, I know you did not accept the boy willingly. He was forced upon you by a man who cared nothing for your wishes, nor those of Philip's family. What harm if we set to rights the injustice Henry has inflicted on us both?"

Richard remembered a time when, if George had put the proposition to him in just that fashion, he might have taken the man up on his offer. But no longer.

Behind him, Richard could hear the rattle of oxen-drawn wagons. A quick check over his shoulder showed him three wagons, all driven by George's men. The account was paid in full, and he could be rid of this irritating little man.

Richard urged Odin forward a few steps, forcing George to crane his neck to look up. "I refuse your offer, George. Take your wagons and go back to Normandy. I will expect a like tribute next year. If it does not arrive, you can expect to see me again, at the threshold to your castle, with a force of Wilmont knights in my wake."

George turned livid. "A warning, Richard of Wilmont. I do not like threats."

"I do not threaten, George. I merely state my intentions should you decide to withhold the goods due. Not only would Gerard back me, but so would the king. I am sure Henry would be interested to know that you feel he has no influence in the dukedom."

George waited until the wagons rolled by before saying, "Then we must see who holds the greater influence with the king—a bastard who owes all to the whim of a brother, or a Norman baron whose heritage goes back far before the Conquest.''

Richard let the insult roll off as he'd done so many times before over so many years. He may be the bastard, but he was the better man.

George intended to contest the wardship, did he?

''You would do well to take great care, George. One look at you and Henry may see Basil, remember the treachery which he lost the chance to punish. Challenge the wardship if you wish, but do so at your own peril. You may end up in the same dank room where your cousin once resided, deep in the subcrypt of White Tower.''

''Henry would not dare!''

''Would that I shared your confidence. I have known Henry to pluck a man's eyes out for the merest offense.'' Richard backed Odin. ''So long as you are off my land within the hour, I care not where you go. London. Normandy. Hell. All are the same to me.''

Chapter Fifteen

Lucinda stood among the goods scattered about the bailey. The men had carried off and stored most of them, but not all. The manor was crowded, the armory squeezed tight, and the storage shed stuffed. Where Connor would put the remaining articles she didn't know.

George had sent every item due, and each of good quality. She'd been surprised, then realized that George would send only the best from his stores. He would expect Richard to inspect the goods before handing over Philip. And her. But she knew she didn't count in George's plans. Only Philip.

A flagon of wine stood near her feet. She blushed each time she looked at it—wondering where from her body Richard intended to sip—so she tried not to look down.

"Philip, come down off those crates," she said, having seen her son's antics on the edge of her vision.

"'Tis a good vantage point, Mother. The better to see the enemy."

"You can barely see at all with that helmet on your head. I think it time to remove it."

"A true soldier must be prepared. I cannot be a true soldier without a helmet!"

Or a sword, or so Philip had informed her earlier when she'd suggested he lay the wooden sword aside before he tripped over it. He'd vowed to protect her with his life should the enemy attack and breach the palisade. A noble vow. But Philip was much too young to take an aggressive stance should the unthinkable transpire.

The longer Richard was gone, the more she fretted. Her stomach ached with worry, her head hurt with visions of what could happen if six men fought twenty. She wouldn't be at all surprised if George tried some devilish tactic to capture Philip and take back his goods.

She glanced up at the wall-walk. Richard had thought of the possibility, too, or he wouldn't have assigned so many soldiers to walk the palisade. Richard wore chain mail, as did all of the men who accompanied him. But chain mail could be pierced if done aright.

Horrible visions of wounds and blood swam through her head, yet mingled with them flashed erotic scenes of how Richard intended to drink his wine when he returned.

A cry of "Open the gates!" came as music to her ears.

Philip scrambled down from his imaginary tower, drew his sword, and took his stance not a foot in front of her.

"Philip, if the gates open, that means Richard returns."

"But what if the enemy sneaks in right behind

him? Richard entrusted me with your care, Mother. I must do my duty.''

Richard rode in at the head of the column, in the same high spirits with which he'd ridden out. He pulled Odin up short and spun the horse in a circle, scattering dust. Stephen shook his head at his brother's antics. The men-at-arms laughed.

The people cheered. All about her they waved their arms in the air and shouted Richard's name.

Richard cut the cheers short. Though he'd refused George's offer and sent him on his way, he informed everyone, he wanted to ensure the man had gone before relaxing guard. With Odin held to a walk, he rode through the bailey and shouted orders to close the gates and commanded the soldiers on the wall-walk to yet keep watch.

He halted the huge destrier near a stack of crates and looked down at Philip. "Still on guard?"

"Aye, my lord, as you commanded."

Richard dismounted. "You may stand down. Put my helmet away and help Edric out of his mail."

"What about yours, my lord?"

Richard's eyes wandered up to peer into hers. She could swear her heart missed a beat. "I will have another remove mine. Go."

Philip did, without argument.

Richard handed Odin's reins to the waiting stable master, then wandered around the piles of goods, peeking into crates, poking at sacks. A warrior inspecting his loot. His chain mail glinted with each movement, hugged his body, encased him in protective metal rings. She'd seen him so garbed on the day they'd first met, thought then that he looked the consummate warrior. He still did. Tall, strong, commanding. Lord of the manor and all he surveyed.

A hint of smug victory teased the corners of his mouth, as if he'd fought some great battle and won. Mayhap he had. Had the battle with George been fought with words, or with swords? If swords had crossed, he wore no sign of it. No blood stained his chain mail or hands.

Beneath the chain mail beat the heart of a mortal man. Along his lower ribs slashed a brutal scar, proving he wasn't invincible.

Ten men, Stephen had said. Richard had held off ten men in the attack in Normandy, and killed or wounded several before Basil's mercenary captain snuck under Richard's guard. Someday, someone might get under that guard again, and she could lose him. 'Twas what she'd dreaded all the while he'd faced George.

He stood before her, whole and unharmed. She should feel relief, but her innards refused to uncoil. Mayhap once she had him out of his armor, stripped down to bare skin, the tightness would ease.

Too, she wanted to hear exactly what George had said, how Richard answered, and what would happen next. His people might believe the danger had passed so easily. She didn't—she knew George.

"I gather all is in order," he said.

"Aye." She gave him the list.

He glanced over it, then asked, "Did you find the wine?"

Lucinda picked up the flagon for him to see.

"Is it any good?" he asked.

"One would need to taste it."

"Oh, aye, one would surely need to taste," he said,

his voice low and suggestive, making her blush once more.

"We have a problem with storage," she said, bringing them back to the task at hand. "Every nook within the manor, armory and shed is full."

"Have we tarp to cover what cannot be put under roof?"

"Some, but I doubt enough."

From across the bailey, Lucinda spotted Stephen, his chain mail disposed of, making his way toward Richard. She sat on a crate, cradling the wine. 'Twould be some time yet before she and Richard could escape to her hut.

Richard studied the list. "Mayhap there are items we could send to my other holdings," he mused as Stephen reached his side.

"Deciding what to do with the bounty?" Stephen asked.

Richard smiled widely at his brother. "I may send you off to Wilmont so I can fill the stall your horse occupies."

Stephen gave Richard a mock aggrieved look. "I am wounded to the core, Richard, that you would rid yourself of my good company so soon."

They both laughed, and Lucinda couldn't help but smile. The two brothers got along so well that they could tease in outrageous fashion. She'd never seen the like among the noble siblings she knew, who more often squabbled than shared humor.

"Actually," Stephen said, "I plan to leave for Wilmont on the morrow. 'Twill give you the space you crave, but not solve your problem." Stephen wandered over to a sack and untied the rope. From within he drew several dried apricots and popped one into his mouth. "I would be willing to take a few of these off your hands. Food of the gods."

Richard crossed his arms. "Been sampling, have you?"

"Naturally. I could not, in good conscience, allow George to send my esteemed brother inferior goods, could I? Nay, I told myself. Only the best for Richard. So I examined the contents of several sacks and crates before we left Normandy, then again when we reached England—just to ensure no spoilage had occurred during the voyage, you understand."

"Oh, I think I understand perfectly well the *sacrifice* you made for me."

"I knew you would." Stephen moved on to another sack. "Taste the raisins. Sweeter than honey," he declared, handing Richard a handful. "And the almonds. Ah, Richard, wait until you taste the almonds. Magnificent!"

"Truly?" Richard asked dryly.

"Truly. Do you think we might have the pheasant for noon meal? Rare pleasant fowl, they are."

Stephen had made his way to where she sat. She waited for him to move on, but he stood still, looking down at her.

"Lucinda, I would propose a trade," he said gently. "My apricots for your wine."

'Twas the first time Stephen had spoken to her without derision. His voice carried no malice. His green eyes reflected no ridicule. Shock held her tongue.

"Come, Lucinda," he chided. "'Tis a treat I warrant you have not tasted for a very long time."

He held out his hand, open palmed, offering the fruit.

Did he offer a truce, or at least an easing of the animosity between them? Whatever Stephen's reasons, if only for Richard's sake, she would accept.

"How could I refuse food from the gods?" she said, holding out the flagon and taking the apricots.

Stephen's smile and slight nod acknowledged the exchange. The encounter left her shaken, yet in better spirits.

Stephen turned to Richard, waving the flagon. "Here is the finest of the fine, the true prize. A bold nectar to sweeten the sharpest tongue. I swear to you, Richard, if you give a flask of this wine to a priest, he will absolve you of not only your past sins but those for the remainder of your life."

"You ask for a miracle," Richard chided, watching Lucinda eat the apricots. He didn't fully understand what had happened between her and Stephen, but the bemused smile on her face was due to more than tasty dried fruit.

Richard wanted nothing more than to take the wine and the woman and hie off to her hut. But Stephen's comment about priests had nudged forth an idea, one that blossomed with the possibility of solving several problems.

"The market fair at Ely is next week, and I have not been up to see Bishop Hervey for some time. Mayhap I should pack up some of these goods and sell them. Better to turn them into coins than let them go to waste." He took the flagon of fine wine from Stephen's hand, glanced about the manor, noting improvements he wanted to make. "I could then hire carpenters to make repairs to the manor, and mayhap build another shed."

"Carpenters?" Stephen asked, incredulous. "Why

not masons? If you choose to make Collinwood your home, expand the palisade and build a proper stone keep. You are a man of great means now, Richard. Why not live like one?''

"A stone keep," he said, almost to himself, envisioning the structure—an armory on the lowest level, topped by a great hall, with private quarters above the hall.

'Twould be practical. Buildings of stone lessened the threat of a devastating fire and provided greater defense against attack. A man could hold out for months against a besieging enemy in a stone keep. Not that he expected an attack in these times of peace, but one never knew when that would change.

Home. The word had always meant Wilmont, the castle where he'd been born and raised. During the past three years he'd traveled extensively among his holdings, but always stayed the longest and made the most improvements at Collinwood. Mayhap 'twas time to make Collinwood his true home.

A cry from the wall-walk interrupted his musings.

"Our men return! Open the gate!"

Within minutes, his soldiers stood before him, smiling.

"The vermin are gone, my lord," one reported. "George moved fast, he did, like 'twas urgent he make time."

"You followed all the way to the border?"

"Aye, my lord."

He waved his men off. George was gone, beating a quick path on the road south, which passed through London and then on to Dover. Would George stop or keep going?

Stephen put a hand on his shoulder. "If it helps, I

believe you might be right in what you told George. Henry has an extremely long memory and a hearty appetite for vengeance. I could go to London and let King Henry know your wishes on the matter. Mayhap tease his appetite by telling him in what low esteem George holds the Duke of Normandy. George will be lucky to leave England with all his limbs."

"Mayhap I should go myself."

"Richard?" Lucinda asked. She'd risen from the crate. He saw her confusion, sensed her fear.

Decisions and strategies would have to wait.

"Come, Lucinda, I have much to tell you," he said, then headed for her hut, knowing she would follow. He secured the door behind them and put the wine and list on the table.

He tugged off his gauntlets. "George is a vile creature."

"I know."

Richard sat on the stool, his back toward Lucinda. She snapped open a fastening on his chain mail.

"George was not content with my refusal to turn Philip over to him," Richard began his tale.

She said nothing at all while he related, nearly word for word, the heated exchange with George. Her only reactions came by way of how she undid the fastenings—slowly or quickly, or when she paused.

"You place a great deal of trust in the king," she said, her tone questioning that trust.

"'Tis Henry's edict. He will not revoke the wardship," he said, getting up to shrug out of his armor.

"Mayhap I should go to London to plead Philip's case."

Over his dead body. He wouldn't allow Lucinda within a hundred leagues of George!

"You will not, nor will I. There are others who can do the task with more finesse than we." Richard opened the flagon and poured the ruby liquid into two cups. "Do you remember Kester, the advisor to whom you appealed for an audience with the king?"

She crossed her arms, her face skewed in thought. "The man who kept the list of supplicants? He made me wait beyond my turn. I was about to take him to task when he finally informed King Henry that I waited."

"One and the same," Richard confirmed her memory. "Kester is well versed in the ways of court, and is a great favorite of Henry's. He is also married to Ardith's sister, so is family. At word from Gerard, Kester will aid our cause."

Richard took a sip of the wine. Ambrosia! His thought must have shown on his face.

"I would imagine George cried when he ordered that wine loaded onto the wagon," she said, then took a sip from her cup, her eyes closing. "Ah, I had forgotten how truly excellent it is. 'Twould bring a grand indulgence, as Stephen said."

"Or influence." Richard swirled the elixir in his cup. "Bishop Hervey is an old friend of my father's and a clergyman Henry respects. For a flask or two of this wine, he might be persuaded to write to Henry and aid our cause as well."

"I dislike having my fate in the hands of others."

Including him.

"Sometimes 'tis best to give a task to those best suited." He shrugged. "Besides, George may change his mind on the matter before he reaches London."

"I would not depend on George changing his mind."

"Stubborn, is he?"

"As stubborn, obstinate, bullheaded and unyielding as any other man who wants something he cannot have."

Including me? He abstained from comment on her low opinion of males. She might give him an appraisal of himself that he would rather not hear. Better to change the subject.

Richard drained his cup. When he reached for the flagon, Lucinda held out hers to be refilled, too.

"These goods that George sent," he said, pointing to the parchment, noting the healthy swig of wine she took. "Sit and help me decide which to keep and which to take to market."

She plopped down onto the stool. "How large a city is Ely? Are there people there who can afford luxuries?"

"A few. I should give the bishop first choice of the goods, then take to the streets whatever he does not want."

She picked up the parchment, studied the list, sipped her wine. "You should surely sell whatever spices you can do without. They will bring a pretty profit."

And on down the list she went. Keep the pheasants, sell the chickens. Divide the barrels of salted meats or fish among his holdings. Mill the grain into flour first—because it would bring a better price—then either sell or distribute. Do not, under any circumstances, sell the wine. Give some to the bishop and his brothers if he must, but keep the rest.

By the time he'd decided what to take to market, Lucinda's eyes had gone dreamily glazed. She removed her circlet and veil, remarking on how warm the day had become.

The woman was fluttered, pleasantly so.

"Does Ely have a large market? With tradesmen and street merchants and entertainers?" she asked wistfully.

"Aye. I think you and Philip will enjoy it."

Surprise rounded her eyes wide. "Philip and me? Truly?"

He chuckled. "Truly. How long has it been since you have been to a market fair?"

"An eternity. Well, nearly forever. Since my youth, anyway."

"You speak as if that were so very long ago. You are not old, Lucinda."

She shook her head. "In years, mayhap not. But in other ways I am ancient. You see, I lost my youth the day I became Basil's wife."

Lucinda had said very little about her marriage. Richard knew he waded in dangerous waters and wasn't sure he wanted to hear more. Still, he splashed more wine into her cup.

"How old were you when you married?" he asked.

"Ten and six, a proper age to wed. I thought it the most horrible day of my life. I learned soon enough that there were more horrible days to come." She rubbed the cup between her hands, and frowned. "Basil lied to my father, you know. He told Father that he thought me lovely and lively, then he spent the weeks following our wedding beating the liveliness out of me because he thought high spirits unsuitable in a wife."

Richard's hand tightened on his cup, and he cursed

himself for prodding her into revealing what he had no right nor wish to hear.

"Do you know what it is like to live in fear?" she asked, very softly, and not really of him. "To continually watch what you say or do because the person who holds sway over your very existence may take offense?"

Under scorn, aye, but not fear.

"Not only my words, but those of others. Once, one of the mercenaries remarked that Basil must surely enjoy bedding such a comely wench as his wife. Basil killed the mercenary, then beat me so no one else would think me comely. I lived through it just to spite him."

By law, a man could beat his wife for whatever offense. Indeed, many thought it a man's duty to strictly discipline both wife and children. Richard knew how a switch felt when applied to a backside. His father hadn't spared the rod when called for. But he'd never been severely beaten, and never due to someone else's heedless comment.

'Twas not hard to imagine why Lucinda never wanted to marry again, why she'd asked him to pay her bride price.

He reached out to touch her.

She drew back, her eyes gone hard, like violet gems. "I have caused you naught but trouble. At court, with your family, with your tenants. Now with George. How can you stand the sight of me?"

'Twas the wine talking. The old fears had come out in the open and she quailed at them, and at the touch of him. He wouldn't have it. He wasn't Basil. She had to know that. Richard cupped her cheeks in his hands, held her still when she tried to turn away.

"I crave the sight, the scent, the taste of you, woman. I see your raven hair and violet eyes in my dreams. The scent of you spins my senses around, but always leads me straight to you. And your taste, ah Lucinda, your taste. 'Tis of the most exotic spice or hardiest wine."

"Stop," she whispered. Tears threatened. She closed her eyes, but otherwise stood rigid.

"Deep inside you hides the lively girl that few have been privileged to see and fewer have appreciated. 'Tis that lively one who wraps me in her warmth and soothes me. 'Tis her summons I will always answer."

She blinked away her tears. Her eyes shone with a deep inner light—her fire. "Words, mere words."

If his words couldn't soothe her, mayhap his body could. A light kiss on her brow led to a longer kiss on her temple. With gentle but firm pressure he kneaded her shoulders and stroked her back. Slowly, Lucinda relaxed. Briefly, he wondered if she responded to him or succumbed to the wine, then decided not to question.

He gathered Lucinda in his arms and held her tightly. He couldn't change the life she'd known, or purge her memories. But he could help her make new ones, better ones, gentler ones.

Hellfire. How pompous of him to think anything that he might do to Lucinda could help. He might even do more harm than good. But damn, he had to try, or never forgive himself.

Richard lowered Lucinda to the furs and, with all that was in him, tried.

Chapter Sixteen

Her brain had swollen and threatened to burst her skull open. The sharp odor of smoke from the cooking fire mingled with the aroma of grease from the goose and churned in her stomach. Everyone spoke too loudly. A yip from one of the dogs sounded like a scream.

She probably should have stayed in her hut, on her pallet.

Lucinda took another small bite of the bread she'd torn from the trencher before shoving the rest toward Philip. The pretense wasn't fooling Richard, or Stephen, though both had the good manners to hold their tongues.

"Are you ill?" Philip asked.

"Nay, just not hungry," she lied, unwilling to tell Philip how far she'd succumbed to the wine's effects.

Never again would she drink more than two cups of wine at a time. Not because of the pain or the sickness, but because her mouth ran loose. She'd told Richard things about her marriage to Basil that she'd never told anyone, horrors she'd intended to take to her grave.

The degradation, the shame, the self-loathing. She'd told him too much, let him see too deep. Merciful heaven, she'd been on the verge of telling Richard that she loved him. Even in her muddled state she'd had the good sense to hold it back.

He'd soothed her with poetic words and tender caresses. Already the man held too much sway over her senses. If ever he mocked her love for him, 'twould destroy her as no fist to her face or insult to her pride ever could.

For all he'd tried, Basil had never broken her spirit. Richard could if he knew how she yearned for his words and caresses. All he would have to do is withhold them.

Richard picked up his goblet and quaffed down his wine. The potent drink seemed to have had no effect on him. "True ambrosia," he said.

"Agreed," Stephen said. "Far better than what Gerard manages to obtain, and I always thought his good. Our brother will be jealous when he tastes yours. Did you get everything you wished to take to Ely loaded on the barge?"

"Aye. All is ready. All we need do on the morn is get on and shove off."

She'd missed the loading of the barge. Richard had slipped out of her hut and handled the sorting and loading while she slept the afternoon away.

Lucinda prayed that her stomach calmed by morn, or she would suffer a miserable voyage. A misery she would gladly endure for the sake of the adventure up the river Granta. Through the marshy Fens, to Ely, to market. Far from Connor's harsh disapproval and farther yet from George.

She didn't take the time to identify the pungent

odor that wafted under her nose and coiled in her
innards. She rose gingerly.

"Your pardon," she said quietly to Richard, then
walked slowly to the manor's door, seeking the fresh
air necessary to keep down the little food she'd eaten.

Once outside, she continued to walk while the
breeze of a gentle spring evening worked its magic.
The sun had already dipped below treetop level, leaving in its wake a glow of brilliant orange. A sign of
a good day on the morrow.

Feeling better, her head clearing somewhat, she
climbed the steep earthwork to the wall-walk. She
stopped at the V between two of the spike-pointed
timbers of the palisade and absorbed the beauty of the
flowing, sparkling moat. The road arrowed between
newly plowed fields and the tenant farmers' thatched
huts. Beyond them the forest loomed tall and thick.

She heard soft footfalls. Expecting to see one of
the guards whose turn it was to walk the palisade, she
glanced left to see Stephen come up beside her. A
slight smile tugged at the corner of his mouth.

"I brought you a mint leaf," he said, holding it
out. "'Twill not cure what ails you, but may give
relief. Bite off a small piece and let it lie under your
tongue."

Chagrined, but grateful for any remedy, she followed his instructions. "My thanks. I gather you have
fallen victim to this malady."

He laughed lightly. "Too many times, I fear." He
glanced out over the scene she'd been admiring. "The
sky promises nice weather for the first day of your
journey. You should have smooth sailing—good tidings for your stomach."

The mint washed the sourness from her mouth.

What effect it would have on her stomach she had yet to find out.

Lucinda twirled the leaf in her fingers, searching for further words. She hadn't been prepared for Stephen's kind words earlier, and wasn't sure how to converse with him now. "You, too, leave on the morrow."

He nodded. "At first light. I hope to reach Bury St. Edmunds by nightfall."

"A long journey for one day."

"Aye, but that will allow me to reach Wilmont early on the following day. I have much to report to Gerard. So, I will say farewell to you now and make for my pallet. Have a pleasant trip, Lucinda."

He turned to leave.

"Wait," she said, gathering her courage. If she didn't ask him now, she might never have another chance. She held up the leaf. "Why bring me the mint, Stephen? Up until today, you would not have given it to me, but let me suffer and hoped I suffered greatly. Today you offer me apricots and mint."

His smile widened. "Because today Richard made a spectacle of himself on his horse, faced George with the iron will of a true lord, and allowed his people to cheer him. 'Tis a tidbit I cannot wait to tell Gerard. Good journey, Lucinda."

With that, Stephen strode off toward the manor, leaving her more confused than before. She would try to sort it out later, when her head didn't hurt. Her stomach, surprisingly, no longer roiled.

Lucinda warily eyed the barge that rested partly on the bank of the Granta. 'Twas no more than a raft of ten logs lashed together with rope. A tarp covered the sizable mound of goods piled in the center, yet left ample room around the edges for the men to push and steer the barge with long poles.

"'Tis safe," Richard said, extending his hand to help her onto the barge. "It has not come apart from underneath us yet."

"Yet," she said, putting her free hand in his. Her other arm was wrapped around her thrice-folded bearskin that Richard had told her to bring along as a soft mat to sit upon.

Philip, she noticed, hopped from log to log with the grace of a deer. She just hoped she wouldn't disgrace herself by falling into the river before the barge left shore.

With her balance none too steady, her hand clutched in Richard's, she gingerly stepped as far into the center of the barge as she could get. She bent to sit down and made a rather ungraceful landing.

"Comfortable?" Richard asked.

"I am fine, Richard. Go about your duties."

To his credit, he did so without another comment on her nervousness or clumsiness. Not until his back was turned did she brace her hands on either side of herself and shift her backside to a better position. Just when she thought her body stable, Richard shouted for the men to shove off.

She grabbed the tarp and held tightly.

The barge glided away from the bank. On a command from Richard, the men lowered their poles into the river and set the barge in motion. The last she saw of anything familiar was Connor, growing smaller with distance, his arm raised in farewell.

She loosened her grip on the tarp. Richard plopped down beside her.

"What think you of my ship?" he asked, a wide smile on his face, the river breeze ruffling his long, blond hair.

"'Tis like no other ship on which I have sailed."

He chuckled. "I imagine." He tapped on a log. "'Tis sturdy, and unless we have a storm, a smooth sailing vessel."

"And in a storm?"

"We seek the bank and shelter."

Six men—three on each side—worked in a coordinated pattern of lowering a pole into the river at the front of the barge, walking along the side to the back, then returning to the front. Edric stood at the front, correcting where needed, keeping half an eye on Philip.

"I should call Philip," she said. "His curiosity will soon get the better of him and he will distract Edric from his task."

"Very little distracts Edric, not even Philip. He is good with the boy."

Lucinda couldn't disagree. Edric was extremely patient with her son, as was Richard. Both took care to answer his questions in a calm and thorough manner, not brushing him aside. Lately she'd learned, from Philip's stories of his adventures each evening, that others about Collinwood had been patient with her son, too. And Philip had also made a friend of the blacksmith's son, a year younger than himself.

Edric's doing? Richard's? She didn't know, but was grateful. Her son, at least, had a chance of having a true home with Richard.

"Since coming to Collinwood," she said, "Philip has told me that he would like to be a soldier, a tanner, a blacksmith, and a great lord. Care to wager that he will now wish to be a sailor?''

"Hmm. After sailor will come merchant or monk. He will find Ely a delight.''

"What is Ely like? A large city?''

"Nay, merely a Benedictine monastery, atop a hill rising out of the marsh. The last time I visited the place, the cathedral had just been begun. I am anxious to see how the work progresses.''

He also wished to talk to the masons about the process and costs of building a stone keep. Lucinda thought it an ambitious and costly project, but kept her opinion to herself.

"And the bishop?''

"Hervey?'' Richard considered for a moment. "He is one of the few churchmen I know who deserves a bishopric. A good man with few vices.'' He glanced at the mound of goods. "I believe I have managed to play into each of those vices, sinner that I am to tempt him so. I will be surprised if he does not buy most of this.''

Lucinda couldn't imagine that Richard would have many sins to confess. Except tempting a bishop to excess. Or perhaps his liaison with her. She shoved that guilt-burdened thought aside, refusing to feel guilty of any sin for expressing her love for Richard in the only way she could.

Richard's fingers tilted her chin up, turned her face slightly. He frowned. "You are pale. Are you still ill?''

"Nay, merely tired.''

He brushed her cheek with his knuckles. "Well then, rest if you can. 'Twill be a long day before we stop for the night.'' He looked to the front of the barge, then rose. "I will rescue Edric. Mayhap Philip and I can snare some perch."

Lucinda pushed at the tarp. Behind it were stacked sacks—of what she didn't know—not crates. More accustomed now to the movement of the barge, she twisted around so she could lean against the sacks.

Despite her illness, sleep had come hard last night. The hurt in her head hadn't kept Stephen's words at bay. At sometime in the wee hours, she thought she'd finally understood what the man had meant.

She'd wondered, when first coming to Collinwood, why Richard's people hadn't greeted him with more enthusiasm. Now she knew that Richard hadn't allowed them to.

Richard *had* changed, even in the short time since she'd known him. Stephen had noticed, too. He'd implied that Richard's confidence had grown and that he seemed more at ease with his role as lord.

All well and good, except Stephen thought that she had something to do with that change. She didn't. Richard's growth into his role had been a natural one. She'd done nothing to aid or hasten it.

Lucinda closed her eyes and listened to the lap of water against the timber vessel, floating along on a peaceful current. Her last thought before falling asleep was that Stephen had been wrong.

When she again opened her eyes, the barge had slowed to nearly a stop. Several boats and barges now shared the river with them, going both directions.

The wharves of Cambridge came into view. Lucinda tossed off sleep with the blanket, and dared to rise to her feet. The bulk of Cambridge stood on the east bank. To see it, she must move around the goods.

Log by log, using the tarp for hand-holds, she moved to the front of the barge.

Richard stood on the very corner, Philip snug at his side, Edric a few steps off.

Richard pointed forward. "There is where we will pay our toll. See how we line up behind this fishing vessel?"

Philip nodded.

"Look up the bank and you will see Cambridge Castle on Castle Hill. A fine, stout place it is. Built by the Conqueror to secure these lands against the northern English who resisted his kingship."

On Richard went, pointing out a fishery and a wharf-side alehouse that served particularly good ale and victuals. Her stomach grumbled at the mention of food and drink, despite the odor wafting back from the fishing vessel.

For a long time the barge inched forward in the very busy port. Richard dug coins from the leather pouch secured to his girdle.

"Here now, Lord Richard!" a man called out. "'Tis not a hunting trip you make this time, I see."

"Nay, not this time. We make for Ely." The barge bumped against the pillars of the wharf. Richard handed over the coins. "How goes the Granta?"

"Reports of smooth sailing all the way to the Ouse, so I hear. Up to see the bishop?"

"Aye. Any sins you wish me to confess for you, Thomas?"

"Nay. I have too many to burden you with. A good voyage to you, my lord."

The men bent hard to the poles, spiriting the barge back into the current, setting them on their way once more. The excitement over, Richard turned around and spotted her.

He nudged Philip. "Your mother has found her sea legs."

Philip giggled.

She smiled. "Not quite, but I work at it. I have also found an appetite. I assume that food lurks under the tarp."

Richard ruffled Philip's hair. "Fetch your mother some of the apricots you uncovered earlier. 'Twill keep her stomach quiet until we stop for a proper nooning."

Philip needed no further urging to duck under the tarp.

Richard walked over to her. "There is a pretty place not far up the river. We will stop there to rest and eat, let you use your land legs again."

She ignored his teasing about her legs.

"You have made this journey before."

"Not all the way to Ely, but nearby. You will see why when we reach the Fens. 'Tis a glorious marsh, ripe with waterfowl. A spectacular place to hunt."

As Richard promised, a short while later the men guided the barge to the bank, and after a short nooning they were underway again.

The farther north they traveled, the fewer trees marked the bank. Tall rushes took their place, until Lucinda had a hard time marking land from marsh. The Fens were uninhabitable to people, but provided a home to countless swans, heron, terns, geese and lapwings—and a myriad of other fowl she couldn't begin to name.

Richard called a halt to the day at one of the lonely little islands of land that dotted the marsh.

"Is the land like this all the way from Cambridge to Ely?" she asked of Richard.

"Mostly. We will turn onto another river on the morrow, the Ouse, though you will hardly know the difference. One can walk the Granta's bank from Collinwood to Cambridge, but not much beyond."

Ely did appear a magical place. On the west bank of the Ouse rose a great hill. Atop it stood the monastery. Richard had taken a jar of wine and a length of fine white linen—most appropriate for an altar cloth—to the bishop.

She, Philip and Edric had spent the past two hours wandering among the merchants' stalls and viewing the wonders of the cathedral. They now stood outside of the chapel where Saint Etheldreda, a Queen of Northumbria and founder of the community some 400 years ago, rested in peace and glory.

Lucinda listened as the bells rang the canonical hour of terce, echoing over the wildness of the marsh, calling monks—and Bishop Hervey—to prayers. Richard should be coming to fetch them shortly.

She couldn't wait to see him simply to tell him that Philip didn't wish to be a merchant or monk. He'd taken one look at the shrine to Saint Etheldreda and decided he wanted to be a saint. Richard would find it humorous, as she had, though she hadn't said so to Philip.

A simple thing, a shared jest. Sharing it with Richard seemed natural, as though the jest wasn't complete until she told it to him. As other things weren't complete until shared with Richard.

She could tell the man almost anything without fear of being brushed aside or laughed at. He didn't always agree with her opinions, but he never belittled them.

So why was it so hard to tell Richard that she loved him?

Because she wanted to hear the words back, and doubted that he could honestly give them to her.

Lucinda spotted him coming across the courtyard, paying more heed to the parchment in his hands than where he walked. As he neared the spot where she waited for him, he looked up, and smiled.

"Edric," Richard called. "Have the men haul all of the goods up from the barge to the bishop's residence. Leave only the supplies we need for the trip home." He rolled the parchment and tucked it into his tunic. "The bishop's men will give you further directions on the evening meal and where to bed down for the night."

"Talked old Hervey into all of it, did you?" Edric said.

"Aye, told you I would. Be quick, Edric. I passed by the kitchens on my way over here and whatever is roasting over the pit smells like heaven."

Edric chuckled as he took his leave.

"As for you two," Richard told her, "I will take you over to the ladies' court after we eat. Apparently you will have the whole place to yourselves. They do not receive many female visitors here."

"Must I stay in the *ladies'* court?" Philip asked, disgruntled. "Could I not sleep with the other soldiers?"

Lucinda crossed her arms. "Saints do not whine over where they are asked to sleep. They accept it as God's will and are thankful for whatever shelter is provided."

"Truly?"

"Aye, my son. Truly."

"Oh."

At Richard's puzzled look, she briefly told him of Philip's aspiration to sainthood. To his credit, Richard managed to squelch the laughter that threatened to burst through his smile.

Richard ruffled Philip's hair. "For tonight, you must be content. Edric and the others will be far too busy to keep an eye on you. I will be with the master of the masons until well after you should be asleep. Come, let us be off to the refectory so we can eat."

Lucinda grabbed Philip's hand.

"You had a good day," Lucinda commented as they walked.

He nodded. "Bishop Hervey decided that he cannot live without everything I brought. Blessed be."

"Did you happen to tell him that you chose all of those goods with his vices in mind?"

"I did not have to. He knew the moment I began describing what goods awaited him on the barge. 'Twas the linen that caught his interest, and the wine that sealed the bargain."

"Does he pay you enough to build your stone keep?"

"Nay, but 'twill make a good start. I will find out more this eve when I speak with the master mason."

"Then your business will be done here."

"We can leave for home on the morn with a much lighter load than we came with," he said, then turned to Philip. "So, you wish to take the path to sainthood do you? Have you considered the hardships necessary to obtain such a high place in heaven?"

Richard began describing a life of haircloth, and callused knees, and continuous prayers.

While Lucinda thought of returning home.

Home. Collinwood. Richard's home. Philip's home until he reached his majority, the place he would always think on fondly.

Lucinda wished it were hers, but knew it could never be. Her place at Collinwood was temporary. In less than two years she would be free of the king's restriction that she remain with Philip, and would be expected to move on.

She glanced at Richard. At some time in the past weeks she'd stopped thinking of home as a place, but as a state of being. As peace. A peace she'd found with only one man, a man she could never call her own, to whom she would never belong.

Chapter Seventeen

Lucinda picked up a spindle and distaff, took a seat near the pile of carded wool that lay on the far side of the manor, and began the deft twirling motions that would turn the wool into yarn. In the two days since returning to Collinwood, she'd worked as hard as any of the women to turn the spring fleece into cloth.

She hadn't asked permission, simply done it. The women had watched to see if she did the task correctly, until the oldest and best of them nodded her approval. Though none spoke to her, none had sent her away.

Spinning required little concentration, the movements ingrained and habitual. 'Twas also a task she performed well. The yarn she made would weave into smooth cloth with no nubs or weak threads.

Richard sat at a table with a wax tablet and stylus. The master mason had given Richard the costs of both stone and labor to build his keep. Wanting to get the most for his coin, Richard labored over alternate designs and reworked costs.

A commotion in the bailey drew Richard's head

up. He put down the stylus. Before he could rise, Connor came into the manor.

"A messenger from Wilmont, my lord," Connor said, walking hurriedly across the floor. He handed Richard a rolled parchment. "The messenger is asked to bring a reply immediately."

Lucinda's stomach clenched. She'd tried not to worry about George contesting Philip's wardship, but couldn't think of a more urgent matter. Gerard probably didn't think her worries urgent, however. Too, word of the king's decision would likely come by royal messenger, not Wilmont's.

Even as she told herself that the baron's missive had nothing to do with her or her son, was merely an important message from brother to brother, she couldn't dismiss the foreboding feeling that the message brought ill tidings.

Richard unrolled the parchment and leafed through the pages before starting to read. A missive indeed, of four pages. Richard read without revealing any reaction, until he reached the third page. His visage skewed into a harsh scowl.

Unable to sit still anymore, Lucinda put down her work and walked over to the table. She sat across from Richard and waited impatiently for him to finish reading. When he finally did, his scowl had faded, but not vanished.

"Is there news of George?" she blurted out.

"Henry told him to return to Normandy and leave the boy with me, as I believed all along would happen."

So great was her relief that she closed her eyes and blew out the breath she hadn't realized she held. "Thank the Lord."

"Aye," he said, with an edge to his voice that brought her up short. Something else in that letter upset Richard.

"All is not well at Wilmont?"

"'Twould appear not. They seem overly concerned over what is happening here. Apparently Stephen's tales caused some alarm."

"I cannot say that I am surprised, Richard. Had Stephen had his way, you would have given Philip and me over to George. I imagine Gerard feels the same. Does he advise you to do so?"

"Nay. Among other things, however, he does advise me—" Richard glanced up at Connor, who yet hovered nearby. "Give the messenger food and drink. I will have a message for him anon."

Miffed, Connor did as bid. Lucinda couldn't blame Connor for his pique. Once, Richard would have discussed with Connor whatever he was now about to impart to her. Furthering the injury, Richard kept silent until Connor left the manor.

"Lucinda, did Stephen say anything to you about our…liaison?"

So that was what Gerard advised against.

"Stephen must have heard about it shortly after he arrived the first time he was here." She told him about both conversations, about Stephen's initial concerns, and then his remarks when giving her the mint.

"It took me a while to sort out what he meant," she said of Stephen's last statements. "I'm sure he gave Gerard the impression that I had something to do with your increased confidence as lord of Collinwood. We both know that is not true, but Stephen left before I could tell him that I deserved no credit, that your confidence was there all along and had just come to the fore.''

Richard put the letter aside, knowing she deserved more credit than she knew. He was a better lord because he felt better about himself as a man. His pride no longer required that he prove his worth to the nobles, only to himself.

Stephen had taken one afternoon to see the difference, and correctly place the cause of it squarely on Lucinda's lovely shoulders.

He'd done a good job in some areas, but an arse-poor one in others, especially with his vassals. He'd let Edric stand as a model for the soldiers, let his other vassals continue to look to Connor for guidance. He'd thought he needed to win their loyalty—the loyalty and respect they might have given him all along if he'd let them.

Not until he'd watched Lucinda struggle to earn simple respect did he realize how much respect he'd already earned.

And therein lay Gerard's concern. Gerard worried that Richard had fallen too far within the influence of the widow of Basil of Northbryre, hated enemy of Wilmont. Gerard had gone so far as to suggest that Richard should expect treachery from so beautiful and cunning a woman. After all, did not women use the wiles of their sex to bring a man low?

This from a man who so doted on his wife out of pure love and devotion that anyone who didn't know better would swear Gerard bewitched, under some spell of Ardith's that didn't allow him to treat her otherwise.

'Twas Gerard's warning that Lucinda might somehow be in league with George, in some scheme to steal away everything that Richard had fought so hard to gain, that caused his anger to flare.

Ludicrous. How dare Gerard accuse a woman he didn't know, didn't *want* to know, of such a low purpose? Obviously, something Stephen had told Gerard had planted the seed of suspicion. Richard wished he knew what.

"Why did you not tell me about your talks with Stephen before now?" he asked Lucinda.

"I thought Stephen would surely come to his senses before he reached Wilmont." She pointed to the letter. "I gather that Stephen overstated the depth of our liaison."

Stephen couldn't overstate because he had no idea how deep Richard's feelings ran. It hurt that Lucinda didn't either. But she wouldn't, because he hadn't told her, and never would. She wanted nothing to do with a permanent relationship with a man again, and he couldn't blame her. When the time came, he would pay the fee necessary for her to avoid another marriage, and set her free.

If she chose to remain at Collinwood, for Philip's sake, so be it. If she chose to go, he would help her—and miss her from the depths of his soul.

'Twas the least he could do for the woman who'd given him so much—so much more than a tumble in the furs when his desire for her became unbearable, so much more than a warm smile and sympathetic ear when his spirit needed reviving. She'd shown him how to love, even though she didn't want his.

"What will you tell Gerard?" she asked.

"That he should send Stephen on his way to the Lady Carolyn."

Richard rose to fetch quill and parchment.

Lucinda rose to return to her work. She glanced once more at the letter. She didn't mean to read any of it, but 'twas impossible not to, given Gerard's clear script.

Gerard's suspicions and warnings about the conniving widow of Wilmont's most hated enemy fairly leaped off the page. Richard had made light of the letter's contents, but Gerard was his beloved brother and liege lord. How could Richard read Gerard's words and not give them credence?

If Richard ignored them, or refuted them, Gerard would be angry, and may force Richard into the untenable situation of defending Lucinda. 'Twould cause a rift between them, no matter who won.

What Gerard had given, could Gerard also take away?

Two days later, Richard stared out over the palisade in disbelief. Within sight marched an army of about fifty men, under George's command. Villeins from the outlying farms were racing to make the safety of the palisade before the gates closed.

Within the hour, Collinwood would be under siege.

Impossible. Incredible. But George had returned, disobeying the king's command, obviously intending to take Philip by force. With too few men.

"Mercenaries." Edric spat out the word, an unnecessary explanation of where George's army had come from. Men who fought for whatever lord paid their fee. Richard hoped the men had asked a high price, and already spent it, because many of them were about to die.

"The man has lost whatever wits God gave him," Richard declared, then turned his attention to the defenses. "Have the men fill whatever containers they can get their hands on with water from the moat. I want as much within the palisade as we can get before we are forced to close the gate."

Edric obeyed immediately. 'Twas no secret that the manor's greatest enemy was fire, and that George would use the weapon to force a surrender.

"My lord," Connor said, climbing the bank to the palisade. "The tenants worry for their farms and cattle and possessions. Do you truly intend to fight?"

Richard didn't need the message that would surely come from George, stating his demands, to know what those demands would be. Turn over Philip and George would desist. Even if Richard handed the boy over, which he wouldn't do, he doubted that George would simply turn around and go home.

George might be looking for revenge for Richard's callous treatment, and try to burn them out anyway.

"George will not give us a choice, Connor. Tell the tenants that I will replace any possessions that may be lost."

And thereby end his plans for a stone keep, for there would surely be losses, and no matter how much he economized, he wouldn't be able to afford both. Not this year anyway. Such was the price of lordship.

And people would be killed. An inevitability he couldn't ignore and would have to deal with, and be held accountable for. Such, too, was the responsibility of lordship.

"If you would just hand the woman and boy over—"

"I will not!" Richard shouted. "I will never hand *one* of my people over to an enemy without a fight, from Lucinda and Philip, down to you, down to the lowest scullery maid! Now, have the bailey cleared of anything that might burn and tell the women and children to take cover."

Unable to stand the sight of Connor any longer, he turned back to check on the approaching army. They had stopped a good distance off. Soon a rider would come with George's demands.

He paced the wall-walk, his attention divided between George out in the fields, the men bearing water from the moat back into the bailey, and the women and youngsters who followed Connor's directions.

Richard looked for Lucinda and Philip, saw neither. Did Lucinda know what was happening? She had to. No one could miss the frenzied activity happening all over the bailey. So where was she?

"A rider, my lord!" came Edric's cry from near the gate.

Richard saw the man coming, one he recognized as one of George's men, riding hard. He bore no weapon that Richard could see.

"Let him approach, but stand ready."

The man pulled up far enough away from the gate so no one could rush him, then shouted the demand for Philip in return for sparing Collinwood.

"Tell George I have received his demand," Richard answered. "Then tell him I refuse, and that the next time I meet him face to face, I intend to shove his head up his arse to reunite it with his brain! Also inform him that I will hold his hide responsible for any damage he causes to Collinwood."

Richard's soldiers cheered and banged swords against shields as the red-faced rider spun around and galloped back to report to George.

"Well said, my lord," Edric said. "'Tis a shame your whole message will not be delivered."

A shame, indeed. The messenger wouldn't dare repeat the whole of it for fear of reprisal.

"I go for my hauberk. Next will come an arrow or two, to test for range. Get everyone inside and close the gate when the arrows get close. I should be back before the first fire-arrow flies."

Richard climbed down the inner embankment and headed for the armory, glancing around for some sign of Lucinda or Philip. Not finding them, he quickly donned his chain mail and went in search of them.

He found them both in the manor. Lucinda, apparently, had taken on the job of readying the manor for wounded. Two tables stood ready. On each had been placed a flagon of water and a variety of creams and oils. Some of the women tore linen into strips for bandages. Two others stood over kettles bubbling at the fire pit. Yet another bunched carded wool into pads to use for poultices.

The scene staggered him. Lucinda rushed around, checking the tables, stopping to give an instruction, then hurrying on to recheck the pots, adding an herb to one and leaving the other alone.

She'd taken command as if she were the lady of the manor and had every right to assume control. To his knowledge, the manor had never been attacked before, and the fear in the women's eyes explained why they'd allowed Lucinda free rein. She knew what to do, they didn't.

The older girls helped their mothers; the younger ones tended the toddlers and infants—except for five boys, Philip among them, who stood grouped in a corner. Philip held his wooden sword, the rest clutched stout sticks.

Fascinated, Richard walked toward them. Philip was giving the boys instructions on how to wield the sticks should an enemy break through the manor's defenses.

"Go for the knees," the boy said, demonstrating with a mighty swing. "When your man is down, bash him over the head."

He made it sound so simple, as though a boy with a stick could bring down a man with a sword.

Richard crossed his arms. "What the devil are you about?" he asked, drawing the attention of the boys and everyone else in the manor.

In the hush that followed, Philip came forward.

"My lord," he said in a calm, resolute voice, "since the men need to protect the palisade, and the older boys are needed to douse fires, we—" he indicated the boys with a sweep of his sword "—will protect the women."

This was his fault, of course, for having given Philip that duty once before when there had been no danger. Now danger had arrived at his gates and these little boys—*hellfire*—were just little boys, not soldiers. A glance at Lucinda told him that she, too, thought the whole thing his fault and that he had best do something about it.

Richard noted the boys' eagerness to be of some service. Having some duty would keep their fear at bay, too. He couldn't disappoint them, but couldn't let them have their way completely, either.

"Protecting the women is a serious duty," he told them. Every little head bobbed in swift agreement. "This means you must stay within the manor, close

by your mothers in case you are needed. You are not
to wander out into the bailey, under any circumstances, to see what is happening.''

"Should not we stand in the doorway, to give
warning?'' the blacksmith's son asked.

'Twas Richard's greatest fear that they would be
drawn into the bailey, and likely the fear of their
mothers, too.

"Nay. Should the enemy breach the palisade, I will
send warning. You must stay clear of the doorway to
allow the wounded passage—and to best protect our
women. Those are my orders and I expect you to obey
them.''

Their heads didn't bob in agreement so quickly this
time.

"You will also heed your mothers' commands.
Should any one of them give you an order, and I hear
that you did not obey straightaway, 'twill vex me
sorely. Understood?''

The boys looked from one to the other.

"Understood?'' Richard said more forcefully.

Several weak "aye, my lords'' followed.

He looked to the one mother who might yet give
argument. Lucinda seemed satisfied.

"Good,'' he told the boys. "Take care that you
bash no one with those sticks but the enemy.''

With that last warning, he left the boys and beckoned to Lucinda. She wore the old peasant-weave
gown in which she'd arrived at Collinwood. Her
raven hair was tightly plaited, then wound around her
head like a crown. She wore no veil or circlet—or
smile.

Still, Lucinda was the most beautiful woman he
had ever seen. The most courageous.

"You have done a good job here," he told her.

"The women thank me now for giving them something to do with their hands and minds. That will change when the first husband or son comes in bleeding. Then they will hate me again for being the cause of their loved one's pain, or death."

"You are not to blame, George is."

"When one's loved one is in pain, 'tis easiest to blame someone close at hand. Go, you must be with your men. I will be all right."

Richard knew she would get through the day in whatever way she could. She would see that the wounded were cared for no matter if the women helped her or railed at her.

From outside he heard the creak of the gates. Edric must have ordered them closed because arrows were getting close. Soon would come the test of his leadership and resolve.

He tucked a finger under her chin and raised her face. "Since you have assumed command, I now give it to you. Do whatever you must without fear of reprisal from me. Scream, bully, beat heads together if you must."

"Have a care, Richard. We need you," she whispered.

In the manor, the women chattered in soft voices, peppered with an occasional nervous laugh. Outside Connor shouted orders to the older boys who placed water near buildings.

Lucinda's eyes sparkled. Her lips parted, beckoning. He bent to her silent plea, to the need encompassing his own soul. The kiss was light, and warm, and not enough. When she broke away, a tear trickled down her cheek.

"Down in the bailey!" Edric cried from the wall-walk.

Richard heard the whiz of the single arrow, which thudded into the earth in front of the manor door.

He grasped the back of Lucinda's neck, kissed her soundly, then fled the manor. On his way to the palisade, he snatched up the enemy's arrow.

George's army formed a long line along the edge of a field, the men down on one knee behind kite-shaped shields. George and two other men sat on horseback behind them. They couldn't possibly overtake the manor. Not with a mere fifty men. But they could harass, and do damage, and take lives.

Richard took a bow from one of his archers. "'Tis time to let them know who is truly vulnerable here, hey Edric?"

Edric chuckled. "Have at it, my lord."

Richard notched the arrow and chose his target. 'Twas too much to hope that he could knock George off his horse, end it all now. The distance was too great. But he could get close. He drew back and let the bolt fly. The arrow flew true, in a high arc. It bit into the earth behind the wall of shields, so near to George that his horse reared and skittered backward.

The wall of shields backed up several yards. The farther back the archers, the fewer arrows would fly over the palisade, and even fewer of the heavier fire-tipped arrows.

Richard handed the bow back to its owner.

The enemy line stood up as one.

"Volley!" Edric shouted. "Shields up! 'Ware the bailey!"

Most of the arrows landed in the moat, a few bounced off the palisade, two stuck.

"Answer, my lord?" Edric asked.

"Aye, we must," he said, then turned to shout, "Put some muscle into it, men. Send them back!"

The return volley sent the enemy back, finding three human targets. So it went for the next hour, the testing of strength and distance, taking each other's measure.

Richard strode the walk, talking to each of his defenders, encouraging them, preparing them as the enemy built a fire.

The volley, when it came, was a sight to behold and deadly in its beauty. Balls of fire streaked through the sky. Again, most fell into the moat. Several hit the palisade and were quickly extinguished by the men on the walk. Three flew over the palisade. Two fell to the dirt, but one found the roof of the blacksmith's hut.

Boys scrambled to put it out, drowning the threat with two buckets of water. 'Twas quickly out, the thatch barely singed, but had the effect of sobering all.

"'Twill be a long day," Edric commented.

An understatement. Edric knew as well as Richard did that the siege had just begun, and only God, or mayhap George, knew when it would end.

Chapter Eighteen

Lucinda wrapped the young man's burned hand while his mother hovered nearby. The mother fretted, but not her son. He smiled at the bandage as if it was a sign of his courage and usefulness to his lord.

They'd been lucky thus far. Two burns. One arrow wound—a mere scratch. No deaths, not yet, but they would come.

The tension in the manor rose with each shout of "volley" from the walk. Then came the endless minutes of waiting for the arrows to fall, the shouts for water, the fear that someone would suffer serious hurt.

Between the volleys, men drifted into the manor to grab a bite to eat or a drink of honeyed mead before heading back to the walk or to the armory for rest. Soon night would fall.

Neither Richard nor Edric had appeared as yet.

Lucinda tied off the bandage and tucked the ends into the folds. "Let your mother fuss over you for a moment before you go back out," she whispered to the young man.

"''Tis naught to worry over and I am needed without."

She patted him on the shoulder. "I know, but if you do not let her fuss she will continue to fret and be of no use to me in here. 'Tis a mother's lot in life to fuss. Give her a moment so we will all have peace."

He sighed his resignation and did as she asked.

She looked around for her own son. Philip and his band had soon wearied of standing guard. They now sat in a circle and played some game.

Lucinda walked over to the table filled with food and drink. Richard and Edric should eat. If they couldn't find the time to come into the manor, someone should deliver a meal to them.

'Twas probably a dangerous thing for her to do, and Richard would likely toss a fit. Still, she loaded a clay platter with bread, cheese and dried fruit, filled two cups with mead, and slipped out of the manor.

Richard was easy to locate. His chain mail glinted, touched with the fire of the setting sun. He stood on the walk near the gate, peering out over the palisade at the enemy beyond. A warrior. The man in command.

No one stopped her from walking across the bailey or climbing the inner bank to the walk—though Edric spotted her and nudged Richard, who turned and scowled.

"Woman, I swear—"

"Do not trouble yourself, Richard. I have heard it all before. Here," she said, handing over the mead. "If you do not take time to feed yourselves, then someone must feed you."

"I am not hungry."

"Wonderful. Eat anyway, as an example to your men. You would not want them falling faint with hunger, would you?"

"The men are on shifts, instructed to eat and rest—"

"Rest. A splendid idea. On which shift do you rest?"

Richard and Edric exchanged a look that Lucinda couldn't misread.

"Neither of you can remain awake during the entire siege," she scolded. "It could take days, weeks!"

"Not so long," Richard said, plucking a piece of cheese from the platter. "He has not the means, I think, for a prolonged siege. The mercenaries will stand with George only as long as he can pay them. He needs to come up with a plan of attack."

Lucinda looked out over the palisade at the enemy camp.

A good number of years had passed since she last saw George, but he was easy to pick out, not by his features—the distance was too great—but by his portly form, garbed in rich robes. He paced along the edge of the camp, behind a line of soldiers whose shields faced the manor.

The man had a mean streak as wide as Basil's and deep as the devil's. Cut from the same cloth as his cousin, George obeyed laws and played the honorable noble only when it suited him. Did he make war on his neighbors as often as Basil had? Did he win as rarely as Basil had?

"What will he do?" she asked.

"Build ladders," Edric said around a bite of bread. "Try to scale the walls."

She shivered. "Tonight?"

"Nay, not tonight," Richard said, grabbing a handful of fruit. "He has yet to cut trees. Soon he will run out of daylight, then the rain will come and drive him to shelter."

Lucinda scanned the sky. No cloud marred the expanse.

"What rain?"

"'Twill rain tonight, heavy," Edric said. He winked at her. "My knee, it never lies."

Richard consumed the last of the bread. Edric devoured the chunk of cheese. Both had been hungry as bears but unwilling to leave the wall-walk.

"Edric, Lucinda has the right of it," Richard said. "Get a few hours' sleep, then you can relieve me. I doubt George will try anything fancy tonight."

"As you wish, my lord. Mayhap I will have another cup of mead first."

Lucinda saw through the ruse. "You may go straight to your pallet, Edric. I managed to come here on my own and can certainly manage to find my way back."

"Of course you can, my lady. I never had a doubt."

Yet he waited. Edric wasn't about to budge until she moved. He would escort her to the manor whether she wished him to or not.

She drank in another draught of Richard's beloved visage. "Is it over for the day then?"

He shook his head. "Another volley or two, perhaps."

Another volley or two to worry over him, to still her shaking hands whenever the call to take cover thundered through the bailey. When the arrows flew,

Richard would be here atop the walk, too easy a target.

She forced herself down the inner bank, Edric at her heels. At midbailey, Richard's call rang out. "Volley! No fire! 'Ware the bailey! Run, Lucinda!"

Lucinda dropped the platter, hiked up her skirts, and sprinted for the manor door with Edric right beside her. They ran so hard her lungs burned. Overhead she heard the whiz of a downward-arced arrow—too close. The door was too far away.

Edric slammed into her and knocked her to the ground. She landed facedown in the dirt, Edric atop her. All around her she heard screams and men shouting. And the heavy thumps of her own laboring, but beating heart. Then silence.

Edric eased off. "Are you all right?"

She felt no pain except the scrapes on her hands. She lifted her head. Two feet in front of her an arrow quivered, the tip stuck in the dirt.

She blew out a relieved breath. "I am fine. You?"

"Unharmed."

He held out his hand to help her up. She no more than made her feet when Richard swept her off them. She flung her arms around his neck, ignoring the bite of his chain mail.

"Dear, sweet Lord," he uttered the prayer into her neck.

Aye, she silently agreed. Someone besides Edric had been watching over her. Another step or two and...merciful heaven, that arrow had come far too close.

She'd heard screams. Someone must be hurt. She should find out who and go back into the manor and treat the wound.

For the life of her, she couldn't speak, couldn't move. So she tarried within Richard's comforting embrace, as if by some magic he could infuse some vigor into her suddenly weak body and tired mind.

"She goes pale as cream," she heard Edric say before the world went dark.

Lucinda's body went limp. Richard's first terrified thought was that she'd died, but she breathed. She'd fainted.

He gathered her in his arms and carried her into the manor. All eyes turned to watch as he carefully laid her on a table.

"Mother?" Philip's small voice trembled.

Philip's eyes, huge and round, glistened. Richard understood the boy's terror.

"She lives, Philip. See, she breathes."

"Then why does she not wake?"

"Your mother had a bad scare and fainted, is all," he said, trying to keep his tone light for Philip's sake. "She will wake when ready."

"'Twas my duty to watch her."

Sensing the direction of the child's misguided thoughts, Richard scrunched down and grasped Philip's shoulders. "You did your duty. You were to guard her while in the manor. If there is any blame here, 'tis mine. I did not guard her well enough while she was outside the manor."

Edric huffed. "As captain of the guard, 'twas my duty. And I think I did a damn good job of it!"

Richard rose and faced Edric. He would never be able to thank the man enough. "That you did, Edric. A damn fine job. If you hadn't knocked her over..."

Hellfire, he couldn't say it aloud. The scene replayed over and over in his head. Lucinda and Edric running toward the manor, directly into the path of a downward spiraling arrow. His heart had lodged in his throat, watching death descend on one he held dear.

On the woman he loved.

He'd never prayed so hard, so fast, so earnestly in his entire life. If God truly held him to every promise he'd made in those terrifying moments, he would qualify for sainthood at his life's end.

Of all the promises he'd made, he would keep one promise above all others. If Lucinda would have him.

Richard picked up Philip, hugged him, then set him on the table next to his mother. This woman, this boy, meant the world to him. No stone keep, no holding, no riches would fill the lonely, empty hole in his life if he lost them. He picked up Lucinda's hand and placed it in her son's.

"Watch over her for me for a moment, will you?"

"Aye, my lord. She is back in the manor. 'Tis my turn to watch over her."

Richard ruffled Philip's hair. "It is at that."

He took a deep breath and brought himself back to the task at hand. In order to have a future with Lucinda and Philip, first he had to secure that future. George was still without, threatening everything Richard held dear.

Sweet heaven, what he wouldn't give to have Gerard make a surprise visit right now. Come up on George's backside and mow his forces down the middle like a scythe through a field of wheat. Of course, then when Richard told Gerard of his intentions toward Lucinda, Gerard would toss a fit. Best that Gerard remained at Wilmont.

Richard knew his best plan of defense was to sit

tight and let George expend his supplies. But, hellfire, the sitting irritated since he would rather take an aggressive offensive.

"My lord, with your permission, I will return to the wall," Edric offered. "There are other wounded you may wish to attend before you return."

Other wounded? He'd focused so hard on Lucinda he hadn't noticed.

Richard cuffed Edric on the shoulder. "My thanks, my friend. I will return shortly. And Edric, that arrow. I want it so I can send it back to George."

Edric left. Richard gave a last glance at Philip, who clutched Lucinda's hand and watched her intently, then moved off to where Lyle, one of the older boys who manned the water, sat on a nearby stool. He sported a large, nastily colored bruise on his head. The boy would have a headache, but seemed fine otherwise.

"Tripped over my own big feet, my lord," Lyle said, chagrined. "'Tain't nothing. How is the lady?"

"Lucinda had a scare and fainted." The more he said it, the more he would believe it. Her brush with death had frightened her into fainting. She would be fine.

Lyle held up his linen-wrapped hand. "She bandaged my burn earlier, right and tight. I am glad the arrow missed her. I saw it coming down, right in her path." Lyle glanced over to where Lucinda lay. "I tried to get to her, but..."

Lyle had tripped trying to run to Lucinda. At least one person of all his tenants thought her worthy, and that gave him hope. If one could, mayhap the rest could too, someday.

Richard clasped Lyle's shoulder. "You have done

me good service this day. You are now off duty until the morn.''

''But my lord—''

''Until morn. I catch you outside of this manor before then and I will take a strap to your backside.''

Richard didn't give Lyle a chance to argue further. He moved on to where one of his soldiers lay on the rushes. The man had taken an arrow to the gullet— and died. The first death, and probably not the last.

A farmer's wife covered the soldier's face with a bandage and crossed herself.

''Has he family here?'' Richard asked, unable to remember.

''Nay, I believe not.''

''I will have to ask Connor. He will know.''

''Then you had best ask quick, my lord,'' she said, pointing to a table. ''He bleeds heavily.''

Hellfire. Richard strode over to where Connor lay on his left side, very still. An arrow pierced him completely through the right side of his body, under the ribs. The women had packed wads of bandaging around both wounds, yet the blood seeped through.

Connor opened his eyes. ''Too old to run fast, my lord,'' he said weakly.

''You had best not die, Connor. Collinwood needs you.''

The light touch on his arm could only be Lucinda's. Her face had regained some color, but not enough. Philip stood at her side, clutching his mother's hand.

''The arrow needs to come out,'' she said.

Connor's eyes widened. ''Nay, do not let her touch me. I would rather die in peace.''

Lucinda's eyes flashed with anger. She bent over until her face hovered mere inches from Connor's. ''I bear you no great love either, Connor. But by all that is holy, I will not let you die, if only because Richard wishes you to live. Say a prayer for courage, old man, because what I am about to do will hurt like hell.''

She rose. ''Richard, can you snap off the arrowhead? I do not think I have the strength.''

''Not enough protrudes to allow a good grip,'' he said, willing to do whatever she asked of him. ''Will breaking off the fletched end do?''

''Aye,'' she said, and turned to one of the women. ''Prepare two pads, heavily coated with alum. If he stops bleeding, I can stitch him shut. If not, we will need a hot iron to cauterize the wounds.''

''She will kill me for sure, my lord. I beg of you—''

Richard wrapped his hands around the shaft and snapped the arrow in two, just ahead of the feathers. Connor's body jerked and he passed out. A blessing.

''Trim the end,'' Lucinda said, handing him a large knife from the supplies at the head of the table. ''We do not wish to leave any stray pieces within him.''

''Fine,'' he said. ''You sit on that bench behind you before you fall down. You direct, we will do the work.'' Philip reinforced his order by pulling Lucinda backward. ''When was the last time you ate?''

She shrugged a shoulder.

''Philip,'' he said, tossing his head toward the food table. The boy scurried off.

Richard trimmed the arrow to a clean point, then cut away the tunic surrounding the wounds. A woman stood by with the treated pads.

''Pull slow, steady and straight,'' Lucinda said.

''You do not ask much, woman,'' he said of her dictates.

"Want me to do it?"

"Sit."

She turned to the woman with the pads. "Flush the wounds with water, then press the pads on tight. Do so quickly. He has already lost more blood than he can afford to lose."

Richard braced a hand on Connor's back and grasped the arrow's shaft with the other. He pulled it out, steady and straight, just as he would pull his sword from its scabbard. Holding the bloody arrow, he stepped out of the women's way.

Blood oozed from the holes in Connor's already too-frail body. The women worked quickly and soon had the pads in place.

They waited. Lucinda nibbled on bread. Richard washed the blood from his hands. Still they waited, but no more blood seeped through the pads.

Lucinda got up and very gently eased away the pad from Connor's back. "'Tis ready for stitching. I will need needle and thread."

"Let another do it," Richard ordered. "You are to rest."

"Volley! Fire!"

"Hellfire," Richard swore and headed for the door.

Lucinda grabbed his arm. Her eyes held no fear, only concern. "You can do naught until the arrows fall. Wait. Please."

She had the right of it. No sense going out until the worst had passed. But he could watch.

"Come," he said. Richard took Lucinda's hand and led them to the manor door.

Night had fallen. Against the black sky, the flaming arrows streaked though the night like falling stars. As always, because of the distance, most of the arrows drowned in the moat. Only two arrows flew over the palisade, both landing in the dirt in the bailey, where no one wasted water to douse them. He watched them burn out, hoping George would burn out soon as well.

"Mayhap now we will have a peaceful night," Lucinda said.

"Mayhap," he said, hoping Lucinda was right.

"Then again on the morn, we will dodge arrows and fire, and treat burns and wounds, and more people will die."

"'Tis the way of a siege, as you well know. We are safer within the palisade than without on the field. If George had not so many men, or if I had more..."

She squeezed his hand. "It irks you to wait and do nothing to hasten the outcome."

"True. I give George a sennight. If he does not leave by then, I will take action. I do not know what as yet, but I refuse to let him sit out there overlong." He kissed her forehead. "Rest."

"You go back to the walk?"

"Aye. I intend to find the stoutest bow in the place and send the arrow that almost hit you into the very center of George's camp. If I do not find fortune and hit George, then pray I hit one of the men whose strength sends fire over our walls."

On the third day of the siege, George changed his tactics. He burned the home of a tenant farmer. Thick, pungent smoke curled up into the wind and drifted high over the manor.

Lucinda tried not to listen to the sobs of the woman whose home burned to ashes, but each sob struck like a knife in her heart. Though Richard assured the family that the hut would be rebuilt, they mourned the loss of the old.

The grumbling had also begun. Too many people

in too little space, beset by too much strain, made for short tempers. Two fresh graves reminded all that more was at stake than loss of a home.

They blamed Lucinda and Philip for their misfortune. Not outright, and not to Richard—at least not that she knew of. Among themselves, in corners and whispers, with sidelong glances from angry faces, they pointed out and cursed the source of the troubles.

Two men lay cold in the ground. A family had lost its home. If George didn't desist soon, more would die, more would suffer losses. The longer the siege lasted, the more they would question Richard's reasons for holding on to the outsiders. And the greater the chance they would rebel, or a group of them would take matters into their own hands and give her and Philip over to George.

Richard's vassals were good people, but even good people could be pushed to rebellion. Though Basil had mistreated them, they'd never had their lives directly threatened, never seen death come at the point of an arrow or a spark of fire.

Given time, Richard would win out over George, but his people might not give him the time. Richard would lose everything he'd worked so hard to build if forced to fight both an enemy without and a rebellion within.

Lucinda thought back to the day when she'd asked the king for a wardship for Philip. Such dreams and hopes she'd held for her son! After the first fortnight under Richard's care, she'd begun to believe it could all come true.

Then she and Richard had become lovers, and she'd even begun to think she could find a measure of happiness for herself. And she had, truly. For a few short weeks she'd been happier than she'd ever been in her entire life.

All because she'd fallen in love with Richard.

Slowly, she climbed the inner bank to the wall-walk, where Richard and Edric spent most of their days and nights. They were there now, staring out over the countryside.

No cries of "volley" had sounded this morning. The sounds of saws felling trees and hammers pounding nails had taken the place of whizzing arrows.

"There," Edric said, pointing out through the V of the palisade's timbers. "They bring up a second pavise. 'Twill not be long now, my lord. Tomorrow, perhaps."

Pavises. Huge wooden shields that could be wheeled close to the palisade. From behind them, men could rain fire on the manor with little fear of injury to themselves. With the fire would come fear, confusion, destruction and death.

"At dusk, have the men refill all of the water containers. 'Twill be a long, hard day on the morrow, but victory will be ours," Richard declared.

He was probably right. But at what cost?

Collinwood lost to a fire arrow not immediately put out because there were too many fires to douse? How many people would die because of George's greed? And what of Richard, high upon the palisade, too easy and clear a target?

Richard might be killed, all because she'd made the selfish mistake of thinking that she and Philip were entitled to more than the hardships of a peasant's life.

Her arrogance, her selfishness, had brought him to this. 'Twas her duty to end it.

She could prevent the bloodshed by leaving, taking Philip with her out the postern gate and melting into the night. With no prize to fight for, there need be no fight.

She wasn't fooling herself. 'Twouldn't be easy. She would need help, and knew who to ask. Connor would be pleased to aid her disappearance, for the simple promise to never return.

"Lucinda? Is aught amiss?" Richard asked.

She stepped under his arm held outstretched in invitation.

"Nay," she said honestly, coming to terms with what she must do tonight if none were to die on the morn. Including the man around whom she now wrapped her arms.

He leaned to whisper in her ear. "Did you think to drag me away to your hut, distract me from my duty?"

In the face of all to come, he teased. Incorrigible man.

"I came for a dose of courage before I go to examine Connor. I may even grant his fondest wish and let him walk about some tonight."

"He is strong enough?"

"For a frail old man, Connor is tough as leather." For what she would ask Connor to do, he would find the strength. To be rid of her, he would do anything she asked.

Once before, she'd set out on her own with a young child to care for and managed quite well. She could do so again.

Leaving Collinwood, however, would tear at her as leaving Northbryre hadn't. Nor would all of her leave Collinwood. Her heart would remain behind.

Chapter Nineteen

"But I do not want to go," Philip said with a pout. He carried his wooden sword and dragged his sack behind him—the same sack in which he'd carried his spare garments on their last journey.

"Neither do I, darling, but 'tis for the best," Lucinda said, wondering who she most wanted to reassure, Philip or herself.

'Tis for the best. Lucinda refused to reconsider the decision she'd made after a mighty struggle. She'd set her resolve, devised a plan, and would carry through.

Everyone was in the manor, sitting down to evening meal on this dreary, mist-enshrouded evening, except the guards at the wall-walk, who looked outward, not inward. And Connor, who stood near the postern gate.

"He will be angry," Philip warned.

He being Richard, and Lucinda couldn't disagree.

"His anger will fade when he sees the sense in what we do," she said as much for Philip as for Connor, who hadn't cooperated with her scheme with the enthusiasm she'd expected. Still, he'd gathered up the food she'd requested and would distract the guard above the postern gate long enough for her to slip out and reach the river.

Connor glanced from her to Philip and back again. "You have all you need?"

"Aye. You know what to tell Richard and when?"

"I dislike deceiving him."

"It cannot be helped."

As long as Connor waited until full dark—too late for Richard to come looking for her, but early enough for him to inform George that the prize had fled—she didn't care how Connor felt.

"What if George does not believe his lordship's message and attacks anyway? Why not just go to George and have done?"

She'd thought of it, and rejected the notion as quickly.

"Because I, too, want to live," she said. "As for George, he will demand to come have a look, and when he finds us truly gone, he will be too busy searching for us to harass Collinwood further. The man's greed drives him. He wants Philip, nothing more."

Connor nodded. "No doubt. Where will you go?"

She almost told him. Cambridge. One could walk the banks between Collinwood and Cambridge, Richard had once told her. The teeming port city seemed her best destination, full of travelers, where no one would note a strange woman and child. From there, she could board a ship or head overland.

But she wouldn't tell Connor. She couldn't risk his telling Richard—or George. Both men would ask him because both would search. Richard out of duty, George out of greed.

"I have not decided," she answered. "Rest assured 'twill be far away. Take care of Richard well, Connor. He is the best lord this holding will ever have."

She tossed her pack over her shoulder.

"Godspeed, my lady."

She almost laughed. "Come now, Connor. You have wished for this day from the moment I arrived. Surely you have no misgivings now!"

"Nay, no misgivings. You have never fit in here, should never have come. However, I...I owe you my life. I would have no harm come to you."

So that was it. Obligation bothered Connor. How appalled he must feel that he owed his life to a woman he so hated.

Damn the man! Why did he go soft on her now when she needed him to believe the very worst of her and so uphold his part in her plans?

"Set your mind at ease, Connor. You owe me nothing. If Richard had not wanted you alive, I might not have worked so hard to save your worthless hide."

His spine stiffened at her false, harsh words. "I will call to the guard as you slip out. Good journey."

The meal dragged on to an interminable length without Lucinda seated beside him. He'd been telling her, for days now, to rest. Apparently tonight she'd taken his advice, chosen to eat her evening meal in her hut with Philip.

Everyone's mood was subdued, thinking of the five pavises that menacingly faced the main gate, and of the battle the morrow would bring. Even having Connor on the mend and back at table brought no one any joy.

Lucinda might wish to rest, but he had a question

to ask her before she took to her pallet for the night. He needed an answer, yea or nay. And after all, he'd promised God. Richard rose from his stool, gathering his courage.

"I will be with Lucinda and Philip for a while if you or Edric need me," he told Connor.

"She is not there, my lord," Connor answered so quietly that Richard strained to hear.

A cold chill crept up Richard's spine. "Then where is she?"

"Gone. About an hour ago, she and the boy left through the postern gate. By now she is well on her way to wherever she is going."

Stark fear held him motionless and speechless, but not for long.

He grabbed Connor by the front of his tunic and pulled his steward off the bench. "An hour ago? You knew and kept it secret?"

Connor quaked, but managed a nod.

"In God's name, man, why?"

"'Twas her wish, my lord, to save us from further death and destruction. She removes the prize, the boy, so there need be no battle."

"No battle?"

"We must send a message to George, my lord, so he knows there is no reason to harass us further."

Richard let go of Connor, if only to keep from strangling the man. He glanced down the row of tables, noting relief on many faces. His vassals thought their trouble over.

Rage, pure and cleansing, bubbled up and overflowed. He grabbed the table and upended it, sending food, drink, dogs and people scattering.

"No one eats or drinks of what I provide for you

until Lucinda and Philip are safely recovered! She puts herself in peril. For what? To save your thankless arses? Do you truly think I will put her at further risk by informing George that she is wandering around in the dark? Fools! Let George attack. Let him burn the whole sorry place to ashes for all I care.''

He pointed at Lyle. "Get Edric."

The young man scrambled to obey. Richard advanced on a trembling Connor.

"Tell me everything," he commanded, and listened to Connor's tale of Lucinda's request for food and help in distracting the guard in exchange for saving Collinwood.

His rage burned all the brighter. "Hellfire, man! Lucinda pulled you from the brink of death and this is how you repay her?"

"'Twas her wish, my lord," Connor wailed.

"And yours! You fairly leaped from your pallet to be rid of her. From now on, 'tis *my* wishes you will heed. You will not eat, or sleep, or take a piss without my permission. Nor will anyone else!"

Edric came running in, Lyle at his heels. "My lord, we must find them before George does."

Richard rubbed his aching temples, but the rage held him captive. "I know, but 'tis night. We cannot go stumbling around in the dark! Use of torches would give away our whereabouts to George."

And give away Lucinda's location, if he found her.

"Then let me go alone," Edric proposed.

Edric worried for Philip. Richard couldn't fault him for wanting to do what Richard yearned to do, but neither could he let Edric go.

"Nay. We must wait for daylight. At first rays, we will find them."

His gaze swept the manor, the havoc he'd wreaked, then he stormed out of the manor and up onto the wall-walk. He looked out into the mist, unable to see much more than the dim fires of George's camp. Somewhere out there Lucinda would be huddled down, hiding.

He could almost be glad that she had some idea of the danger she faced. Once before she'd escaped a bad situation with little more than the garments on her back, with a toddler in her arms. For three years she'd remained hidden, raised her son in the best way she knew how.

But unlike when she'd left Northbryre, a band of ruthless men camped on Collinwood's doorstep. Hellfire, if one of the mercenaries found her...he refused to complete the thought. He had to trust that she wouldn't be captured, or he would drive himself witless with worry.

How far had Lucinda gone? In which direction? Up river? Down? Across, somehow, and overland? The mental exercise gave some relief, but not for long.

He wanted to yell and beat on something, someone—mostly himself for not anticipating her move.

Richard's hand smacked against the palisade. He'd been so proud of Collinwood, of the fortress built for protection, of the new farms and recently acquired wealth. Of his plans to build a stone keep. Yet none of those things brought him the joy he'd found in loving Lucinda, none of the satisfaction he'd found in caring for Philip.

His head pounded with pain, but he held on to his rage, for despair lurked behind it.

All night, Richard haunted the wall-walk, even when the mist gave over to rain and back again. He paced, and watched, and paced some more. When light brightened the sky, Richard peered outward at George's camp.

The fires had gone out during the rain. The three supply wagons stood off to the side of George's tent, the oxen milling about nearby. Several tents dotted the campsite. The pavises stood in an eerie row, ready to be rolled forward. Yet, no one stood ready to roll them.

Not a man could be seen. Nor George's horse.

George and his force had snuck off during the night.

"Open the gates!" he shouted, already on the run, the knowledge running along with him that George wouldn't leave unless he had Philip.

Richard forced himself to calm down, to read the signs about the camp that would tell him something, anything, about the situation he now faced. Finding George. Philip. Lucinda.

They'd left in groups, headed in several directions. Only one group, the largest, had taken the road south, led by a horse. George's horse.

Richard turned to go back to the manor, then stopped. On the drawbridge, near the gate, and on the wall-walk stood nearly every man and older boy. All armed with a spear or sword, or bow or club. A lump threatened his throat. He managed to swallow it before he reached the drawbridge.

"I thank you," he said, "but I take only ten men." He spied Edric near the gate. "Choose those most skilled with bow and sword, and who can long sit a horse. George has a good start on us, and we must assume he has Philip."

And Lucinda. George had captured Lucinda. Richard ignored the sweat that broke on his brow, and the tremble that threatened his composure. He headed for the armory to fetch his chain mail, to lead the company that would free the woman he loved and the boy he adored, and give him back his life.

Lucinda walked beside the man assigned to guard her, stiff and sore, and so angry she could spit.

She'd almost reached the river. A few more steps and George's patrol wouldn't have spotted her. She'd fought, to no avail. Philip had better luck. She would have to commend whoever had taught him to ''go for the knees'' and then ''bash the man on the head'' with his wooden sword. But that had worked only once, and the two of them couldn't fight off five men.

Lucinda glanced over her shoulder. Philip marched along behind her, as if he hadn't a care in the world, secure in his belief that Richard would find and rescue them. Philip still bore a red splotch on his cheek where George had hit him last night for expressing that opinion.

George had also believed it. He'd paid off and dismissed the mercenary captains, then taken to the road in the dead of night, to escape Richard and to reach Dover as quickly as possible.

And so they marched—she and Philip, and fifteen men—while George rode up ahead.

Richard. Would he come? Most likely. Out of duty. She didn't want him to risk his life yet again, but he probably would. Damn, she'd made a mess of her escape. Not only had she been caught, but no message of her leaving had been delivered to George's camp.

George looked back, a smug smile on his pudgy

face. The toad. How she would like to scratch his eyes out! Except her wrists were bound together with rope.

"How do you, Lucinda?" he asked sarcastically.

"Quite well, George. And you? Is your arse sore yet?"

He raised a surprised eyebrow. His surprise matched her own. Merciful heaven, she should watch her tongue. Yet she longed to spit venomous words, lash out and sting him though it would do no good.

"As an ugly wench who is of no use to me, you had best amend your insolent manner if you wish to set eyes on Normandy."

She had no desire to set eyes on Normandy, and intended to do whatever she must to avoid boarding the ship. This road ran through London. A crowded city. A place where she and Philip could get lost in the throng and find sanctuary in one of the many churches or abbeys.

He threatened her with death, which she expected from him. If the wretch thought she would die easily, the man had best think again.

With a start, Lucinda realized she didn't fear George. She *should* fear him. He came from the same rotted mold as Basil, that devil's spawn who'd tried his damnedest to beat her into meekness, berate her into believing herself unlovable.

In the past weeks, she'd learned differently. While she might never lie in Richard's arms again, she would always feel his warmth, hear his tender words. By loving Richard so thoroughly, she'd gained strength and healed.

No man, not even George, could wound her soul ever again.

* * *

Richard's man-at-arms beamed as he reported his sighting.

"They have stopped for the night, my lord. Two leagues ahead. George, Lucinda and Philip, and fifteen men. No sign of any of the mercenaries."

George was a dimwit. A smart man would have retained the mercenaries as escort; the greedy man had decided to save his coin.

"Lucinda and Philip all right?"

"The boy's tunic is torn about the sleeve. The lady wears no veil and her hands are tied in front of her. Both moved smartly, though, as if uninjured."

If George had ordered Lucinda's hands tied, she must have given him trouble. While he inwardly cheered her boldness, he prayed she wouldn't test George's patience too hard.

Lucinda had certainly tested Richard's patience, to the point of rampage. He'd lost his temper before, but never to the severe degree that he'd tossed a table around the room. He tamped down the rage that threatened his composure at the memory of his reaction to her leaving him, putting herself and Philip in danger. He would save his rage for later, when he confronted George, and later still, when he informed Lucinda of his disapproval of this exploit.

Then, when she clearly understood that she was never to leave him again, he would take her in his arms and keep her there—forever.

Hellfire, he was starting to act as Gerard did toward Ardith. Overbearingly protective. Eager to please his wife's merest whim. He'd often teased Gerard, but no longer. Not now that he understood the pain and joy of loving someone so much it hurt.

Gerard. His brother would likely toss a grand fit

when told of his plans to wed Lucinda. Dealing with Gerard might be harder than dealing with George. Richard didn't give a damn about George, but did care, very much, about his relationship with Gerard. He'd never crossed Gerard before, not in anything of importance, never in any way that might cause a rift. But even if it caused a rift, Richard would still make Lucinda his wife.

That is, if she accepted him, which he wouldn't know until he rescued her.

"We leave the horses here," he began his instructions for a surprise attack, assigning a man to watch them. Three others would comb the woods, stalk any guards surrounding the camp, and do whatever necessary to keep them from raising an alarm.

His men were tired from having ridden all day, but not nearly as tired as George's men, who'd walked. He was counting on that weariness, as well as the element of surprise, to carry the day.

Getting close enough to the camp, undetected, to discover Lucinda and Philip's exact whereabouts within the camp was the most important duty. He assigned it to Edric and himself. Edric also volunteered to protect the precious pair during the fighting.

"No one touches George but me," Richard said, reserving the right to put the noble to sword point if necessary.

Lucinda sat at the base of an oak. Philip knelt beside her. She opened her mouth and Philip popped in another piece of bread, the first food they'd had all day.

George refused to unbind her wrists, even to eat. He punished her for not cowering, which she refused to do. She'd stopped trying to loosen the rope, had only succeeded in rubbing her skin raw and hastening the swelling, thus tightening the rope.

George and most of his men sat around a fire, waiting for snared hares to finish roasting. She doubted that she or Philip would be invited to partake.

"Another piece?" Philip asked.

"The next is yours. You need the food more than I. You are still a growing boy. How are your feet and legs?"

"Sore," he said with a grimace.

"Mine, too."

They finished the bread in silence. Her stomach still felt empty, as she was sure Philip's did, too. She squirmed a bit and leaned against the tree, making the best of an uncomfortable seat.

"Come," she told Philip, who wiggled under her upraised arms and settled in her lap, his head on her shoulder. He sighed and closed his eyes.

"Mother?" he whispered.

"Hmm?"

"I do not like George."

She rested her cheek against his brow. "Neither do I."

"Was my father truly like him?"

Poor Philip. No matter how many times he heard of how bad Basil had been, he still wanted to believe his father hadn't been *all* bad. Unfortunately, Lucinda couldn't think of one good quality that Basil had possessed. "I fear so, Philip."

"Will I be like them? Connor thinks so."

She snuggled Philip in closer. "Connor is a...well, he is wrong. What does Edric think? Or Richard?"

Philip's shoulder shrugged.

"They think you quite special, as I do," she assured him.

He opened his eyes. His bottom lip trembled. "I want to go h-home."

Back to Collinwood. Merciful heaven, 'twas where she wanted to be, too. With Richard. Lying in his arms on a bear pelt. Safe. Warm. Loved.

"Mother?" he whispered, but the tone had changed.

"Hmm?"

"I see Edric."

Every nerve in her body came alive. She wanted to spin around and look, but knew she could give Edric's position away if she did so. "Do not move, Philip. Not a muscle. Do you see Richard?"

"They hide in the bushes behind us. Richard looks very angry."

Let him be angry. Furious. Enraged. So long as he was here, she didn't care.

Lucinda heard the arrow before she saw it fly across the campsite and spear one of George's soldiers. She pulled Philip close and lurched sideways, landing facedown with Philip tucked safely beneath her.

She counted the arrows whizzing over her head. Six, she thought. George's men screamed in pain and shouted in anger. Soon swords struck swords, and shields. Richard's voice rose above the din, barking orders.

Out of the corner of her eye, she caught a glimpse of boots. Edric's boots. He stood near her head, standing guard. If he wanted her to move, he would tell her so. Until he did, she would hug the ground. She closed her eyes and prayed for a quick and successful end of the skirmish.

Beneath her, Philip wiggled, pushing her away. She moved sideways—enough to give him air but not enough to let him up.

The longer the battle raged, the more she worried. Had Richard brought along enough men? Had the element of surprise worked in Richard's favor? Had he worn his chain mail?

She was about to look up to check when she heard Richard shout. "Come back here, you filthy swine! I have seen enough of your backsides. Face me if you dare!"

Someone ran past her, crashing into the underbrush.

Were George's men fleeing?

Edric chuckled. "Come, my lady, 'tis all but done," he said. "Flip over and we will have you loose."

Lucinda gently rolled, bringing Philip with her.

"Hold still, Philip, while I cut your mother's bindings," Edric said. His sword cut through the rope like a hot knife through butter. As her arms separated, he plucked Philip from atop her so she could sit up.

All around her men lay on the ground, dead or wounded, only one of them Richard's man. Groans of exertion had turned to moans of pain. The fighting went on but most of George's men either lay on the ground or had fled.

Richard fought like a demon possessed. Chain mail gleaming, sword flashing, he blocked the slash of an enemy sword. Then he ducked under the man's guard and punched him in the face, sending his victim off his feet and backward.

At the edge of her vision she caught a flash of red silk. She jerked her head up to see George, sword raised, coming straight at Edric.

"Edric, behind you!" she shouted, and tried to get up.

But George never got near Edric. From behind, Richard grabbed George's tunic, and with a mighty heave, flung him aside. George rolled in the dirt, and by some miracle, got his pudgy body back upright.

Enraged. Richard was definitely enraged.

"Spawn of Satan," Richard taunted, waving his sword at George, advancing.

"Bastard!" George took a swipe at Richard. Richard put his own sword up to deflect the blow.

"Ah. But at least I know who my father was. Tell me, George, did your mother tarry with the stable hand? 'Twould explain the stench about you."

Swords clashed, but no one could doubt who was the better swordsman. Richard played with George, as a spider toys with a fly before the kill. He didn't play long. Richard took a step back, then lunged. Lucinda closed her eyes, tight.

When the sound she heard didn't match the vision in her head, she dared a peek. George's sword lay several feet away, and Richard had George backed up to a tree, a hand around his throat. Richard wasn't going to kill George. Oddly relieved, Lucinda got to her feet.

"Would you like to know why I am not going to stick my sword in your fat gullet?" Richard asked.

George couldn't speak, or move his head.

"Because I truly think that Henry would like to see you again."

Richard let go. George nearly fell.

"I will go back to Normandy," George said hoarsely. "I swear, I will send all your goods due and never bother you again. You may keep the boy, with my blessing."

Richard scoffed. "Come, man, do you think I need or want your blessing for taking back what is mine?"

He looked over at Philip, then reached out and touched her son's bruised cheek. "How did you come by this?"

Philip glanced at George. "He hit me."

"Did he?"

Lucinda shivered at the menace she heard, but knew without a doubt that she had nothing to fear.

Then Richard looked her over. He took his time, and she felt the burn of his gaze from head to toe. When he focused on her wrists, his eyes narrowed to slits.

"Edric, tie the prisoners up, bind them to each other," Richard ordered, then with a swift, mighty blow, backhanded George. The man went down with a thud. "But this one—truss him up, ready for the spit, like the pig he is."

"Aye, my lord." Edric handed Philip to Richard, whose expression melted slowly from rage to soft concern.

"You all right?" Richard asked.

"May I help Edric? I know how to tie a knot."

"A tight knot?"

Philip demonstrated by pulling on an imaginary rope with straining arms and a contorted face.

"Then have at it," Richard said, and put her son down.

He sheathed his sword, dusted his hands and crossed his arms.

The moment she'd longed for and dreaded had come. Did Richard have it in his heart to forgive her?

Chapter Twenty

Richard watched Lucinda walk toward him, slowly, nervously twisting on the rope that had rubbed her wrists raw. Her plait had come partly undone, her raven hair mussed and sprinkled with twigs and dead leaves. Dirt smudged her cheek. She wore the old gray gown that she'd been wearing when they met.

Beautiful. Alive. Soon to be his, he hoped. He longed to take her in his arms and kiss her senseless…but not yet.

"'Tis a remarkable sight you make when enraged, Richard of Wilmont. I do not recall seeing the like before," she said.

He'd loosed most of his anger and frustration during the short-lived clash with George and his men…but not all.

"What you saw is the style in which I fight. The rage? That happened last eve, shortly after evening meal, when I gave Connor a tongue-lashing and up-ended a table."

Lucinda's eyes widened slightly. "Truly?"

"Aye. You see, I had just been informed that the mother of my ward had whisked him off to God knew where. At night. With a besieging army sitting outside the gates. And no way to go after her until daylight. I lost my temper. People scattered, cups and trenchers flew, even the dogs crawled off to escape me. 'Twas a remarkable sight. You should have been there.''

Lucinda crossed her arms. "Of course I left just before dark. Late enough so you would not come looking, yet not too late for you to send a message to George that I had fled with Philip. Instead of sending that message, you fly into a temper and toss tables around.''

Richard leaned forward. "I was not about to let George know you were out there!''

"Why ever not! He would not have believed you until he had thoroughly searched the manor. By that time we would have been too far away for either of you to find us.''

She had a point, except...

"But he *did* find you!''

Lucinda waved a dismissing hand. "Pure happenstance. A patrol snooping about for the postern gate. Had we left the gate a few moments earlier, we would have reached the river and they would not have spotted us.''

He blew out a long breath. Nothing in her tone or attitude indicated remorse for leaving, just irritation at being captured.

"Where did you intend to go?''

"Up river to Cambridge, for a start. I knew I could get there by walking the river. I thought a port town a good place to hide until I felt that you and George were no longer hunting us. From there, to a small village or mayhap another city. I had not decided.''

To his chagrin, he admitted her plan a good one, still...

"You had no right to take the boy away, Lucinda. Henry's edict names me his protector—"

Lucinda grimaced, bent over, and put her hands on her knees. "Oh, dear."

"What is wrong?"

"My legs. I fear they were not made for walking so far, so fast. Could we continue this argument while sitting?"

Hellfire. She'd been on the march for a good part of the night and all day, and he stood here yelling at her while she was in pain. Richard swept Lucinda up and carried her over to a log. He sat, setting her on his lap.

Lucinda's arms stayed wrapped around his neck. He didn't let her go. He couldn't.

"My thanks," she said, her breath warm against his neck.

"For?"

"Coming to our rescue. Arguing with me."

The first he understood, the latter he didn't. "You like arguing?"

He felt her chuckle. "Aye, because I can, with you, without fear of reprisal. 'Tis a wondrous feeling." She backed out of his embrace, only as far as needed to look him in the eye. "You have given me so much, Richard. I merely wished to give you something in return."

"By leaving? I fail to see—"

She hushed him with a fingertip to his lips. "I could not bear to see you lose everything you had worked so hard to build. George was about to burn Collinwood to the ground—"

He grasped her hand and returned it to his shoulder. "There are ways to defend against pavises, Lucinda. 'Twould have been harrowing, but George would not have succeeded."

"Your vassals were on the verge of rebellion."

"Vassals grumble against their lords—and ladies. 'Tis their nature. You should not have taken their complaints to heart." He put his hand on her cheek. "I *can* protect you, Lucinda, both you and Philip. You truly had no reason to leave."

She turned her head, pressed her lips to his palm. "You might have been killed, and that I could not bear most of all."

Hellfire. Should he shout with joy or smite her backside? She'd risked her life for his sake, and damn near sucked the life right out of him!

"I can fight, and win, my own battles, woman," he said sternly, then slid his thumb over her parting lips, hushing any words. If he didn't say his piece now, he might lose his courage later.

"Your leaving nearly brought me to my knees. I could think no further than of bringing you and Philip back to where you belonged. With me. I love you, Lucinda. Should you ever ponder pulling such a reckless stunt again, I will...well, just do not. My poor heart might not survive."

Lucinda let the words wash over her, gladden her heart and bring peace to her soul. She heard every word he'd said, wondered if he wouldn't come to regret them, but couldn't dwell on anything beyond his declaration of love.

He loves me.

Her smile couldn't hold all of her joy. Fingers trembling where she stroked the strong line of his jaw, she swallowed hard. All that she wanted to tell him had jumbled up in her throat. Most could wait, but not the most important words, those she'd once thought she could never say to any man.

"I love you, too, Richard."

He whooped as he picked her up and swung her around. Lucinda held tight to her gentle warrior, giddy with glee, wishing she could whisk Richard off to some private bower to show him how thoroughly she loved him.

When he finally set her down, she yet clung to him, too dizzy to stand on her own.

"Say it again, Lucinda. Tell me you love me and will never leave me again."

So easy this time. "I love you, Richard, and will never, ever, leave you again. I am yours for as long as you will have me."

"Forever. We will be married as soon as I can arrange it."

Marriage. Merciful heaven. If there was one man in the entire kingdom that she was willing to—wanted to—marry and spend the rest of her life with, 'twas Richard.

"There is no need to rush," she said. "Patience, my love."

"I suppose," he said on a sigh. "'Twill probably be more than a month. I need to get this rabble on their way to London. Then we need to visit Wilmont. 'Twill take us at least a sennight."

Wilmont. Gerard. Her joy plummeted.

"Gerard could take it all away from you, could he not? You could lose Collinwood. Your stone keep. All of your wonderful plans for—"

"Ah, Lucinda. He could but he will not." Richard

shrugged. "And even if he did, I need no stone keep or vast empire to ensure my happiness. All I need is you at my side."

A lovely sentiment. But would he feel the same if Gerard truly stripped Richard of all he possessed? She tightened her hold on Richard's neck. She couldn't make the confrontation with Gerard easier for Richard. The brothers needed to work this out in their own way, on their own terms. *Richard's battle,* she inwardly repeated over and over.

Surrender came hard, but it came. She trusted Richard, and his love.

Richard sat across from Gerard at a table in Wilmont's great hall. He'd nearly finished his fourth—fifth?—cup of ale, and came close to the end of his tale.

"So, I sent Edric and three others to deliver George and his remaining men to King Henry. The two men of mine who were wounded I sent back to Collinwood. The rest of us came here."

The two days of travel to Wilmont had been wonderful. Lucinda had ridden with him, on his lap, snuggled contentedly in his arms. Philip thought the trip a delight.

The boy didn't yet know that Richard intended to marry his mother. At Lucinda's suggestion, Richard had agreed to not tell Philip until after dealing with Gerard. Not because she feared her son would object, but because she knew Philip would rejoice and might blurt the news at an awkward moment. Richard bowed to a mother's wisdom.

"Let us hope that Henry deals with George in better fashion than he dealt with Basil!" Gerard said.

"'Tis hoped. I wrote a note to Henry that gently reminds him to deal with George quickly and thus avoid the vexation of having yet another prisoner escape him."

"There is nothing quite so vexing as waiting on Henry's whims, is there?"

Except, perhaps, dealing with Gerard. He obviously didn't want to talk about Lucinda. He'd barely glanced at her when Richard brought her into the castle. He hadn't objected when Ardith whisked an obviously travel-weary Lucinda off to the solar for a bath and change of clothing. Nor had he stopped Daymon from taking Philip to meet the falconer and view the mews' many hunting birds. But he hadn't liked it, either.

"Henry can do what he wishes with George. I truly do not give a damn if the vermin lives or dies, so long as he goes back to Normandy."

Gerard chuckled. "And sends all of those wonderful tributes due. The wine you sent with Stephen is long gone. Could I talk you out of a barrel or two?"

"I have my doubts. 'Tis really too good to share."

Gerard leaned forward. "Mayhap, then I could win one. What say you, Richard, to a bout in the practice yard? Winner gets the wine."

Ardith was busy with Lucinda, and might be for some time yet. And getting Gerard into the best possible mood seemed a good idea.

Richard got up. "Last one to sweat gets the wine."

They went out the massive oak doors, and down the steps into the bailey. So many times he'd walked this path with Gerard to take part in their favorite pastime. Would today be the last? Richard hoped not.

All depended on Gerard, on whether or not he could accept Richard's marriage to Lucinda.

"Stephen tells me you intend to build a stone keep at Collinwood," Gerard commented.

"Aye, I have the means now." And good reason. He would soon have a family to protect. Lucinda, and Philip, and any other children they might be blessed with. "I assume Stephen has gone to see the Lady Carolyn."

"Hah! More like flew off. I wish him well in his pursuit. I hear tell she is a strong-minded woman. Mayhap she can tame him."

"Tame Stephen? 'Twould be like harnessing the wind."

They stepped into the armory, and as was their custom, stripped down to breeches and boots. Both preferred to shun the weight of hauberks—a great annoyance of Ardith's. Gerard took his broadsword from its scabbard. Richard drew his, too, from right where he'd left it nearly an hour ago.

As always, whenever they took these familiar steps, word spread of the impending swordplay and a crowd gathered. 'Twas no different today.

"However, marriage to the right woman can do odd things to a man, make him do things he would not have before, just to please her," Gerard remarked.

"Like you do for Ardith. That woman has you tied around her little finger," Richard taunted, because 'twas what Gerard expected, and to emphasize the point.

Gerard chuckled, setting his stance, feet slightly apart, knees bent. Richard did the same.

"I try not to let her take full advantage. But, hellfire, pleasing her pleases me." Gerard's laughter faded. He turned serious. "I would wish the same for you, one day, that you would find contentment."

Richard kept the point of his sword lowered. "I already have, Gerard. With Lucinda."

Gerard's face turned stormy, but the lightning Richard expected to strike didn't flash. "So Stephen warned me. I wish you to reconsider."

"You ask me to do that which I cannot. As you love Ardith, so I love Lucinda. She will be my wife, Gerard, with or without your blessing."

"Damn it, Richard! Taking her as a lover is bad enough, but to wed her! Have you forgotten who she is?"

"I have forgotten nothing! Do you remember, when Ardith was in Basil's hands, what she suffered? Lucinda has suffered tenfold, and survived, and came out the stronger. I love Lucinda for the woman she is now, not for who she might have been. I will marry her, and would prefer to have Father Dominic perform the ceremony here at Wilmont. If you say nay, we will go elsewhere. But by God, Gerard, I will marry the woman."

Gerard grasped the pommel of his sword in both hands. From his mouth came the familiar roar of Gerard's battle cry. He brought the sword up and around in a mighty swing. Richard ignored the horrified screams and gasps of the crowd, his attention fixed on the sharp point of his brother's whirring, oncoming sword.

Richard didn't move a muscle, simply smiled an inward smile. Everything was going to be all right.

Lucinda lounged in the wooden tub, even though the bathwater had cooled. She hated the thought of getting out and possibly rippling the tranquillity of the solar, thus disturbing the budding friendship she'd formed with Ardith.

As if by mutual agreement, they hadn't talked about either the past or the future—the former being too painful, the latter as yet unsettled until after Richard spoke with Gerard. But over the past hour or so she and Ardith had discussed housekeeping methods, traded recipes for roasted boar, and compared the joys and miseries of mothering six-year-old boys.

Lucinda had found ease in Ardith's gracious welcome into her home and solar, and hope in her warm smile.

A loud, bloodcurdling roar invaded the solar through the unshuttered window.

"Merciful heavens," Lucinda exclaimed, turning in the tub to stare at the window. "What was that!"

"Oh, dear," Ardith said, waddling over, a towel in her outstretched hand. "We left them alone overlong. They must have finished talking and decided to play. The roar was Gerard. He and Richard must be in the practice yard."

Lucinda stood up, took the towel, and stepped out of the tub. "They fight?" she asked, her heart nearly stopping at the thought of what they might be fighting about.

"They practice their swordplay," Ardith said. "'Tis truly a spectacle, if you care to watch."

Play? Nay, not this time. The sound of steel striking steel in fast, punishing strokes, reverberated down her spine.

"Can you stop them?" Lucinda asked, praying Ardith could before one of the brothers killed the other. If Richard lost, she would be lost. If Gerard lost,

Richard would be bereft, and may never forgive himself.

"Aye, but I see no reason..."

Lucinda strove to make Ardith understand. "They do not play, Ardith, they fight. Richard...Richard was going to tell Gerard that...that he asked me to marry him. I fear Gerard did not take the news well."

"Truly?" Ardith asked, surprised. "Richard simply told you? How odd for Richard."

"Ardith, *please* stop them before one of them is hurt!"

"Set your mind at ease. Neither of them would ever take up a sword against the other in anger. Come, dress. We will go down and you will see."

Lucinda hurriedly donned the filmy white chemise and midnight black linen gown that Ardith had insisted she wear, laughing that she would have no use for it until after her baby's birth. Lucinda didn't bother with a veil.

Merciful heaven, in all of her wildest imaginings of how the brothers' talk would end, she hadn't envisioned that they would come to blows.

Ardith led the way down the stairs and into the great hall, walking far too slowly. She stopped midhall. "Thomas, come," she called to a young man.

"Aw, my lady, must I?" Thomas asked, reluctantly following her order.

Ardith smiled. "Aye, you must. Lucinda, meet Thomas. He has the shrillest whistle in all the kingdom." Ardith took his arm for support and began walking again.

Lucinda's patience nearly snapped, but she kept still. Ardith simply didn't understand that the brothers were out in the yard to settle a dispute. Over Lucinda.

They crossed the bailey as fast as Ardith could walk, heading for a large crowd.

"You must not be too concerned at what you see," Ardith said. "In truth, they drive me to distraction, but all is well."

All was not well. Couldn't Ardith hear the heaviness of the blows? The anger in their voices? The crowd parted for Ardith, Lucinda following close behind.

When she stopped, Lucinda nearly fainted.

In the center of the yard, Richard and Gerard snarled and circled each other like dogs fighting over a bone. Both hefted large, gleaming sharp swords. Neither wore a hauberk, or even a tunic.

Magnificent specimens of virile male warrior, both.

"Come, Gerard," Richard taunted. "Do your worst."

"I will have you without breaking a sweat."

"Hah! Such arrogance! I keep what is mine. Try to deprive me and I will have your guts for nooning!"

She'd seen Richard fight, but not like this. His bout with George had been short-lived and one-sided. Richard and his brother, however, were equally matched.

Gerard brought his sword up, and around.

Ardith put a hand on Lucinda's arm. "Steady, Lucinda."

Richard spun away and came back at Gerard with a punishing blow.

"They will kill each other," Lucinda said, her heart pounding so fast it threatened to burst.

"'Tis what I keep telling them. They never listen. The worst is, they never even come close. If you are to marry Richard, then you had best get used to this."

Ardith's hand tightened on Lucinda's arm. "'Tis how they play, and express their affection and respect for each other."

Lucinda saw no affection in the flurry of Gerard's attack.

"Oh my God," she whispered, and swayed.

"Thomas, now, before she faints," Ardith said.

Thomas gave a long, shrill whistle.

Richard ducked away and under the swing that Gerard struggled to check. He dropped his sword point to the dirt and turned to where the shrill signal had come from.

Ardith stood there, arms crossed on her big belly, scowling. Lucinda stood next to her, pale and frightened nearly witless.

"Hellfire. Caught," Gerard mumbled.

"Damn," Richard mumbled back. "Why do they become overwrought?"

"Only the Lord knows, and I imagine He wonders. Come on."

They started across the yard. Philip and Daymon came running up. Daymon stopped before Gerard and held his arms out for his father's sword.

Philip stared up at Richard, awed. Richard felt his chest swell at the pure adoration. He ruffled Philip's hair.

"I suppose now you wish to be a soldier again."

"Oh, aye, my lord!"

Richard laid his sword across Philip's arms. "You can begin by going with Daymon and learn how to care for a sword."

The two boys walked off, proudly bearing the swords.

Ardith cleared her throat, a call to task.

"You sweat, Richard. I win," Gerard said, putting an arm around his wife.

He was sweating. Damn. "Aye. You get a barrel of wine," Richard said, gathering Lucinda in his arms. She trembled, but didn't faint. "Mayhap I will send for several barrels, for the wedding."

Gerard's arm tightened around Ardith.

Ardith elbowed Gerard's ribs. "Be gracious, darling."

Gerard sighed. "For the wedding. Come, wife. You should be off your feet."

The two of them headed for the keep. The crowd began to disperse, the excitement over.

"You are alive," Lucinda whispered.

"Of course I am alive."

"When Gerard came at you I thought... Oh, merciful heaven, I thought..."

He wrapped her in a hug. "Gerard would never harm me, though he may curse me to hell and back."

"You told him?"

"He is not terribly pleased, but resigned. I knew so the moment he lifted his sword. 'Tis more than I hoped for."

Lucinda's head came up. "Then what were the two of you arguing over out there?"

"Wine."

"Wine. You fought bare chested with sharp swords over wine?"

He didn't miss the edge in her voice.

"We did not fight. We played."

Lucinda looked at him in the very same way that Ardith looked at Gerard when they argued over the very same subject—one of exasperation filled with love. Lucinda truly loved him. He was one fortunate man.

She sighed and rested her cheek against his shoulder. "The next time you *play,* please don a hauberk."

Richard smiled and leaned down to place a light kiss on her forehead. He couldn't promise that he would mend his ways, but he would think about it.

"You smell good," he said, caught by the scent of the soap she'd used to wash her hair. Fresh and womanly. Arousing.

She laughed lightly. "You smell."

"Any water left in that tub?"

"'Tis cold."

"'Twill do."

He nudged Lucinda toward the keep, intending to dunk himself in the tub then whisk her off to a bedchamber, with an entirely different kind of play in mind. Gerard already had his stone keep, his goose-feather mattress, and two sons with possibly a third on the way. 'Twas time to catch up.

Mysterious, sexy, sizzling...

THE AUSTRALIANS

Stories of romance Australian-style, guaranteed to
fulfill that sense of adventure!

This November look for

Borrowed—One Bride
by **Trisha David**

Beth Lister is surprised when Kell Hallam kidnaps her on her
wedding day and takes her to his dusty ranch, Coolbuma. Just
who is Kell, and what is his mysterious plan? But Beth is even
more surprised when passion begins to rise between her and
her captor!

*The Wonder from Down Under: where spirited women win
the hearts of Australia's most independent men!*

Available November 1998
where books are sold.

HARLEQUIN®
Makes any time special ™

Look us up on-line at: http://www.romance.net   PHAUS5

SEXY, POWERFUL MEN NEED
EXTRAORDINARY WOMEN WHEN THEY'RE

Destined
for
Love

Take a walk on the wild side this October
when three bestselling authors weave wondrous stories
about heroines who use their extraspecial abilities to
achieve the magic and wonder of love!

HATFIELD AND McCOY
by HEATHER GRAHAM POZZESSERE

LIGHTNING STRIKES
by KATHLEEN KORBEL

MYSTERY LOVER
by ANNETTE BROADRICK

Available October 1998
wherever Harlequin and Silhouette books are sold.

HARLEQUIN®
Makes any time special ™

Silhouette®

Look us up on-line at: http://www.romance.net   PSBR1098

COMING NEXT MONTH FROM

HARLEQUIN HISTORICALS

- **BLACKTHORNE**
  by **Ruth Langan,** author of
  THE COURTSHIP OF IZZY McCREE
  A nursemaid shows the Lord of Blackthorne how to love again
  and helps unravel the mysterious secrets that have haunted
  Blackthorne's inhabitants for years.
  HH #435 ISBN# 29035-7 $4.99 U.S./$5.99 CAN.

- **APACHE FIRE**
  by **Elizabeth Lane,** author of MACKENNA'S PROMISE
  On the run from vigilantes trying to frame him for murder, a
  Native American army scout hides out at the ranch of a
  beautiful widow.
  HH #436 ISBN# 29036-5 $4.99 U.S./$5.99 CAN.

- **LOST ACRES BRIDE**
  by **Lynna Banning,** author of WILDWOOD
  A rugged rancher must contend with a young woman who
  inherits the neighboring ranch and ends up stealing his heart.
  HH #437 ISBN# 29037-3 $4.99 U.S./$5.99 CAN.

- **THREE DOG KNIGHT**
  by **Tori Phillips,** author of MIDSUMMER'S KNIGHT
  A shy earl and an illegitimate noblewoman forge a marriage of
  convenience based on trust and love, despite the machinations
  of an evil sister-in-law.
  HH #438 ISBN# 29038-1 $4.99 U.S./$5.99 CAN.

DON'T MISS THESE FOUR GREAT TITLES
AVAILABLE NOW!

HH #431 THE WEDDING PROMISE
Carolyn Davidson

HH #432 HONOR'S BRIDE
Gayle Wilson

HH #433 A FAMILY FOR CARTER JONES
Ana Seymour

HH #434 LORD OF THE MANOR
Shari Anton